𝒴

*is a Path Book*
*offering practical spirituality*
*to enrich everyday living.*

*"Your word is a lamp to my feet*
*and a light to my path."*
*Psalm 19:105*

2006

Shirley –
With every blessing!
Here's to the journey.

D

# Passiontide

a novel by
## Brian E. Pearson

Path Books
A LIGHT TO MY PATH

2002
Anglican Book Centre
600 Jarvis Street
Toronto, Ontario
M4Y 2J6

Text set in Berkeley; display set in Rauch
Cover and text design by Jane Thornton


**National Library of Canada Cataloguing in Publication**

Pearson, Brian E
        Passiontide : a novel / by Brian E. Pearson.

ISBN 1-55126-350-5

1. Christian fiction, Canadian (English). I. Title.

PS8581.E382P38 2002    C813'.54     C2002-901292-9
PR9199.3.P373P38 2002


Printed in Canada

Dedicated to the memory of

*the Reverend*
*Stuart George Schoberg*
*1928 – 1965*

United Church Minister of the
Long Beach Pastoral Charge
1962 – 1965

# Preface

This book is a work of fiction. I hasten to point this out because many readers of my last book, *How the Light Gets In,* a collection of short stories, assumed I was writing auto-biographically.

Perhaps I set the stage for this myself, recalling in the Introduction of that book how a real-life encounter had led to the telling, and then the writing, of one of the stories. But it opened the door to misunderstanding. It caused some to bristle at the audacity of a parish priest offering up as entertainment the stories of people he knew, including some of his own parishioners! Of course, I felt honoured — as a good liar, if nothing else. But the truth is that, while certain stories were *inspired* by real-life people and events, with very few exceptions the characters and circumstances in that book were made up, including (sadly) the mime who preached the Sunday sermon.

Likewise, all the characters and circumstances of this book are made up, though many of the places are not. Toronto, for example, exists, the resentment of some Westerners notwithstanding; Grenfell, Saskatchewan, can be found on any decent map, where there is a lovely Anglican church that gets utterly bypassed in this story; Calgary exists, the indifference of some Easterners notwithstanding; and, most certainly, Tofino and Ucluelet exist.

However, the characters who populate this book are entirely fictional, and I take full responsibility for their actions, both noble and dumb. Some, like the members of the two coastal churches I name, are far less colourful than the real people who fill those pews. This is intentional. They must decrease, that he might increase — "he" being Father David, the main character of the story (who, by the way, is also made up). In fact, I can promise anyone visiting the picturesque churches of St. Columba, Tofino, and St. Aidan, Ucluelet, that you will find a far more lively bunch than is represented in this novel. My apologies to them for this, many of whom (I hope) remain my friends.

While I claim full responsibility for the characters and circumstances represented in this book, I cannot claim full credit. Along the way they have benefited from the interest and the input of others. These include Sam Carriere, Kem Luther, Marni Nancekivell, Robert Maclennan, and Sandra, my wife, all of whom read the first drafts and made helpful comments that have improved the telling of the story; my son, Rob, who gave Father David's car its name; Terry Christensen, who guided me through some of the realities of true-to-life medical emergencies; my friends, who wish to remain nameless but who generously and wonderfully provided me with a writer's space (complete with brilliant sunsets, sandy beaches, and gently lapping waves) for the first re-write; and, again, Robert Maclennan, whose encouragement and enthusiasm are a greater gift than he will know.

As always, I am indebted to Sandra and to our three children, Heather, Rob, and Ben, for allowing me a certain measure of distraction and inattentiveness from time to time, while I focused instead on the people and circumstances living in my head. Their love and support made the novel possible.

This book is dedicated to the memory of the Reverend Stuart Schoberg, United Church minister of the Long Beach Pastoral

Charge from 1962 to 1965. A promising theologian, Reverend Schoberg won a scholarship to Oxford University. He was preparing to leave the charge to begin his studies toward a Doctorate in Divinity when he decided to embark on one final outing.

He loaded up his twelve foot clinker-built boat with the equipment and supplies he would need for a three-day beachcombing expedition around Vargas Island, up in Clayoquot Sound. Warned by seasoned fishermen in the area not to take the hazardous seaward route, Reverend Schoberg set out as planned from Ucluelet on 27 March 1965.

The first leg of his journey was to have been a four-hour boat trip along the rugged coastline up to Tofino. When he failed to arrive later that day, he was declared missing, and a sea and air search was mobilized. The boat was found intact two days later, outboard motor and equipment all still in place. It was July before Reverend Schoberg's remains washed ashore. Some guessed that he had never even cleared the mouth of the Ucluelet harbour. He left a widow and two young children.

# Chapter One

Father David reached out in the dark and groped for the stop button on the clock radio. Dan the Traffic Man was already sounding pretty excited this morning, warning commuters away from a fog-bound tie-up on the Don Valley Parkway. But this was all Father David cared to know about Dan, the invisible man with the chainsaw voice whose only usefulness to the Corcoran household was in cutting through its last minutes of sleep. Father David found the button and gave it a slap, stopping the Traffic Man before he had time to suggest an alternate route.

Father David heard Beverley stirring beside him. Once again, she would be starting the day before he would, though this was a new pattern for them. Ordinarily, he was the one who was up first, making his way downstairs in the dark to his study for morning prayers. But not since their summer vacation had ended a few weeks ago. He had returned from their holidays feeling tired and out of sorts. He had begun clinging to these dying moments of repose, as if it were the end of the day, not the beginning.

He rolled over, bunching his pillow under his head, and tried to go back to sleep. But he could hear Beverley in the bathroom, and found himself following her movements in his mind as she robed and padded down the stairs to the kitchen. He listened as she ran the water for the coffee, opened the fridge, and began mixing up some juice, the wire whisk tinkling on the sides of the glass pitcher. Soon she would come back upstairs to look in on Paul and Catherine, their teenaged children, to make sure they were awake. By then he would have used up this brief period of grace, and the day would come for him.

So he pushed himself out of bed, propelled only by a sense of duty, which nevertheless was strong in him. When all else failed, duty could always be counted on to take him by the shoulders and shove him forward, like his mother used to do when she would guide him purposefully out the door to go play with the other children on the street.

Settling himself heavily onto his prayer stool, Father David muttered his way through his morning prayers. A strict twenty minutes later, he rose, showered and shaved, then joined Beverley in the kitchen. She brought him a mug of coffee and he sat at the table, glancing through the morning paper, until Paul and Catherine presented themselves in the doorway, their coats on, their backpacks slung over their shoulders. Rising mechanically, Father David laid down the paper, kissed Beverley on the cheek, and headed out to drive his children to school.

Arriving a little later at the church, he unlocked the front door and made his way down the long hallway to his office, flipping lights on as he went. He slumped into the chair behind his desk and dialled a code on the phone, then hit the hands-free button, leaned back, and waited for the messages; there were none. So he got up, prepared the communion set, and headed off to the first appointment of the day, the monthly Anglican communion service at the Westview Nursing Home.

As he drove along, an old tune formed in his head, a hymn so familiar that he paid no attention to the words as they flowed soundlessly by, like the neat suburban bungalows of his neighbourhood streets and boulevards:

> When I survey the wondrous cross
> on which the Prince of Glory died,
> my richest gain I count but loss,
> and pour contempt on all my pride.

By the time Father David arrived at the Westview, the early-morning fog had lifted and the sun was breaking through, warm and promising. He sat in his car for a few minutes, collecting his thoughts, preparing himself for what he knew lay ahead: the dark cluster of sad greeters parked just inside the front door, a ghoulish gallery of hollow eyes searching every new visitor for ... what? Escape and rescue? News from the homeland?

He reached down into his emotional reserves, a storehouse filled through almost twenty years of ministry, and found again that delicate mix of pastoral concern and personal charm that allowed him to saunter along the hallway, lined with creeping wheelchairs and outstretched arms, past the nursing station, greeting anyone who chanced to make eye contact with a forced cheeriness. "Good morning!" he called out. "Hello there!" It didn't matter to him that most of the residents did not — or could not — respond. In his black suit and Roman collar he imagined he was to them a sign of hope and consolation.

"Hi everyone," he called out as he entered the Fireside Room. There was no fireside. There was no fireplace! But there were seven or eight residents gathered in the small sitting room, some slouched in chairs or on couches, others parked at odd angles in wheelchairs, brought in hastily and left there by volunteers. These were the bright ones, and some returned his greeting.

"Hello, Father!" It was Arnold, short and balding. As one of only a handful of men in a sea of widows, he seemed valiantly to be trying to hold up his half of the universe by acting as genial host and general *bon vivant.*

"Hi, Arnold," Father David said. "How are you today?"

"Can't complain," he said. "No one listens to me anyway, when I do." Father David forced a smile for this joke that Arnold had told dozens of times. It had become a ritual, their little dance of greeting.

"It's Sylvia's birthday today," a volunteer announced as she wheeled another resident into place.

"Really!" Father David replied with exaggerated interest. "How old are you, Sylvia? May we ask?"

Sylvia's arms were tied onto the armrests of her wheelchair, her thin body propped upright by pillows at either hip. Her bent back forced her head to bow forward, and it bobbed slightly to the rhythm of her faint pulse. But she looked up at the sound of her name, uncomprehending.

"How old are you today, Sylvia?" the volunteer shouted into her ear.

Sylvia looked around. She could hear the sound all right, but couldn't make out where it was coming from. The room looked on without expression as Father David knelt on one knee in front of her, slipping a hand beneath hers, placing his other hand gently on top. "Happy birthday, Sylvia!" he said, looking intently at her. Her head reared back, her eyes widening to take him in. Father David smiled and patted her hand.

He rose and walked over to a small table in the middle of the room where he began unpacking the communion set. It consisted of everything you would find on the altar on a Sunday morning, but in miniature: a small square linen corporal, two tiny candlesticks, and a silver chalice and paten, like toy accessories for Minister Barbie.

Father David lit the candles and began handing out the orders of service. Most of the assembled congregation, he knew, would not be able to read or follow along, but it was his way of making everyone feel included.

Mrs. Sollemby had now arrived and was getting organized at the piano. She was a volunteer who played for hymn sings and church services as needed, though with no discernible joy in doing so. She wore the countenance of someone fulfilling some sort of obligation, paying a debt perhaps, or atoning for a sin. So she never greeted anyone. She just sat down at the piano, got out her dog-eared hymnal, placed it on the music ledge, rested her hands in her lap, and waited.

Father David greeted her anyway, as he always did, in the hearing of the small assembly, thanking her for coming. She acknowledged him with a slight nod of the head, poised to hear what service would be required of her this day.

"I thought, this being a glorious September day," Father David addressed the room, "we might sing, 'For the Beauty of the Earth.'" He looked around the room. "How does that sound?"

His question was greeted by a few nods. "Oh, that's one of my favourites!" someone spoke up.

"All right then," Father David said, encouraged. "We'll just sing the first two verses from your hymn sheets. Got those handy? It's on the second page."

He did a quick tour of the room, helping people find the spot, turning the page where it was needed. A volunteer who had stayed for the service worked the end of the room closest to the door, pressing song sheets open on trays or on laps. "Ready?" he asked finally. "Okay, Mrs. Sollemby."

It was no surprise that his was the only voice heard singing. He had a strong voice, and he tried to restrain himself so as not to overwhelm the room. But, predictably, the hymn became a solo anyway. There was no real expectation that anyone else would sing along.

Father David had prepared a little homily for the service. He used as his text a passage from the gospel of John. "'I am the good shepherd,'" Father David read aloud, "'I know my own, and my own know me ... I came that they may have life, and have it abundantly.'" Father David closed his Bible and looked out at his frail congregation, some of whom had already fallen asleep. "I came that they may have life," he repeated, "and have it abundantly."

"God wants us to have life," he began, "and not only life, but *abundant* life. Some days we may not feel very lively. We may feel sick, or tired, or sick *and* tired. We may look around us and think, 'This doesn't feel very much like abundant life. Who are the people who need me? What is the purpose of my life?' We may even find ourselves wondering, 'What's the point of it all? What good am I doing here?'"

Someone was snoring, long breathy sighs punctuated by sudden pig-like snorts. Father David carried on.

"But Jesus came that we may have life," he said, "and have it abundantly. This life is his gift to us. It is not something we can conjure up or create by ourselves. Even in the midst of sickness and sadness, Jesus gives us the precious gift of life. Suddenly the clouds part, and the sunlight fills the room, and we feel once again the gift of sunshine. Or a loved one comes to call, and we remember that we are known and loved by others. And even on the dreariest of days we can always recall in our hearts the many blessings God has given us. This is one of the special gifts of ageing: that we can rummage back through a lifetime of memories, giving thanks to God for all he has done for us through the years."

Arnold's head had fallen to his chest. Father David decided he'd better bring things round to their snappy conclusion.

"So when Jesus says he has come that they may have life, he is talking about *us*. *We* are his sheep, we who accept his love and walk in his ways. *We* are the ones called to abundant life in Christ. This is his gift. Thanks be to God."

He looked out over his little flock. A deathly silence had descended upon the room, a silence borne less of rapt attention than of sound slumber. He cleared his throat loudly and moved on to the communion part of the service.

He took hold of the bread and wine which had been blessed and reserved for this purpose at last Sunday's service. "The gifts of God for the people of God," he said, and he elevated the chalice and paten. Not expecting any response, he said it himself: "Thanks be to God!"

He stepped forward and began moving around the circle of worshippers, pressing a wafer onto open palms, reminding the communicants to raise the bread to their mouths and eat it. When he got to Sylvia, she looked up at him blankly. "The Body of Christ," he said. Her hands could not rise from the armrests; so he placed a wafer on her lower lip, hoping she would be able to do the rest herself.

He picked up the tiny chalice and went around the circle again, offering the wine to each one in turn, raising the chalice to parched lips, repeating the words, "The Blood of Christ." Each time he wiped the rim with a small linen purificator, though in terms of hygiene this seemed a futile gesture, some communicants losing more to the chalice in drool than they were receiving in wine.

When he got to Sylvia, the wafer he had given her was still protruding from her mouth, stuck now to her top lip. He reached to remove it, but her lips were dry and it would not pull away. He did not want to rip it off like an adhesive bandage, so he simply offered her the chalice, reasoning that the wafer, softened by the wine, would come loose. She could then take it in along with the wine. He had reasoned correctly. The wafer was freed from her lip. But now it came to rest in the chalice, floating on the surface of the wine.

There were still several more communicants. He couldn't very well offer them a chalice with someone else's wafer floating in front of their eyes. So he tipped the chalice slightly, stranding the wafer on one side, dipped his finger in and brought it out, placing it on his own tongue. It stuck to the roof of his mouth like a wad of paper as he completed the circuit, offering the chalice to each of the remaining communicants.

Returning to the table, he said the final blessing, thanked everyone for coming, and began packing up the communion kit. This meant consuming whatever wine remained in the chalice, including, of course, whatever else had been added to it in the course of communion. Unlike some of his less assiduous colleagues, he would not simply dump out the wine, perhaps pouring it down the sink. This was no way to deal with the blood of Christ! It was consecrated to be consumed, not mingled with the dish water. The only dignified solution was to pour it directly into the ground; but he didn't have that option here. So he raised the chalice to his lips and, closing his eyes, drank down its contents.

As he was packing up, Sylvia spoke up. "Is it my birthday?" she asked.

Father David looked up. "Why, yes it is, Sylvia."

"How old am I?" she asked, squinting up at him.

Father David looked at the volunteer by the door, who shrugged. "I don't know, Sylvia," he said. "I don't know." He looked down at her for a moment. "But you take care."

He made his way out of the room, striding swiftly down the dark hallway, past the nursing station, down the long row of wheelchairs and searching eyes, toward the light radiating from the front doors. Emerging into the bright sunlight, he shielded his eyes as he searched for the place where he had parked the car. He reached it, got in, placed the communion kit on the passenger seat, and let out a deep sigh. As he turned the key, the acrid taste of Sylvia's communion wafer lingered on his tongue.

. . .

Father David's next appointment was clericus. Most of his Anglican colleagues in the deanery were able to refer to this monthly meeting of the clergy without resorting to Latin. In fact, most simply called it a "deanery meeting." But for Father David, clericus — the Latin term for clergy — was a reminder of the long and dignified tradition to which they belonged: they were priests in the church of God, a high calling indeed. Using the Latin helped raise their sights, he thought, or it ought to have, if only the rest of them would look beyond whatever new and passing fad was supposed to save the church *this* week.

Since moving to the suburbs, Father David had been disappointed to discover that, even though his clergy neighbours were now no more than ten minutes away in any direction, he felt more alone here than ever he had in his relatively isolated country parish. The truth was, he rarely saw his neighbours; and when he did, he usually regretted it.

It was like that old joke he had heard a thousand times at church gatherings. "Clergy are like manure," some jolly speaker would chortle into a microphone, anticipating the room's riotous approval of this naughty little irreverence; "spread out, they can do a little good." Har, har, har. But brought together in one place, Father David conceded now — in a heap, as it were — well, it was sometimes just about enough to make him gag.

It felt to him as if his colleagues here were all locked in some sort of race with one another, perhaps a three-legged race, some of them improbably bound together through theological disposition, others through ecclesiastical rank. Jockeying for position, they bumped up against one another, each cleric reporting that he or she was "encouraged" by developments in their parish, or "hopeful" about some new innovative program.

On the surface, it appeared that no one could be doing better, that each parish was healthy and growing — an interpretation easily contradicted by the statistics. What was worse, they spoke earnestly of being "brothers and sisters." If that were true, Father David thought, it was only according to the worst and most dysfunctional associations one might have with the word "family."

This month's meeting was being held at St. Mark's, a neighbouring parish, whose rector, Barbara, was also the regional dean. When Father David arrived, a handwritten notice taped to the door informed him that the meeting would take place in the youth room downstairs. This was not a good sign.

There was a perfectly good board room off the church hall, Father David knew. It was well lit and functional, and they could sit like professionals around a table. The youth room, by contrast, was a dark tomb in the basement, lit indirectly through one high barred window. The view through that window, the only visual relief offered by the room, disclosed the cracked concrete walls of a window well and whatever dry leaves and candy wrappers had fallen there, rising up on windy days to swirl about frantically, if pathetically, round and round in the enclosed space.

Throughout the room, on various end tables and coffee tables, were scattered low-lit occasional lamps, including one glowing red lava lamp that was always in motion, appearing to Father David to be radioactive. The chairs and couches were mismatched rec room cast-offs, brown corduroy and blue velour predominating, most resting squarely on the floor, their legs having been removed. The carpet was orange shag. Father David frowned. This meant it would be a "Caring and Sharing" day.

Father David had arrived early, as was his custom. Barbara was just inside the door of the youth room, checking on the coffee pot. "Hi, David," she said, turning and taking him in at a glance, as if scanning for surface cracks. "How *are* you?"

She did everything so intensely. She was one tough cookie, a former nurse whose main contribution to that profession had been to serve as the union representative. Her piercing blue eyes must have struck terror into the hearts of hospital administrators, Father David imagined, that penetrating gaze boring straight through whatever defence or resolve they had plucked up in preparation for her arrival. No doubt she got what she came for every time. Then maybe she got tired of winning, tired of making grown men cower, and maybe that is why she went back to school to become a priest. Only now, he was certain, it must be worse, with cowering clergy on every side.

He looked away, surveying the room for a chair that promised the least discomfort. "Fine," he said at last, without commitment. "How are you?"

"We've got this new youth worker, really neat young woman,

really qualified, and she's just doing amazing things with the youth group. She's planning an inner city exposure trip. It's scaring the hell out of them, but I think it'll be a real eye-opener."

"Hm," Father David replied.

He had chosen his chair, a hard-back wooden stacking chair. Randomly he reached for a book from the nearby bookshelves and turned it over in his hand. It was called, *When the Church is Revolting*. From what he could tell by the cover, it was some sort of call to arms, a challenge to the church to become more revolutionary, to overturn the tables of the moneychangers, to harangue the power brokers. It offered strategies for church-based social change, and you could send away for a booklet of *Peace and Justice Songs* for use in inter-generational worship. He placed the book back on the shelf and sat down, folding his hands in his lap, waiting.

Barbara was still looking at him. It appeared she was preparing to say something, but at that moment two more clergy walked through the door.

One was Bob, fifty-ish and bear-like, with a greying beard. He gave Barbara a hug. They had known each other in seminary. If he was afraid of her you couldn't see it, though his affectionate greeting might just be a calculated defence. The other was Charles, the new young incumbent of the Chinese congregation, who slipped nervously past them both to settle himself quickly into a plush armchair in the corner. No one would be able to hug him from there. He smiled formally at Father David, who nodded politely in return.

The rest arrived in small clumps, milling awkwardly in the doorway, pouring themselves coffee as they exchanged greetings with one another. They lingered there as long as they could, until a new clump arrived, forcing them deeper into the room. They had no choice then but to commit themselves to one of the chairs or couches and lower themselves into the dark folds of overstuffed upholstery, knowing they would not be getting up again without a graceless struggle. There they sat like captive chimpanzees, leaning forward, trying not to be swallowed whole, their arms dangling in front of them. Still, their faces were set to convey a positive attitude as they cast furtive glances around the room.

Today would be a day for "Caring and Sharing," Barbara announced when they were all settled. It would be a chance to check in with one another, she explained (though everyone already knew exactly what it meant), and she hoped they would all be open to do that. The bishop himself had commended the process, she said; he had even recommended it to some of the other deaneries.

It was interesting, Father David thought, that for someone who regarded herself as a renegade, someone who routinely and publicly bit the head off any authority figure who got in her way, Dean Barbara so frequently drew upon her closer association with the bishop to lend weight and credibility to her own plans. If anyone didn't like the thought of opening up to one another in their "caring and sharing," they had to contend not only with Barbara, which would have been enough, but also with the bishop.

So they began to go around the circle, answering her Question for the Day, which was, on this occasion, "What gives you life in your ministry?" Barbara offered to go first herself, to break the ice.

"For me," she said with practised eloquence, "it's seeing Christ through the brokenness."

Yes, of course, Father David thought. She would have prepared for this. Whatever she did, she always made sure she was the cleverest, the one with the most profound insight, the one who was wisest. It was certain, for instance, that no one would prove wiser than she was today, and that, if they tried, they could expect her — lovingly, of course — to point out some flaw in their reasoning, or some inconsistency with their actual lived experience. No doubt about it, she was a master at spiritual one-upmanship! Or was that now one-up-personship?

As Barbara went on to describe in heart-rending detail a recent pastoral conversation with someone who had been abused as a child, Father David's mind wandered. He surveyed the room. If haberdashery were any measure of their professionalism, they were certainly a motley crew. Father David's was the only black clerical shirt among them; he was the only one in black, period. Barbara wore a white clerical shirt with a Roman collar, the kind fitted for women, with darts sewn into the sides. There were only two other clerical shirts in the room — Charles, the Chinese priest, in gray, and Brewster in, of all things, a casual short-sleeved brown shirt with a plastic tabbed collar.

Now what was the sense in that, Father David wondered. What was the point of wearing clerical garb at all if it took on a fashion palate of stylish colours and tones? If it was brown today — which, of course, was already yesterday's colour — then why not pink tomorrow, or green, or why not Hawaiian with pictures of palm trees and surging waves? It was a dangerous United Church influence, he thought, shaking his head, like wearing a stole to match the carpet rather than the liturgical season; it diluted the notion of priesthood.

The point of being a priest at all was that the personality did not interfere with the transmission of God's grace. While priests brought distinctive personalities and distinctive gifts to their ministry, theirs was a ministry of function, not of personal charisma, like the Pentecostals. Any priest should be interchangeable with any other. Unless, of course, they began to pander to passing fads and personal fashion statements. Then, for all the dignity they imparted to the role, they might just as well go to work in plaid shirts and bib overalls.

Which was pretty much what bear-hug Bob was wearing, Father David realized, gazing round the room. With his blue jeans, his casual shoes, and his checked shirt open at the neck, just what was he trying to be? A hip woodsman? An ageing hippy? Father David was sure that counselling sessions with "Father Bob" would be an enlightening business, not to say entertaining. Did he darken the room and light a few candles? Did he burn incense or ring little bells? Did he make young couples — who only wanted to get married — join hands with him and sing a chanted mantra before getting down to business? He could not stifle a small grin at the thought.

"David, is there something funny about any of this?"

He looked up, startled. Barbara was bearing down on him from across the room. "No, of course not," he answered. "I was thinking about something else. Sorry."

A charged silence hung in the air. Father David took in the group with a glance. No one was making eye contact. Only Barbara was looking at him, looking directly at him.

"Well," she said, breaking the spell. "I think that's all I want to share. David, perhaps you'd like to go next."

"All right," he said, recovering his composure, "though I thought you wanted us to go round the circle. But sure, I'll go." He had to think for a moment what the question was. "What gives life to our ministry? Was that the question?"

"What gives life to *your* ministry, yes," Barbara nodded.

"Well, for me, it would be the liturgy. The liturgy gives me life."

"What is it about the liturgy?" Barbara posed, leaning forward now, trying to sound pastoral, but coming off more like a pissed-off talk show host.

*Damn*, Father David thought. Why can't she ever just let something be? He didn't want to open up to this group. He frowned, but pressed on.

"Well, it's the dignity of it, the orderliness of it. It's bigger than the one who happens to be presiding. It's bigger than all of us. And we get swept up into that — into God, in fact, who is loving and, well, orderly. It's like, for this brief moment, we get a glimpse of heaven."

Father David considered the words that were coming out of his mouth. He believed them. He really did love the liturgy, loved leading it, loved standing at the heart of it. The Sunday eucharist was the high point of his week. He would be happy if he could do a eucharist every day, like they used to do at the cathedral when he was an assistant curate there.

"And is that why you like to be called 'Father'?" Barbara asked him.

Father David felt the zinger rip into his chest, a direct hit. It was such a personal question. He struggled to gain control of his breathing, to appear calm and unruffled. But it was not a fair question. It was not a question at all. It was an attack, a public attack. Every eye in the room was now raised to monitor his response.

"I prefer to be called 'Father' because it emphasizes the role, not the person," he said evenly.

"But you *are* a person," Bob joined in from across the room, nodding and smiling encouragingly. The circle of clergy seemed to be closing in, like hyenas crouched on their haunches, holding back for the right moment to leap through the fire and tear him flesh from flesh, bone from bone. How long had they been lying in wait for this moment, he wondered.

Still, Father David kept his head. "I am a person called to play a role," he answered. "When I preach, it is not *my* ideas that matter; it is the Gospel. When I give pastoral care, it is not *my* caring that matters; it is God's. When I preside at the altar it is not *my* person that people want to see; it is Christ's. I don't apologize for this: it is the role to which we have been called. The clerical collar is not a fashion statement," he said, being careful not to look over at Brewster. "It's a sign of office. When I wear my stole, I cross it in front because I am bound, literally bound, by a higher authority than my own personality, than my own likes and dislikes. I am God's representative through his church. I am, in that moment, the role, not the man."

Barbara didn't miss a beat, pushing things farther, upping the ante. "What else gives you life, David?"

But he wasn't going there again. "That's it," he answered, definitively. It might have been taken as, "That's it, I've just told you," or "That's it, I've had it with these stupid questions." He didn't offer to elaborate.

Barbara allowed a brief pause, sat back in her chair, let the moment linger, and then addressed the group, "Okay, then, let's carry on." She turned her body away from Father David and toward the priest seated next to her. "What about you, Claire?"

Something burned within Father David now. He was angry. He knew that on these matters he stood alone. No one shared his high notion of priesthood. The younger clergy approached their ministry through an adolescent need to change the world into their likeness. The older ones, especially those who had been ordained as a second career, saw their job simply as being nice people doing nice things for others. None of them had the slightest comprehension of the deep archetypal resonances of their priestly role.

Father David himself had no illusions about the power of the priesthood, and about the heavy burden of responsibility that fell on those who responded to the call, to take it up. But the church, his church, was going off in some other direction. On occasions like this he felt like a fossil, an object of curiosity, perhaps even of scorn. But it only strengthened his resolve.

As the meeting broke up, Bob strode purposefully across the room, his grinning face filled with interpersonal warmth. Father David saw him coming and tried to escape, avoiding his gaze. But Bob reached out and took hold of his shoulder. "Hey, David," he said. "A few of us are going to lunch. Do you want to join us?"

"No, thanks," Father David replied, shaking him off. "I brought a lunch."

Bob grew serious, looking at him now with what appeared to be deep pastoral concern. "You okay?" he asked.

"Yes, fine, thank you," Father David said. "I'll see you later."

He made his way up and out into the noonday sun. With relief he pointed his car toward Holy Cross, his own church, ten minutes away but a million miles from here. The sign on the lawn had his own name painted on it — "Rector: The Reverend David F. Corcoran, BA, MDiv." — along with the times of the Sunday services. Nowhere did it say anything about "caring and sharing."

. . .

Back at Holy Cross, Margaret, the church's secretary, who worked mornings, had already left for the day. He had the church to himself. He went into his office and sat down at his desk, turning on the CBC from the portable radio he kept on the bookshelf. He opened the lunch Beverley had packed. As he sipped through a straw from the little juice box, he tried to put the morning's meeting behind him.

He was not displeased with what he had said about the role of a priest, though he knew it opened up a chasm between him and the others. But had he trusted them, had he been able to speak the whole truth, what he would have wanted to say was this: It was Beverley who gave him life. She was his wife but also his best friend, the only one who understood — the *only* one.

If it had been Beverley on the hot seat, she would have given clericus an earful. Father David loved this about her. She didn't care what people thought. She said and did exactly what she felt. Even Barbara would have been no match for her.

Maybe *she* should have been the priest, he thought, something that had crossed his mind many times before. She certainly had the training for it, having been for two years a novice in the Anglican Order of St. Cecilia — a nun. She and David had met when he was the assistant curate at the cathedral. He had taken the youth group to the convent for a Christmas retreat. She had been assigned to work with him, supporting him in the daily Bible studies and lending her enthusiastic guitar-playing to their group singing.

Their chemistry was instinctive and immediate. They "fit," though it took her departure from the order for them to be able finally to articulate it to one another. She did not leave the order for him, but she certainly left *because* of him. He had opened up in her the hope, and even the possibility, of finding a life-partner. She had done the same for him, and they were drawn to each other like children in a playground, the rest of the noise and laughter dissolving into the background as they bent their heads together, digging with their fingers in the sand.

But she was the plucky one. He himself was reserved, careful, circumspect — traits that had hardened in the mould of his strict upbringing. He had a sister, Paula, almost six years younger than he was. But he had always felt like an only child, caught up far too young in the serious world of his austere father and his quiet diminutive mother. By the time Paula came along it was too late, he was already one of *them*.

Beverley, on the other hand, was the oldest of five. Hers had been a raucous household, the back door slamming with a constant procession of people in and out, strangers showing up for supper at the last minute (friends of her brothers, mostly). Her mother was unflappable and contributed to the constant commotion by holding down a series of irregular part-time jobs. Her father was prone to falling off the wagon, though he was a happy drunk who filled the house with crude pranks and uproarious laugher. It was a house buoyed by chaotic abandon, every day bringing with it new calamities and fresh adventures. It might have been chosen by a panel of impartial judges as the household least resembling Father David's.

How Beverley ever got the idea of entering a religious order was a bit of a mystery to those who knew her. But it had more to do with the liveliness of the order than with anything retiring or introverted about Beverley. It was true that she saw it as a place to exercise her growing vocation as a Christian leader. But also, as a plump woman with a flushed complexion and a loud voice, whose chances of marriage seemed slim, Beverley found in the religious life a sense of acceptance and belonging that eluded her in the outside world.

So through her years in the order, Beverley came to know the church well and the peculiar demands of being a "public" Christian, of being a "professional" minister marked by odd dress and unworldly practices. This meant that she not only sympathized with Father David's world, she *knew* it, from the inside out, and this made all the difference.

The lunch she had packed him this day was a little sparser than usual, he thought. Sometimes she would throw in a bunch of grapes or a chocolate bar. But today's lunch was pretty standard fare — a ham sandwich (without the lettuce that kept it moist), an apple, two cookies wrapped in cellophane, and the juice box. Father David reflected in passing that, for quite some time now, his lunches had lacked the little extras he had come to look forward to.

When he had finished, Father David rose and took the communion kit into the sacristy for cleaning. As he ran the tap to get the water hot, he could hear it echoing out in the empty church. The water in the sacristy took forever to warm up; so leaving it to run, he wandered out into the sanctuary to survey his small domain.

Holy Cross was an A-frame building, the sharply slanting ceilings exposing red pine, shellacked to a glossy finish. It had been built in the early sixties, when church attendance was already beginning to wain across the land, but when people were still confident and hopeful, their memories fresh with scenes of crowded pews and overflowing Sunday schools, scenes that had characterized churches all across North America in the heady post-war years. The first swells of the baby-boom generation had raised great expectations.

It was not an unattractive church, but in the late nineties it certainly felt dated. And Father David had no particular fondness for the populist influences from which this architecture had arisen. He was a stone and vaulted ceiling man, himself, a proponent of classic architecture that gave expression to a God who was somewhat remote, and certainly larger than life. The God of the sixties, it seemed to him, had crash-landed on earth. Jesus came right down off the cross, doffing his robes and crown in exchange for jeans and a T-shirt, and became everyone's personal buddy. "Oh, Jesus, I just want to thank you," people had prayed in the small breakout groups at the evangelistic conferences Father David had attended as a teen. "I just want to praise you, Jesus...."

He had never understood, personally, why it was that they *just* had to thank him, that they *just* had to praise his name. If they thought that in their heartfelt extemporaneous outbursts they were spurning liturgical prayer, they were wrong. They were merely reinventing it, but badly. If you are going to use a formula to guide your prayers, why not use a formula created by faithful scholars from a former age more devout and learned than our own? In the light of such ditties as "Give me oil in my lamp, keep me burning," is it not somehow more dignified — for both God and us — to sing "Thou whose almighty word, chaos and darkness heard ... let there be light"?

He didn't understand it at all. When he and Beverley had pioneered the requisite "contemporary" services back in his rural parish of St. Jude's, they had drawn on Catholic resources, songs that quoted scripture and reflected actual theology. Sure, the songs had a swing to them, especially as Beverley led them with gusto on her guitar. But they also had meaning and depth: they were *part* of the tradition rather than a departure from it.

As he stood alone in the sanctuary now, looking out over the rows of empty pews, an overwhelming sadness began weighing upon him. He really didn't fit in the new emerging church. He knew this. It tolerated him, with his priestly collar and his old-fashioned views, but that was about all. Even his own congregation. They called him "Father" because he asked them to. They tried to enter into the spirit of his high mass at Christmas and Easter, though inevitably every year someone complained of an allergic reaction to the incense. They accepted his theologically complex sermons and his scholarly Bible studies, believing him to be a bright and competent priest, but failing themselves to have even the faintest idea what he was talking about.

The sad truth was that, after seven years here, Father David's congregation still had no appreciation of the things he stood for. Which meant that some day, when finally he moved on, a new priest would come along for whom the Eucharist was not central, someone in a green clergy shirt, who would throw the gates open wide to rock music in the choir stalls, dancers in the sanctuary, and pablum in the pulpit. And the people would accept it all without so much as a whimper. They would see it as "refreshing," as "contemporary — really appealing to the young people."

Facing down his own forty-fifth birthday, which was approaching in the spring, Father David couldn't help wondering if he wasn't well on his way to becoming a walking anachronism — in plain terms, a joke.

The hot water was still running in the sacristy, a steamy mist now escaping through the door. But Father David was rivetted to his place at the chancel step as he considered this startling new image of himself, a pathetic middle-aged priestly figure fading into irrelevancy. He surveyed the stained glass windows that lined the nave, fourteen coloured depictions of the Stations of the Cross, seven on either side of the church, each a memorial to someone who had died, someone who was otherwise completely forgotten by this new generation of worshippers, just as he himself would soon be.

There, closest to the rear doors, was Pilate condemning Jesus to death. The artist had depicted Jesus with a bloody and tortured body, the result of the beatings of the soldiers, but his face was strong, impassive, unrelenting. That same face recurred in each window. Jesus was suffering blows and indignities to his body, but his spirit was strong, resolute, or so Father David had conceived it in his own mind.

Only in the window depicting the crucifixion itself did the artist fail, he thought. There, Jesus' face grew contorted, pained, calling out to his Father in heaven. It was Father David's least favourite window, though he knew Jesus' pain must have been real. But perhaps the artist had given in too much to the idea of Jesus being like us. Where was his unearthly strength in this depiction? Where was his faith? Sure, he had uttered those terrifying words — "My God, my God, why have you forsaken me?" But we hear these words through the victory of the resurrection. All was not lost. It was in the process of being won!

But Father David was not able to pull himself up by these thoughts. He gazed now upon the tortured face of Jesus on the cross, and heard himself whisper aloud something he had never fully considered before: "But to him ... in that moment ... everything *was* lost!"

Father David stood still, confounded by this strange and unsettling new thought. What did it mean? Was it true? There, on the cross, was everything really lost?

When the sound of running water returned to his ears, Father David did not know how long he had been standing there. He could not recall his last thought. He turned and saw steam now pouring from the sacristy in great clouds. He had to will his legs to move.

Father David went through the motions of cleaning the communion set. He had written in his daily planner "article for newsletter" as his intended task for the rest of the afternoon. But something had now intervened, and he felt too heavy, too tired, to apply his mind to an inspiring piece that was supposed to be both theologically instructive and spiritually uplifting. Who would read it anyway? Who would care? He wanted just to lie down. So he did something he almost never did in the middle of the day. He went home.

. . .

As he approached the rectory Father David recognized a car in the driveway. It belonged to Jill, an old friend of Beverley's from the convent days. She often came over in the afternoons to visit with Beverley, sometimes staying on for supper. Father David liked Jill. She battled depression, he knew, and Beverley was a support to her. But she also had a wicked sense of humour. So her presence often signalled some refreshingly irreverent conversation among the three adults around the table after the meal.

It seemed, however, as he entered the house, that no one was home. He called out. A sudden stirring upstairs indicated that someone was there. He could hear floorboards creaking above his head, and footfalls on the carpet.

He went into the kitchen to start the kettle for a cup of tea. Jill rushed down the stairs and swept past him. "Hi, David," she called out, not looking in. "I gotta go."

Father David walked to the door. Jill was pulling on her boots. Her hair was tussled and she appeared flushed.

"Is everything all right?" Father David asked.

"Yes, fine," she said. "But I have to go," and bolted out the door.

Father David returned to the kitchen in search of the teapot. It was never in the same place twice, Beverley being less concerned than he with order. He found it in the cupboard where they kept the drinking glasses. He then began rooting around for the tea bags, which he knew must be someplace, though not in the stoneware pot on the counter where they were supposed to be. He heard Beverley coming down the stairs.

"The strangest thing happened to me a little earlier," he began to say. She appeared in the doorway, red-faced and wild-eyed. "Is everything okay?" he asked. "Jill was acting a little weird. Are you okay? What were you doing?"

"No, no, everything's fine," she said. "Are you making a cup of tea?"

"Yes," he said. "Is everything okay? What's going on?"

"Nothing," she said, reaching into the fridge for the milk. "We were just ..." her voice trailed off. "So what were you saying? What happened?"

Sitting at the table, he began to tell her about clericus, about how he was attacked by Barbara. He tried to describe his disturbing thoughts later, back at the church. But none of it came out making any sense. And it was clear that Beverley herself was distracted, moving quickly around the room, wiping counters, taking things from the fridge, putting them back again. She was not getting what he was trying to say.

"It's okay," he conceded finally. "I'll figure it out. What time do the kids get home?"

The front door opened almost as the words were leaving his mouth, and Catherine burst in. She was their youngest.

"Mom? I'm home!" she called out from the hallway. They heard the thump of her backpack hitting the floor. As she entered the kitchen she was surprised to see her father. "Hi, Dad. What are you doing home?"

"I came home early today," he said. "How was your day?"

Catherine was like her mother in so many ways, Father David thought, so full of life. As she foraged for a snack, searching the fridge for some juice, and then the cupboard for some cookies, she kept up a running commentary on the significant details of her day in grade eight, none of which seemed to have anything to do with learning, Father David mused, but everything to do with belonging to a group of friends.

Paul arrived just as Catherine was winding down. He slipped silently into the room before anyone realized he was home. He was in grade ten, a good student, and Father David felt proud of the capable young man he was becoming. He too was full of life, but it was more a rich inner life than a boisterous outer one like Catherine's. Because he was so often quiet, he would catch his parents off guard with his quick and sudden wit. At the moment, though, his face registered only mild amusement at the unusual scene of the entire family gathered in the kitchen at this odd hour of the afternoon.

The house soon settled into familiar activity as Beverley began preparing supper. Catherine spread her homework on the kitchen table while keeping up a stream-of-consciousness monologue to her mother. Paul took to the driveway to shoot some hoops. Father David, uncertain where he fit in, retired to his study.

He removed his stiff clerical collar and laid it down on the desk. This was the one room in all the world where he felt completely at ease. He leaned back in his desk chair and surveyed the bookshelves that ran the length of the room, his eyes falling on the decrees of ordination and the two university degrees that hung on the opposite wall. He propped his elbows on the arms of the chair and brought his hands, prayer-like, to his mouth.

Something was happening today, something just beneath the surface, something important. But he could not quite get a grip on it. His mind drifted back to clericus and to his epiphany of sorts in the church. Just what was the message? That his understanding of priesthood had become irrelevant? That he himself was a dinosaur? And just what did this have to do with Jesus' tortured face in the crucifixion window? He could not focus his mind enough to wring meaning from any of this. These were questions bubbling up from some deeper place, a dark place with which he was not familiar. He reached to turn on the desk lamp.

Catherine poked her head in the door. "Whatcha doing, Dad?" she asked.

"Just ... thinking," he responded.

"Hmm," she said, looking mischievous. She entered the room slowly, mysteriously, as if harbouring a secret plan. Then suddenly she lunged forward with both hands and mussed his hair. He tried to grab her arm but she was too quick for him, twirling round and bolting from the room, giggling, the door flying shut behind her. He chuckled at her cheeky impertinence. She was growing up.

Their children were such a blessing to him. Before they were married, he and Beverley had discussed the family they planned to have. She had said she wanted eleven children. He had thought she was joking. He offered a compromise: two. It was as close as they ever got to their first fight. But it never came to that. She had the idea that it was her role as his wife to give in. And he had the idea that it was his role to let her.

Now he wondered what their life would have been like if they had had eleven children! He shook his head. It was simply unimaginable to him — the chaos, the noise, the constant confusion. He could not even imagine having three, their little nest being just big enough as it was, just the right size, and a great source of joy.

He rose, pulled on his sneakers, and went out to join Paul on the driveway.

"You want to play some Twenty-one?" Paul asked him. This

was a deliberate accommodation. Father David couldn't dribble a basketball, couldn't do a lay-up to save his life. But he *could* stand in one place and shoot baskets, and Paul knew this. Paul also knew that, still, this was a game his father was bound to lose.

"Sure," Father David said. "But be kind."

After supper, when the children had gone, Father David rose to start clearing the table. Beverley addressed him, still seated at her place.

"David?" she began. He stopped short. There was a tremor in her voice that was unfamiliar to him. It was quietly urgent, imploring.

"Do you have anything on tonight?" She was looking down at her plate, which, he realized, had hardly been touched.

"No," he said, "nothing."

"Is there anything going on at the church?"

"No," he said, thinking about it for a moment. "Brownies was last night. AA is tomorrow night. I don't think the Sunday school teachers meet this week; I think it's next week. So, no, there's nothing going on." He considered leaving it there, but he was growing concerned. "Why?" he asked her.

"I need to talk with you. There's something you need to know." For a moment neither of them spoke. Something was wrong — it was plain — but Father David had no idea what it was; nor did he really want to know.

"I'd like to go somewhere," she continued. "I was thinking of the church. Would that be all right with you?" Beverley said, looking up at him for the first time, fear palpable in her eyes.

They drove over to the church in silence. Father David felt a tightening in his chest, a tell-tale sign that he was distressed. He didn't know what was coming, but he knew he wasn't going to like it. Why else would she want to meet him like this?

He unlocked the front door and proceeded down the hall toward his office. "No," she said. "Can we meet in the church instead? I don't want to feel like you're counselling me."

Father David turned on a few lights and opened the doors to the church for her. Beverley chose a pew near the front. She entered it and sat down. Father David, feeling too exposed out by the main aisle, walked around to the side aisle and joined her from the far end of the pew. They sat together, a small distance between them.

"David," she said finally, turning to him, her eyes brimming with tears, "there's something I just have to tell you. I hope you'll hear me out, because this isn't easy for me."

The rest of what she had to say came to him in fragments, the words registering in his ears but not in his understanding. She and Jill ... not an ongoing thing ... it had only happened this once ... not sure what it all meant ... confusing, upsetting ... maybe mid-life crisis or something ... it would never happen again ... nothing's changed ... everything's changed ... could he forgive her ... they could work it out ... was he okay ... was he okay?

Father David looked at her.

"I know how awful this must be for you to hear this," she was saying. "But are you all right?" She was looking alarmed. "David?"

He didn't know. He barely knew who he was, or who she was, sitting there in the semi-darkness. He felt paralyzed. He couldn't move, he couldn't speak.

She reached out to touch him. Involuntarily, his arm shot up to block her.

"David, don't!" she cried. "Don't do this! We can work it out!"

He turned away from her and found himself staring into the

glass-shard face of Jesus, his twisted body writhing in pain on the cross, backlit by the burning lights of the parking lot.

At this moment, he knew without a doubt, he was losing everything. Everything.

. . .

"No, you're right," Bishop Hovey was saying. "I don't need to know the details. But are you sure you're doing the right thing?"

"Yes," Father David replied evenly.

"Have you considered accessing our Employee Assistance Program? They're very good, I'm told. And it's totally discreet. I could get Judy to give you the number."

"No, I think I'm doing the right thing," Father David replied.

"I mean, David," the bishop persisted, "the two of you are going to have to work this out someday, somehow."

"I know that," Father David replied.

"I don't want to tell you what to do, David. But this just doesn't feel right."

"Bishop Hovey?" Father David struggled to contain the quivering in his chin as he considered what he was about to say. "I almost hit her," he said, his voice breaking. He looked away, holding back tears.

"Okay," Bishop Hovey said. "Okay." He leaned forward across the coffee table and patted Father David on the knee. "It'll be okay. You'll work it out, I'm sure."

The bishop rose and returned to his desk. "Well, since you called this morning I've been able to find a number of interesting possibilities." He shuffled through some papers on his desk. "The thing is, there's nothing here, nothing close by. But I think you aren't looking for something close, are you? So I've called Doug Long. He was a classmate of mine. His diocese takes in Vancouver Island and the Gulf Islands. He's been having trouble filling an interim position in a relatively remote part of the Island, up the coast."

Bishop Hovey found the paper he was looking for and held it up to the light, inspecting it as if it might contain secret writing. "Have you heard of the Pacific Rim National Park? Well, it's the parish of Tofino and — I don't know how to pronounce this — Uclueclic? Ucuelic? Apparently they're the two coastal communities at either end of the park. He thinks he can have the position filled by the spring, but he needs someone to move in and take services till then. It's six months, David. And it's the other side of the country. I'm not sure we could do any better, if you really think that's what you want."

Father David's heart was pounding. His parachute was gaining definable features. He had only to take the leap. "Vancouver Island?" he mused to himself. But the alternative was unthinkable. He had not been able to talk to Beverley since their conversation in the church last night. He had not been able to look at her. Eventually she had left. He had spent the night at the church, praying and wrestling with what all these new revelations might mean. But his brain kept short-circuiting. He couldn't make sense of it. All he could think of was getting away, getting far away. Even now that pull was too strong to resist.

"How would it work?" Father David asked.

"If you could get yourself out there within the next week or so, you could start the first of October. There's a rectory in Uclueclet, Ucuelit — whatever — that's partially furnished; you could live there; and Doug would pay you a living allowance of $1,000 a month. We would continue your salary here so that

Beverley and the kids would be looked after. I'd have Barbara take your services at Holy Cross this Sunday; she would read a pastoral letter from me, explaining you are on stress leave for six months. They don't need to know anything else, though it would be a good idea for you to say something to your wardens before you go."

"Why would it have to be Barbara?" Father David asked.

"She's your regional dean, David," the bishop replied. "She can handle it."

They fell silent for a few moments.

"So?" The bishop was ready to wind up the deal.

"All right," Father David said.

"I'll call him back. But you're to call him yourself when you get there." He wrote down the number on a piece of paper. The bishop looked across at Father David. "So, you're sure about this?" the bishop asked again.

Father David nodded.

"Here, then take this." The bishop went to the closet that held his vestments. He groped far back on the top shelf and brought out a liquor bottle. "This was a gift to me. But I don't drink scotch. You're not a drinker either, are you? Well, here. Apparently it's pretty good. It's not for the road. It's for whenever you need it. And, David, at some point I sense you're going to need it."

David took the bottle from the bishop. The unadorned black and white label said it was Laphroig, sixteen years old, a single malt whiskey from the Isle of Skye. He had almost no idea what any of that meant.

"Sorry I don't have a bag or anything for you to take that in," the bishop said.

"Bishop?" Father David said, rising to his feet.

"David, this once, couldn't you just call me 'Jim'?" the bishop said.

"No, I'm sorry," Father David replied, "I couldn't. Bishop Hovey — thanks."

"Okay," Bishop Hovey said. "Let me know how things go. And don't worry. I'll look in on Beverley."

As Father David left the bishop's office and made his way through the little maze of secretaries' workstations in the outer office, he knew he must appear quite a sight. His eyes were red and swollen, his clothes had been slept in, and he gripped in his hand a bottle of whiskey. But this was only one of several hurdles to be faced, he knew, so he had better just plant one foot in front of the other. He left the building without looking up.

The next hurdle was to get himself a car. He and Beverley had only one between them, but it was not thoughtfulness that prompted him to seek out his own transportation; he didn't want to have to negotiate with her about anything. He just wanted to leave.

So his next appointment was with Harv, his sister Paula's husband. He was an auto wholesaler, a broker of trade-ins before they got to the used car lots.

"Christ, David," he said as he rose to meet him at his office, thick and bulky behind his enormous walrus moustache. "You look like hell! What's going on?"

Father David didn't want to talk about it. He just wanted to buy a car. Cheap.

"How cheap?" Harv wanted to know.

"Three thousand dollars?" Father David replied.

"That's not a lot, David. What's it for? Is this, like, a second vehicle for Bev? For groceries, running round the city, that sort of thing?"

That was as good an explanation as any, Father David thought; so he nodded. Harv scratched his head but was soon on the phone, turning up an old model Ford Escort wagon. Not a lot of pep, but good for groceries, he said. Did he want to go see it?

No, that would not be necessary, Father David said. He asked when it might be ready, later that day perhaps? That was a stretch, Harv answered. But if they got all the paperwork done now, he could have it by tomorrow.

"You sure you're okay?" Harv asked as they rose and shook hands.

With those arrangements now completed, Father David had to reconcile himself with returning to the house to pack. He didn't want to deal with Beverley, this being the most formidable hurdle of all. But on the other side lay some promise of relief, some vague liberation, and this next step was necessary. So he drove home, plotting out what he would need to pack.

He made it to the study before Beverley realized he was home. She came and stood in the doorway as he began placing books in a cardboard carton.

"David, can we talk about this?" she said. "We need to talk!"

"No," he said, without looking up.

"Well, what are you doing? Are you leaving?" she was sounding angry. "Just tell me what you're doing, David."

"I'm going away for a while," he said. From his crouched position he turned his body toward her but still did not look up. "I'm taking an interim ministry somewhere. You'll get my paycheque."

Beverley was incredulous. "You're leaving the parish? David, I can't believe this! You're leaving?"

"It's only a leave of absence," he replied, glancing quickly up at her. "I'm not leaving the parish."

"Why? Why, David?" she pressed him. "You don't think we can work this out? I don't believe this!" She stormed out of the room. He could hear her pacing the kitchen, throwing utensils into the sink.

He continued placing books in a second carton, his mind racing. He'd need his twelve-volume biblical commentary, though that would take up a full carton itself. And he'd need some of his church history texts, and also his pastoral theology. His other reference books — *The Oxford Dictionary of the Christian Church*, *Encyclopaedia of Theology*, and *Bible Atlas* — these he'd have to pick up from his office. He could hear Beverley building up a head of steam in the kitchen. She returned to the doorway.

"Well ... were you going to tell Paul and Catherine?" she demanded. "Or were you just going to walk out? Is this how we're going to deal with this? I'm so sorry I said anything to you. I thought we could work this through. I thought maybe we loved each other that much. Well, I guess not! You're just going to walk away! Great! Just great, David!"

He steeled himself as he rose to his feet, taking up a carton in his arms. He walked past her. He didn't want to get too close; this could get physical, he thought. Just keep moving, he told himself, placing the carton by the back door. He climbed the stairs to their bedroom, two steps at a time, and began pulling clothes from his dresser drawers. Beverley followed him.

"I told you I was sorry," she said, growing frantic. "I told you it was a mistake. So what's changed? What is it we can't talk about? Have you never made a mistake? I made a mistake, all right? So what's the problem?"

He turned to face her. Without warning, a legion of pent-up demons released itself, spewing across the room. "IT'S EVERY-THING!" he screamed at her, his face contorting, spittle spraying from his mouth. "IT'S EVERYTHING! IT'S NOT JUST YOU! IT'S EVERYTHING!" He sat back onto the bed, shaking, throwing his face into his hands. "God!" he said, sobbing. "It's just everything, okay?"

"Okay," she said carefully, backing slowly out of the doorway. "Okay. But, David, you have to tell us what you're doing. And you have to talk to the kids."

He nodded, his face still in his hands.

Paul and Catherine were alarmed before their father said a thing. They had never seen him like this. He had been angry before, and depressed. But this was something else. This was frightening.

Beverly had called the two into the living-room after they arrived home from school. Father David was standing by the fireplace. Beverley said simply that their father had something to tell them. Paul sat down on the couch, his face expressionless. Catherine stood behind him, her hands gripping the back of the couch. Beverley sat leaning forward on a chair between David and their children.

"Some things have happened," he began. "Your mother and I are going through something, and I have to go away for a little while. Only a few months ...."

"A few *months*?!" Catherine exclaimed. "Why a few months?"

"I just ..." Father David tried to clear his mind. "I just need to go away, okay? I can't explain it. I'm going to take an interim ministry someplace where I can be alone. I've got to work some things out."

"*Where?*" Catherine demanded, getting shrill.

Father David took a deep breath. "British Columbia," he said.

Beverley's jaw dropped. "British Columbia?!" she said. "David!"

Catherine ran over to her mother and broke down, falling at her feet and sobbing into her lap. Paul's eyes dropped to the carpet.

"I'm ... I'm sorry," Father David tried to say. "This is nothing you've done. I just need to work it out. By myself."

"But why British Columbia, David?" Beverley asked him.

"Will you be coming back, Dad?" Paul asked, looking directly at his father.

"Of course." Father David tried to sound firm, but his attempt failed.

Paul got up and left the room. Catherine and her mother were both crying now. "Why is he doing this?" Catherine was asking. "Why?" Beverley held her daughter to her, stroking her hair.

"I'm sorry," Father David said. "I'll write. I'll phone. It'll be ...." His voice trailed off.

A car horn blew from the driveway. "That's my ride," he said. He took a step toward Beverley and Catherine. But Beverley's eyes narrowed at his approach. *Bastard!* she mouthed over top of Catherine's head. So he turned and left.

· · ·

The taxi took Father David to his mother's house, where he would spend the night. This would be the last hurdle. Soon there would be no turning back.

As he lifted his suitcase and his cartons of books from the trunk of the cab, piling them on the curb, he wondered what sort of reception he would receive from his mother. He paid the driver and turned to face the house. She was already standing in the doorway.

He greeted her with a kiss on the cheek. She moved back into the house as he made several trips from the curb to the vestibule.

"Do you want a cup of tea?" she asked him, when the last carton was brought in and he had closed the front door.

"Thank you, Mother," he replied, taking off his coat and wandering into the living-room. He was still feeling shaky from the scene he had left at home, and was not anxious to open the whole subject again. She did not try to start a conversation with him from the kitchen — it had always been a rule in their house not to talk between rooms. But there seemed something deliberate in her leaving him alone while the tea was made.

This had become a familiar house to Father David, though he had never lived in it himself. It was the house she had bought with the insurance money when his father died, twenty years ago. David's father, Franklin Corcoran, had been a parish priest, and Father David had grown up in a series of draughty rectories. So had his mother, Lucille, whose own father had been a priest, and then a bishop. She had no intention, when the opportunity arose, of cheating herself out of a proper home, this small but stately bungalow set on a winding tree-lined street in Leaside, a pre-war Toronto suburb. She had lived comfortably since Franklin had died of a heart attack, in his study, while preparing his Christmas sermons.

It had been a shock, of course. He had been so vital and alive right up to the moment of his death. But his passing also became a source of liberation for Lucille. After a period of mourning, it seemed that she began to blossom. Her clothing became, if anything, more colourful, more cosmopolitan. She began moving in an active social circle of widows and couples her age, and appeared, over the years, actually to be growing younger.

She attended the local Anglican church, making sandwiches or baking tarts when called upon by the ACW. But she kept her distance, and joined no committees or guilds. Much to Father David's frustration, she did not have an opinion on the present rector, and seemed to be oblivious to the various tensions and problems with which the parish was known to be plagued. She had managed somehow to rise above it.

If her husband's death had released her from the role of dutiful rector's wife, it also gave her a new perspective on her grown children. They were living their own lives now, making their own decisions. She was no longer required to will them through each new phase of their lives. She could now begin willing herself through her own. As she was able, she went on cruises and signed up for courses and attended symphony orchestra concerts.

So when she asked Father David about his plans, she was interested, but not as a mother who felt she had to interfere to set things right. She was interested as one adult to another. As she set the tray on the coffee table before them, she simply wanted to know his plans.

"Well," Father David began. "I've accepted an interim ministry. It's in British Columbia." He looked over at her for a reaction. Seeing none, he continued, "Vancouver Island, actually. It's for six months. I hope we'll have figured some things out by then."

"What things, David?" she asked him, handing him his cup of tea.

"Things. I don't know. Beverley and I seem to be going through something right now, I don't know what it is. I don't know, Mother. Everything just seems so confusing."

"And Beverley?" she asked. "What does she say about this ... separation?"

Father David frowned. He put his tea cup down. "It's not good, Mother. She's not very happy about it. Neither are Paul and Catherine. They think ... they think I'm running away or something."

"Are you, David?" she asked him. "Are you running away?"

He felt his emotions rising to the surface again. But she did not look away. He struggled to gain control of his cursed quivering chin and to hold back the tears that were welling in his eyes. He tried to speak, but couldn't. She had her answer.

"You know, David," she said pensively, "you were always such a serious child. I used to call you my 'little man.' You always wanted to know what was expected of you, and then you tried to do just that. You wanted to please everyone. And you got ever so mad if you were playing a game with your friends and they didn't play by the rules. It used to make me feel sad for you. You seemed such a lonely little boy. Like your father, in some ways."

She sipped at her tea, placing the cup back on the saucer she held in her hand. "You won't know this, I suppose," she said, looking amused. "But since your father died, I have had several suitors."

Father David looked at her, surprised.

"It's true," she said with a smile. "And not just two."

"They wanted to marry you?" he said.

"Is that so hard to believe?" she asked.

"No. Not at all, really," he said. "I just never really thought about it."

Lucille smiled again, nodding slightly. "Well, it's true. But I didn't want to get married again. Once was enough. I loved your father. He was good to me and good to you and Paula. There are days I miss him terribly. But I don't miss being married. I don't know if you can understand that. While we were married, it would never have occurred to me to leave your father. I was happy, as far as I could tell. And besides, there simply wasn't the time to think about it. But when he died, I guess I just didn't want to have to work so hard again."

Father David thought about this for a moment. "Why are you telling me this?" he asked.

"I don't know," she said. "But do you want to know what I think? I think this plan of yours is not about you and Beverley. I don't think it's about your marriage. I think it's about you. I might wish you didn't have to do this — I mean, poor Beverley. And the children ...." She shook her head. "But I don't suppose at this stage there is any other way." She looked at him. "So you just do what you have to do."

Father David was confused by her words. But he raised his eyes to hers. "Thank you, Mother," he said.

"Well, I'll get supper started," she said, rising. As she carried the tray into the kitchen she called over her shoulder, "You should phone your sister. She's worried about you."

That night, settling deep into the soft mattress of the single bed in the guest room, Father David slept soundly. And as he slept, he dreamed.

It was the dead of night. Silhouettes of winter trees framed the hillside, their bare branches swaying in a soundless wind. His mother, wearing an apron, stood beneath one of those trees, waiting for him. As he approached he saw that they were in a cemetery, a gothic cemetery with tall monuments surrounded by low wrought iron fences. She watched him as he made his way between the headstones and the fresh mounds of earth. He felt frightened, but her presence strengthened him for what he had to do.

He arrived at an old grave site, unmarked and set with concrete walls deep into the ground, like a large bathtub. He climbed down into it. It was larger than he expected. At one end, where the drain should be, was a small door-like contraption. He had to turn a handle to remove the door. It exposed a deep hole containing a series of similar contraptions. Removing each one in turn, he came finally to a small tin. He reached down, grasped it by a handle on the lid, and hauled it all the way up from the bottom. Peeling back the lid, he saw a moist living substance, like pressed ham. He knew it to be the heart of a great and revered saint. A tiny fork, concealed inside the lid, permitted him to withdraw one squared piece that had been cut the length of the heart. It slid out easily.

Father David awoke with a start. The sun was rising. It was time to leave.

# Chapter Two

Mid-morning, Harv brought the new car around. He asked what Father David thought of her. The Ford Escort wagon was a metallic baby blue, but Father David didn't care about its aesthetics. It had almost 200,000 km on it, but that kind of number didn't mean much to Father David. So he said it looked fine.

He immediately set to filling the wagon with his belongings. He had been up and out early, using his mother's car, taking what he needed from his office before Margaret got in. He left a note for her, trying to explain what was happening. But he knew there was no way she, or anyone else, would understand. He would just have to leave a few loose ends, though this was so unlike him. The bishop would be making some sort of provision for Sunday supply, so in a matter of weeks they would have moved on without him anyway.

He wasn't in a mood to chat. So he gave his full attention to packing the car, turning his back on his mother and his brother-in-law as they stood by the curb, watching him. He did not wish to endure Harv's dismissive smirks, especially as it was now plainly evident that he himself had lied the previous day, suggesting the car had been for Beverley. But what did it matter now? In half an hour he would be on his way. He trained his mind on the task at hand.

The cartons of books fit easily into the back, though they didn't leave room for much else. He stuffed his suitcase into the space behind the passenger seat, and laid out his robes carefully across the back seat. At the foot of the passenger's seat he placed his boots and his duffel coat. On the seat itself he placed a road map of Canada he had bought earlier that morning. Overhead, on the under side of the visor, he found a place for a small pad of paper, a few pencils, and a thin emergency flashlight.

He placed the requisite car registration and insurance forms in the glove compartment, closed it up tight, and sat for a moment behind the wheel. It would be courteous to offer Harv a ride back to his office, but he was beyond courtesy now. He rose from the wheel, kissed his mother on the cheek, asking, as he did, if she would mind returning Harv to his office. He shook Harv's large hand and thanked him for helping him out.

Then he started the car, waved, and pulled away. Harv had already turned toward the house by the time Father David checked the rear-view mirror. But his mother remained at the curb, watching him go.

The highway was busy with crosstown traffic. Father David slid in and out of lanes, as he made his way toward the northbound turn-off that, in his mind, would launch him on his journey. He knew there were thoughts to be thought — bad thoughts — about his leaving Beverley and the kids, about walking out on his parish on such short notice, about doing something so reckless he would surely pay for it one way or another the rest of his life. But there would be time for those thoughts later. For now, an intoxicating excitement overruled everything else. He felt almost giddy. He was on his way. He didn't know where he was going, exactly, but he was finally on his way.

As he turned onto the northbound highway, he thought of all the school children who at this moment were sitting at their desks in classrooms all across the city. He thought of office workers at their workstations or in their windowless cubicles. He thought of the snarled traffic he was leaving behind. He thought of Beverley who would be ... what? *No, don't go there!* he reprimanded himself.

He drove on, as the apartment complexes and industrial parks at the edge of the city gave way to tracts of new suburban development, curbed roads and stooping street lamps appearing in the midst of empty fields like a mirage, surrounded by dirt and swept by dust. Just beyond the city's grasp, he surveyed the beginnings of open farmland, with its rows and rows of feed corn swaying dryly beneath a cloudless blue sky. Tall maple trees, their dying leaves turned brilliant red and gold, lit up the wood lots.

He knew this part of the road well. It was the way to his old parish of St. Jude's. He told himself to be sure to give a nod in its direction when he passed the turn-off, to acknowledge the honest farming community that had informed those early years of his ministry. But he was well passed it when he finally remembered, and it was too late.

As the highway began taking him into Canadian shield country, with its rocky outcrops and bent coniferous trees, Father David was amazed at the excellent time he was making. He could drive all day, he thought, and into the night too. He was being propelled by more than the gas in his tank. "I'm travelling on a wing and a prayer," he said out loud, and the sound of it pleased him.

It was not until he had left behind the familiar signs of cottage country — the numbered county roads, the hamburger joints, the gravel turn-offs — that the enormous extent of his journey began to dawn on him. He had travelled in his life. But he had only ever travelled east, which meant he had only ever travelled *back*.

In the summer before he was to begin divinity school, Father David had gone alone to Britain. It turned out to be a "family roots" tour, taken over by relatives so pleased at last to meet one of Frederick and Lucille's children. He was the first of the Canadian relatives to visit. So he stayed in the homes of distant aunts and even more distant cousins several times removed. They would have it no other way. They took him on tours, extravagant outings that required hours of preparation to drive a mere ten miles to sit in a tea shop overlooking a gray overcast beach, or to buy ice cream and post cards from a vendor's stand beside a misty field, some derelict abbey way off in the distance. His relatives passed him among themselves, countering every suggestion he made for something he might like to see on his own with a cheery, "We'll make a day of it then."

So he had seen the requisite sights — the crumbling remains of Hadrian's Wall, the crowded Tower, the tomb- and plaque-lined cathedrals. But the memories that predominated were of sitting around kitchen tables, sitting in back seats of cars, sitting in stuffy parlours, sitting around tiny pub tables, drinking endless cups of tea and draft beer, all the while draining the very dregs of small talk, trying to patch up the tenuous connections since his parents' departure twenty-five years ago. It was not like heading out; it was like going home. And it helped Father David appreciate all the reasons his parents might have left.

Israel had been more of an adventure, but it was a journey even farther east, and even farther into the past. He and Beverley had gone the spring after they had been married, a kind of belated honeymoon. They went on a guided tour that was filled with older people, not unlike the aunts and uncles he had left in Britain, who fawned over the newly-weds — a young priest, no less, and his bride who used to be a nun, don't you know. It seemed so romantic to them all, and they teased the couple mercilessly.

Still, the locations they visited were exotic: the bright turquoise hews of the Mediterranean; the lush Jordan River valley (and here, the "very spot" where our Lord was baptized by John); the fishermen, after all these generations, still plying the waters of the Galilean Sea; the wild and formidable desert spreading out from the salt-rimmed shores of the Dead Sea; and then the teeming city of Jerusalem, with the magnificent Dome of the Rock overlooking the Kedron Valley, and the maze of streets with shops and crowds, here and there signs indicating stations on the Via Dolorosa, the Way of Sorrows. It was thrilling, and the guide was forever making the biblical connections to places Father David had heard and read about all his life, places he had imagined, but never quite like this. It was a journey back to his more distant roots, a spiritual home-coming of sorts.

But now this — this was entirely different. He had never before ventured west. Nor had members of his family. It was the open way, the undiscovered land, the uncharted future, as it had been to countless pioneers far more rugged than he. He had no relatives west of Toronto, and he himself had never been north of Parry Sound. He had already passed that by now; the road signs had begun counting down the mileage to Sudbury, the next major destination. As he continued rolling northward, there were fewer and fewer cars on the road. He was entering new and unfamiliar territory.

At Sudbury he decided to stop. It was late afternoon. The car needed gassing up, and he was starting to feel pretty empty himself. A garish strip of fast food outlets was mildly reassuring, not unlike some of the less attractive parts of his own parish. So he entered under the familiar sign of the bucket and found an empty spot by the window. The hard moulded seat was attached by a bar to its matching table, part of an overall design to get him in and back out again quickly, "fast food" having less to do with the time of preparation than the time allotted for eating.

He tried to take some measure of comfort from the fatty chicken, the greasy fries, and the watered-down pop. The Israelites had been given manna in the morning, quails in the evening; this, he ventured, might be the sad modern day equivalent. He filled up the car and was soon on his way again, following the sun as it declined ahead of him in the western sky.

A couple of hours out of Sudbury, the sun now low on the horizon, a rosy splash radiating from behind a bank of clouds, Father David could feel his bowels stirring within him. The quail and the manna were not sitting well. On this stretch of the journey he had grown quiet, his random thoughts languidly turning up and over before giving way, each to the next. But now he grew focused on something else that seemed to be turning up and over. He'd better stop soon.

He was on a gently curving stretch of highway, bordered on his right by an irregular string of tall willows, on his left by the North Channel of Lake Huron. It was pretty, but it offered little by way of rest stops. He was approaching Sault Ste. Marie, he knew, where the neon lights would draw weary travellers to the same predictable fast food chains and economy motels. They promised only bland familiarity, not quality. His body felt the truth of this acutely now.

He might not make it that far, he found himself thinking, as he calculated the mileage from the billboard advertising. His insides were gurgling, giving voice to a roiling mass of half-digested chicken and fries that was flowing, chamber by chamber, down to the dark sewers below. He was going to have to pull over, whether a service station appeared or not.

But he rounded a curve and saw up ahead a hand-marked

sandwich-board sign with an arrow pointing to a gas station selling "CHEEP GAS." He anticipated the driveway by several feet, bouncing through the edge of a shallow ditch and lurching up to the side of the building.

Leaving the car running, he bolted for the washroom door. It was locked. He tried the women's. It was locked as well. He raced around to the front door which opened into an empty grease-smeared office lined by calendars displaying half-naked women. An inside door led to the repair bay. Clenching pelvic muscles he had not exercised in years, he thrust his head into the bay.

"I need the key to the washroom!" he called out. "Quite badly, actually!"

After an agonizingly long moment, a voice called back, "It's hanging by the door!"

Father David made a grab for it and rushed back round the corner. Fumbling frantically, he got the key into the lock, turned it and burst into the dank washroom, just in time. Relieved, he sat in the dark, catching his breath. The blood had drained from his face, leaving him cold and clammy. He began to shiver. He leaned forward and pressed his forehead against the cold edge of the porcelain sink. *Oh, God,* he whispered to himself, shaking his head.

He waited until he felt steady enough. Then he rose, found the light switch, returned the key, and made his way back to the car. It was still running, making a strange but pronounced ticking sound he had not noticed before. He put the car in gear, and headed back onto the highway.

It was dark now. As he approached the outer ring of the Sault, the city's lights beckoned just as he had imagined them. But he chose to drive on, following instead the signs for Wawa. The thought of stopping, of taking a motel room, of sitting alone in front of a fuzzy television screen — this was less bearable than the thought of pressing on, though the springs in the driver's seat were rising up now to greet him in new and tender places. He adjusted his position, with no effect.

His car was one of the few heading north. He saw signs advertising the Agawa Canyon and its spectacular fall-colour train excursion. By driving at night he would be missing this natural wonder, missing what many had described as awe-inspiring: the deep-cut valleys exploding in fall splendour, the sudden trestle bridges, the craggy outcrops of Canadian shield.

But this was not a sight-seeing tour. It was ... well, what was it? A journey of discovery, he told himself, a spiritual pilgrimage, a ... a cowardly escape; that's what it was! He was running away. He knew it. But he also knew that he was not able to stop himself. Even now, as the headlights probed deeper into the lonely night, and as the racing yellow line measured out the distance between himself and home, he knew he could not turn around. Wherever it led, this road, for the time being, was one-way. Though the ticking sound from the engine did seem to be getting worse.

Somewhere south of Wawa his distracted stream-of-consciousness was shattered when a long-legged animal slunk past the edge of his headlights back into the darkness. He fancied that it had been a timber wolf, though it might have been a dog. He told himself he was entering the wild Canadian northland, and the thought excited him.

It was past midnight when Father David pulled off the road for gas in Wawa. His joints were aching, and his eyes were feeling strained. Still, he could not reconcile himself with the thought of a lumpy bed in a bad motel. But it was more than that: he could not reconcile himself with the thought of staring into a mirror and facing whatever it was he thought he was doing. He brushed aside the mental picture of Beverley and Catherine, huddled together in the chair in their living-room, and of Paul, looking straight ahead, asking if he were coming back. Father David bought himself a pop and a chocolate bar, and pressed on into the night.

The drive became dreamlike after that, mile after mile, coasting down the long hills, dragging slow motion up the other sides, the engine tick-tick-ticking, the shadowy tree line sailing past, sometimes opening to vistas that were themselves swallowed up by the darkness. As he grew more and more fatigued, he felt more numb than sleepy. He permitted himself thoughts of home now, for they failed to rouse in him any emotions whatsoever. Nor were his frail rationalizations worthy of cross-examination, for they flowed along in a ceaseless stream of images, unconnected and imprecise.

It was like a drug, this endless highway. He could command the wheel and keep the car on the road almost without effort, and certainly without thought, allowing his mind to wander at will. The car simply carried itself along, now whizzing down long hills, the speedometer coaxed to its upper range, now chugging up the next — ticka-ticka-ticka-ticka — requiring only that Father David keep his foot wedged sideways on the gas pedal, his eyes resting vaguely on the two elliptical circles of light that, moment by moment, delivered him to his unknown future.

Hours later, he slipped into Thunder Bay just as the city was beginning to stir beneath a blanket of wet darkness, a heavy dew having formed in the night. He felt the pre-dawn chill when he stopped for a coffee and a muffin at an all-night doughnut shop, its early morning customers shuffling silently up to the counter, uttering their first words of the day, like mantras: "Large, double-double." "Medium, with milk."

Father David felt tired now. He sipped at the coffee, the steam curling up into his face from the hole in the lid, as he followed the signs that led him through the city and out the other side. The sky was lightening in his rear-view mirror. It was time now, he realized.

Without a struggle, he pulled off the road at a campground at Kakabeka Falls, parking the car adjacent to the little warden's booth at the entrance. He felt for the lever down at the base of his seat, pushing the seat back with his head until he was more or less reclined. Bunching up his sweater for a pillow, and spreading out his duffel coat on top of him for a blanket, he twisted his body sideways, pressed his cheek into the headrest, and fell asleep.

. . .

He awoke several hours later. The sun was up but still low in the east. There was activity now at the warden's station. Through the narrow slits of his eyelids Father David could make out a couple of recreational vehicles pulled up to the window, checking out. His eyes felt dry and irritated; so he closed them tight as he lay still, allowing his breathing to catch up with the rest of his body as it awoke, registering an ache in his lower back and cramps in his joints, the result of having remained too long in the same position.

Finally he rubbed his eyes, forced himself to sit up and look out onto this new day, and climbed out of the car. It was a crisp clear morning, the dew still thick and shimmering on the ground. He pulled his sweater over his head and slid his arms into the sleeves of his coat, wandering off to find a place to wash up.

His unshaven face looked drawn and haggard in the metal mirror above the row of stainless steel sinks in the campground's wash station. He found he didn't really mind the look, though he was usually scrupulous in his appearance. There was the possibility of a new man emerging here, if not exactly the cigarette ad variety, then certainly someone who appeared more "lived in" than his soft — and recently jowly — city persona. He splashed water on his face and brushed his teeth, deciding to remain, for the time being at least, unshaved.

He pulled back onto the highway, his body heavy and his head still in an early morning haze. The road sliced now through bush country, with long stretches between the towns. Father David realized with a start that he was still in the province of Ontario! Almost twenty-four hours had still not brought him to the province's western boundary. It would be another day's drive before he emerged onto the open prairie. What must that be like, he wondered.

Being a Toronto-centric Ontario boy, he had not often thought of the prairie provinces. His imagination had rarely carried him west of Mississauga. But he had studied the prairies in high school geography classes; he had watched recent television footage of the devastating floods around Winnipeg; he had read the complaints of prairie wheat farmers, demanding increased government support. Now he grew eager to find out what it was like to actually be *on* the prairies.

He stopped for a mid-morning break in Dryden, at a roadside diner that promised home-style cooking, a pulp and paper plant within sight, belching its plumes of sulphuric stench into the air. He had the Big Breakfast. It delivered what it promised: a lean steak with two eggs over easy, home fries and toast, and a bottomless cup of coffee, which the waitress kept filling without even asking.

Country and western music played from speakers hidden in the ceiling panels, real C&W, not the pop mulch that passed for "new country" music on the city stations. Like the strong bitter coffee, burning on its way down, this was music with a twang, music that stung at the same time that it soothed. Father David found himself mildly interested. The words were hard to make out, though he was pretty sure they were about someone who was hurtin'.

He paid up, leaving a two dollar tip for an eight dollar meal, gassed up, and was on the road again, his little engine tick-ticking constantly now, struggling against even the gentlest rise in the road.

His mind had grown clear again. He realized that he had succeeded in putting a safe distance between himself and whatever it was he was leaving behind. Cautiously, he began pulling the fragments of the last few days out from the shadows, as if they were old photographs strewn about the glove compartment. He reached in and took out the first that presented itself to him.

It was a picture of his empty church and of the stained glass windows telling the story of Jesus' Passion. He found he was not able to stick with any one thought for long — sustained theological reflection was too much work right now. But he turned over in his mind this new notion of Jesus losing everything on the cross. Of course, it could not be otherwise. If Jesus had fully expected that somehow the Father was going to spare him this pain, and this tragic end, his dying would not have been a real death; after all, which of us dies with such assurance? No, in the moments of his dying, Jesus — like us — must have felt that all was lost.

How we linger at the portal, Father David thought, terrified of letting go — he had seen it so many times at the bedside — knowing that in death there is no retrieval of things lost. Everything really *is* lost to us the moment we lean back, close our eyes and let go. Whatever else there is, waiting for us beyond the grave, it is something brand new, something not available to us here, not until the old is utterly relinquished.

So it must have been for Jesus. It must truly have seemed to him that he was losing everything, not only life as he knew it, but also his great mission, which was scattering to the four winds even as he hung on the cross, the disciples disappearing into the crowd.

Father David let the thought linger. It was starting to grow fuzzy, starting to slip from his grasp. Okay, he thought, just let it go. It's okay. Like death, there's nothing you can do but let it go — let it all go. If it has any truth it will return.

He stopped again in Kenora. It felt strangely familiar to him, this northern town set amid rocks and lakes, like some of the towns he knew in the Muskokas, but rougher around the edges. Some native men sat together on a park bench overlooking the river, one playing a guitar. At first Father David assumed they were drunk, like so many he had seen in the city parks. But they were not drunk. They were just enjoying one another's company over this sunny noon hour, making music and trading stories. It reminded him of bright fall days like this at college, when students would spread themselves out on the lawn in the quad under a cacophony of music blaring from stereo speakers propped in the open residence windows overhead. It represented a measure of freedom he had never allowed himself. He had always had something important to do.

As he carried on, the rocks and lakes soon gave way to lower deciduous groves — aspen mostly, the silver leaves trembling in the breeze — and to roadside scrub brush. The topography was changing, flattening out. The sky was opening up around him.

Soon after he passed the sign saying, "Welcome to Friendly Manitoba," the roadside trees vanished altogether, and he pulled out onto a flat limitless expanse. The flatness was oddly exhilarating to him, though at some darker level also disconcerting. He had never been surrounded by so much ... space!

He was suddenly reminded of a nightmare he had suffered as a young child, something he had not thought of for years. It was among his earliest memories. There were no characters in the dream, and there was certainly no plot. There was only the growing perception of a vast yawning emptiness opening up before him, like the screen of their old television set in its dying moments after it was turned off. Everything just went gray. Except, that is, for a tiny diminishing dot at the very centre of the screen.

David would watch that dot as it got smaller and smaller, as the surrounding grayness of the screen grew darker and darker, swallowing it up, until there was nothing, nothing at all but his own reflection staring back in the glass, nothing but the helpless sensation that he, little baby David, was drowning in the sea of his own expanding consciousness. His breathing would stop. Then he would suddenly gasp, sucking air into his tiny lungs, and wail with all his might into the dark night. Amazing, that he could recall all that now. And the sheer terror of it.

Without noticing it, Father David was speeding up, flowing along with the afternoon traffic bound for Winnipeg. He opened his window and stuck his elbow out into the breeze with an assumed nonchalance, as if he had driven this patch of road all his life, as if the world opening up before him was not, in some mysterious way, terrifying to him. But there was an autumn chill in the air, and after a few minutes he retrieved his arm and wound the window up again.

The road stretched on and on. He reached for another mental picture from the dark glove compartment of his mind. It was clericus. He smiled slightly, shaking his head with recognition. It was not so much that he didn't like his brother and sister clergy.

Well, okay, it *was* that he didn't like them. But that seemed so — he didn't know — petulant or something, something not worthy of him. Perhaps it was more that he just couldn't trust them. That had been his father's view.

Archdeacon Frederick Corcoran had not been a joiner. Otherwise, Father David was certain, his father would have been a bishop. He was hard-working and sincere, giving to his ministry whatever was required, which was just about everything. He had no life outside of the demands of his job and the obligations of his family. Father David had known his father only as the rector of large churches, with important people occupying specific pews, looking up at him as he preached.

His father worked for days on those sermons, locked up in his study, reading biblical passages from the original Greek and Hebrew, trying out sentences aloud before committing them to paper. Then, on Sunday mornings, those same sentences were lifted directly from the page and once again given voice, magnificent voice. His father was a good preacher.

But on more than one occasion Father David had heard his father complain to his mother about his colleagues. This one was lazy, that one was unscrupulous, the other one was ambitious. He had high standards, his father, and none of his ordained brethren seemed capable of measuring up.

Father David recognized those same feelings in himself about his own colleagues. Theirs was a high calling, after all. It was not good enough to approach one's ministry as if it were a career, climbing the ladder, telling people what they wanted to hear, ingratiating oneself to the rich and influential. His father never pandered to anyone. Father David admired that in him.

Yet his mother had found life with his father to be difficult. This was a new thought altogether. He wondered how he could have missed it. They had never fought; at least, he was unaware of it, if they had. They had had their disagreements, it was true, and he could remember his mother on one occasion crying softly in their bedroom. But his father had gone to her, and they had spoken together in hushed tones. Eventually they re-emerged and everything carried on as usual.

But the price for holding to one's principles is necessarily high. People may not like you. People may take advantage of you. People — even those closest to you — may tempt you to compromise. His father had not compromised. He had brought dignity and integrity to his ministry, and it spilled out into his family as well, into the orderliness of their day to day life, into their standards of honesty and hard work.

Sometimes, Father David now realized, he had felt sorry for his father. The man had had no friends but his mother. Father David couldn't remember him laughing very much. And he died far too young, before either he or Paula were launched into their adult lives, leaving something undone, something unsaid. Father David wondered now what that might be. What would he want to hear his father say to him, if he could? He allowed the thought to trail off as he adjusted his position on the hard seat.

Late in the afternoon, Winnipeg suddenly appeared to the north. From the bypassing ring road, the city rose up in the distance as a small cluster of skyscrapers and high-rise apartment buildings. He was sure that it was peopled, that Canada's Gateway to the West was all there, intact. But he wasn't about to deviate from his course to find out. He stopped only long enough to eat a limp Caesar salad and a dry piece of garlic bread from a gas station restaurant, and then he drove on.

Again Father David found himself driving into the setting sun. He followed it as long as he could, along this open highway with its vast expanse of sky in all directions. But the sun beat him to the horizon and, after a torrid sky-lit farewell, Father

David was once again left alone in the dark. Mile after mile, hour after hour, he wedged his foot onto the gas pedal and plunged deeper into the night.

As midnight approached with not another vehicle in sight, Father David pulled over to stretch his legs. He gathered his duffel coat around his shoulders as he wandered down toward the ditch. A split railed fence marked the edge of a farmer's field that stretched off into the darkness. The farmhouse was nowhere in sight. Leaning on the fence, he gazed up at the night sky, pulsing with stars.

In the distance he heard a strange sound, like the humming of power lines when they are wet with snow. How odd, he thought; the sky was dry and cloudless. He relieved himself in the tall grass, looking furtively up and down the highway for headlights. He walked back to the car and stood by the driver's door. His breath misted up in front of his face. Then in the corner of his eye he saw a flash off to the north. Descending from a great height, there danced an impossible curtain of shimmering green, unlike anything he had ever seen before.

He wondered if it might be the reflection of a town's lights. But this luminous display was too fluid, too heavenly, to be of any earthly origin. It was as if the angels were ascending and descending from their celestial home, ringed in radiant splendour, their tinted hues meeting and mingling like waves crossing and criss-crossing on a beach, casting hue upon hue, each one more brilliant than the last. The fantastic display turned suddenly red now, brilliant red, spreading across the entire northern horizon. He could detect again a faint hissing, like the sound of the wind in the trees. But there was no wind; and there were no trees.

Father David held on to the roof of the car to keep his balance. He felt he might otherwise be lifted up to simply float away with the incredible wonder of this sight. He remained still for as long as he could, until the night chill entered his joints and he began to shiver. He climbed back into the car and, in his first real prayer since beginning his journey, whispered, "Thank you, Lord. I just want to thank you."

He put the car into gear and drove on to the first motel that displayed a vacancy sign. He pulled up, registered at the desk, found his room, and crawled into bed.

. . .

It was well into the morning when he woke. The motel provided a continental breakfast in the tiny lobby, which meant a pot of drip coffee and an open box of small sugar-dusted doughnuts. He ate three, gulping down the coffee from a Styrofoam cup. He was preparing to leave when a thought struck him. He rang the bell on the counter. A pleasant-looking middle-aged woman appeared. She might have been the same one who had been on duty the night before, but he couldn't remember.

"Is there a service station in town?" he said.

"You need gas or repairs?" she asked in return.

"I need to get something checked out, a sound coming from under the hood," he said.

"Then you want Al's," she said, and gave him directions.

"What town is this, by the way?" it suddenly occurred to him to ask.

She smiled, but it was a wry smile. "This is Grenfell, Saskatchewan," she said.

He thanked her, and left. He was in Saskatchewan.

Father David found Al in the service bay, a lanky humourless man wiping his hands on an oily rag as he stood, pensive, before an open hood. He appeared to be about Father David's age, but with the no-nonsense look of someone who had been around a lot longer.

Father David explained to him the "ticking" problem.

"How is she on pick-up?" Al asked.

Not very good, Father David explained, and it seemed to him it had been getting worse.

"Where you headed?" Al asked.

"British Columbia?" Father David answered, though he hadn't intended it to sound like a question.

Al took off his cap and scratched at his temple, running his hand around to the back of his head. He replaced his cap. "I don't think so," he said.

"You don't think so?" Father David asked.

"I don't think she's going to British Columbia," Al said, matter-of-factly. "I doubt she'll make it."

The problem, Al explained, was that it was a four-cylinder car that was probably running on only three cylinders. The reason for that, Al suspected, was a cracked cylinder head, a problem that was only going to get worse and that would be putting pressure on the other cylinders in the meantime. Father David could wind up with a two-cylinder car.

"I'm not sure I'd be wanting to drive through the mountains on two cylinders," Al concluded.

"Well, can you fix it?" Father David asked.

"Yup, I think so," Al replied.

"Great. So how long would that take, do you think?" Father David asked, feeling hopeful.

Al thought about it out loud. Today was Saturday (Father David had quite forgotten what day it was); he wouldn't get the parts until Monday, earliest; it would take the better part of a day, maybe a day and a half, to do the work; so, barring any unforeseen problems, maybe Wednesday. But you never know what you're going to find when you do a job like this. It could get pretty expensive.

How expensive, Father David wanted to know.

Again Al did his figuring out loud, naming all the parts and adding up the labour. "So that would be something close to two thousand dollars," he concluded. "If we don't find anything else," he added flatly.

Two thousand dollars! Father David let this sink in. He would have to use a credit card. But he and Beverley shared the account; so that would leave *her* having to figure out how to pay off *his* bill. This was not what he wanted.

And the timing, too — that would be a problem. Okay, Wednesday, Father David thought. Thursday to Calgary, Friday to Vancouver, Saturday to find his way onto the Island, Sunday to do the services — no, it wouldn't be enough time!

"I can't do it," he said. "I can't afford it, and I don't have the time. I have to get to a new job by the weekend."

The two fell silent.

"Okay," Al said finally. "Here's what I can do for you. I'll offer you a trade, a straight trade. You see that little number over there?" He nodded in the direction of an old compact, badly spray-painted a shocking lime green. The layered applications of bright paint were too thin in places to cover up the former dark colour of the car, resembling some sort of camouflage job gone terribly wrong. It looked more like a cartoon car than a real vehicle.

"That's a Chevy Sprint," Al said. "Ten years old. Over two hundred thousand clicks on it. It's not too peppy, but it'll get you to British Columbia. Meanwhile I can fix up your wagon here and sell it for my labour costs."

Father David felt he didn't have much else to barter with — well, nothing at all, in fact. So they shook hands, exchanged some paperwork, and within half an hour Father David was transferring his belongings from the Escort to the Sprint. The problem, he soon discovered, was that the Sprint, even with its hatchback door, had not even half the luggage space of the Escort wagon. He mentioned this to Al, who nodded without saying anything. The papers had already been signed.

He could fit his suitcase and robes in the back seat, as in the Escort, but there was room for only two cartons of books in the trunk. Father David had brought six! Oh, man! He closed his eyes. He just wanted the whole situation to blow away, standing here on this dirt lot in the middle of nowhere, the dry wind whipping up from across the open prairie, slapping him in his foolish face, half way to God knows where.

"Is there a church in town?" he asked Al, finally opening his eyes.

"Sure, several," Al said.

"How about an Anglican church?"

"No, I don't think there's one of those. How would United do?" Al asked.

"Oh, all right, that'll do," Father David answered, vexed. "Where do I find it?"

Father David removed his belongings and loaded the four extra cartons of books into the Sprint, filling the trunk and the back bench seat.

He trundled off to the United church. Finding no one there, he turned to what he assumed must be the manse next door. No one answered when he knocked, so he left the cartons piled up on the porch by the back door. He had nothing else to write on; so he wrote a note on the side of one of the cartons. It read:

My name is David Corcoran. I am an Anglican priest. I am on my way to Vancouver Island to start a new ministry, but my car broke down here in [he went back and scratched out *the last two words, unable to recall the name of the town]* and I have had to get another. But there isn't room for all my books. Would you be able to keep them for me until I return in six months or so? I would really appreciate it. I will phone you from my new *[he thought for a moment, trying to recall what they called it in the United Church]* pastoral charge when I get there. My thanks!

He returned to Al's, packed the rest of his stuff into the car, and headed back onto the highway. It was almost noon.

The Sprint represented a marvel in modern marketing. You think of a word like "sprint" and you think first of "speed." But that was not the defining characteristic of this little car, Father David soon learned. The defining characteristic was "short distance," the other half of the word's definition. Perhaps that explained the little green frog that was appliquéd to the corner of the driver's seat — a frog prince, no less, with a crown on its head — a symbol made all the more poignant by the car's new swampy colour.

The Frog Prince, as Father David dubbed his new acquisition, had almost no power at all. When Father David put his foot to the floor it produced only a *pffffft* sound and then a slow agonizing acceleration that, at best, only brought him up to speed with the flow of traffic. Passing another vehicle was out of the question. He had to settle for falling into line behind the sluggish transports and the careening camper trailers, biding his time until finally those vehicles left the road, giving him a brief open run — hence the "short distance" — up to the next slow-moving vehicle.

Fortunately the road was relatively straight, with few hills to climb. But the landscape did seem to be changing again. If Manitoba had been unremittingly flat and flaxen, southern

Saskatchewan was rolling and grassy. The sky was still open and vast, the distant horizon offering puffs of white cloud that vaporized by the time he thought he should have reached them. It made Father David feel that he had never really seen the horizon until this trip. In Ontario the skyline was forever etched in square buildings silhouetted against the sun or, in the country, by lone trees and rounded wood lots. Never had he actually experienced the horizon as a straight line — as, in fact, the slow distant curve of the earth.

But he did so now, humming along in his little green machine, the road ahead rising in hopes of meeting the sky, the sky never quite stooping low enough to fulfil the road's desire. It was a landscape that taught you to be patient, to just keep moving and not get too anxious, because some things may not come together any time soon, perhaps not even in a lifetime.

This is, of course, the natural pessimism of the farmer. Father David had encountered it among Ontario's dairy farmers, who didn't even have the false promise of such a big sky on which to pin their hopes. But, like people of the land everywhere, they had had to reckon with the fickle patterns of the weather, and even more, with the fickle world economy, in which they had no choice but to be small-bit players, mere dust particles in the wider scheme of things, blown and buffeted about by swirling winds over which they had no control. Every day they were reminded just *how* small and insignificant they were against the odds thrown up by these vast unpredictable forces.

No, the road and sky may *look* like they are destined to meet, but you would have to go a long way and wait a long time to see it, maybe forever. Better just attend to the chores, oil the machinery, do the books, keep the operation going. There's no promise that tomorrow will bring anything better than what we've got today. Get used to it.

Well, today *had* brought something better than yesterday, Father David mused — at least for Al. He got rid of a lime-green lemon that had been rusting on his lot! This had been his lucky day, yessiree-boy. Wait around long enough, bide your time, and one day some new sucker will pass through on his way to that false horizon, scattering in the dust his last few coins, all for Al to come along and pick up after him.

Father David's mood darkened as he thought just how ill-prepared he had been for this journey. Of *course,* he had been an easy mark. People can tell when you are at the edge. All it had taken was one thing to go wrong, one thing to fall out of place, and all of a sudden he was panicking, accepting a prognosis for his car when the guy hadn't even listened to the engine himself, for God's sake, being cornered into a deal for a car that was probably no better than the one he left behind. And he had NOT EVEN TAKEN IT FOR A TEST DRIVE! What an idiot! What an absolute idiot!

He thought then of the books — his books! His heart sank deeper still. Good God, what had he done? Those books were precious to him, every one: the biblical commentaries, the liturgy handbooks, the studies in systematic theology, the church-related dictionaries and encyclopaedias. He had chosen them precisely because he couldn't imagine doing his job without them. Now they sat in cardboard cartons abandoned, orphaned, on the back porch of a total stranger! It made him sick to think of it. He would have to call as soon as he arrived on the coast.

Father David wondered if this was how the Hebrews had felt in their wilderness wandering. So much had to be left behind. They ate on the road, or they didn't eat at all, figuring it out as they went along. But then, God was with them: a cloud by day, a fiery pillar by night. He would be hard-pressed to defend his own journey as having been God's idea to begin with. In fact, even as he had prayed in the church through that long fateful night, God had never really committed himself, one way or another. The only image Father David had — and it was certainly no consolation — was the anguished face of his Lord in sharp-edged stained glass.

So where *was* God in all of this? Was God leading him, making provision for him? Was this sad-eyed little excuse for a car really a gift from God? Or was it his, Father David's, just desserts for having done something rash and incredibly stupid? Where was providence in any of this?

He pulled over at a truck stop outside Regina for lunch. It was a large noisy place with the clashing of cutlery coming from the kitchen and cowboy music blaring from bad speakers, the base lines booming, severed from the tinnier upper sections. Conversation was loud and pervasive. He had almost to shout to give his order, sitting alone in a booth by the window.

If he drove through to Calgary, it would make for another very long day. He wasn't sure he was up to it. But tomorrow was Sunday, and he wanted to be somewhere he could find a church to go to. He unfolded his map on the table. He traced the road ahead with his finger, stopping two-thirds the distance between Regina and Calgary. Maybe Medicine Hat would be far enough. He folded up the map, taking care to maintain the original creases. The thought of the day's drive still ahead exhausted him. He felt stiff and achy. His tailbone was sore and his eyes were itchy.

The afternoon sun *seemed* friendly, beating down upon the car as Father David made his way westward. He reached for his clip-on sunglasses. But as he looked out on the world through the tinted light, he could feel himself relaxing, settling deeper into the driver's seat. He could feel its warmth, the warmth of his own body, the air around him matching the warmth of his skin, like a womb. He was growing sleepy. His joints and muscles just seemed to be letting go, pleading with him. "Oh, just a quick nap, *pleeease*," they seemed to be saying, "a few minutes, that would be all." But his mind would not give in.

He searched the radio for the loudest most obnoxious music he could find and turned it up. Somebody was screaming into a microphone against a rhythmic backdrop that sounded like a train crashing. He rolled his window all the way down and stuck his head out into the bracing breeze until his eyelids flapped. He tensed up one hand into a fist, then released it; then the other, and released it. He did the same, as best he could, with his toes. He rubbed his face, hard, getting some blood flowing. He readjusted his body in the seat, straightening his back. He drove on.

What do lesbians do anyway, he asked himself. It was more a dare than a question. Surely this would wake him up! He couldn't attach a face to the mental pictures that were summoned, not a familiar face anyway. He began imagining the possibilities, with and without skimpy costumes, with and without various "toys." He found himself getting aroused. Okay, now we were getting somewhere. But the steamy scenes that had begun rolling from the dark projection booth in the back of his mind were cunningly erotic, taking him farther than he had actually planned to go.

It was when he forced himself to think of Beverley, just Beverley alone, that his mind snapped back. He could not bring himself to think of her with Jill; so the film came to an end, the loose end slapping as it rolled to a stop.

This much was true, he knew: she *had* always been the adventurous one, the passionate one. He had envied her this. That passion was what had sustained him. Her love of life and of living flowed out from her into him. She was his life. This might be the closest he could come to understanding why he loved her. But somehow it hadn't been enough. Not for her. And, apparently, not for him either. Though, for the moment, that was as far as he dared to go.

. . .

It was a brilliant Alberta morning as Father David rose in his small room at the Highwayman Motor Hotel just outside Medicine Hat. He shaved and showered, the rumble of the occasional transport passing just outside his door. It was Sunday and he was feeling hopeful about the day, a day that would deliver him both to the Blessed Sacrament and to the Rocky Mountains!

He pulled on a black clerical shirt, poked the studs through the two slits in the neckband, and attached the stiff white collar around his neck. He buffed up his black patent leather shoes until they shone. At his wrists he inserted silver cufflinks, which had been his father's, a formal touch he reserved for Sundays. He slipped his arms into his black suit jacket, pulling at the cuffs as he studied himself in the mirror. He looked presentable for church.

The drive to Calgary was clear sailing along an open highway under the same expanse of blue that had accompanied him through the prairies. The pasture land and the fields of wheat stubble on either side of him were turning brown, but the bright sunlight was still able to eke from them glints of gold, hints of their former wind-blown glory. Putting behind him yesterday's darker moments, Father David was inclined to believe today that the trip was going rather well. He was making good time, he was being judicious with his money and, above all, he was enjoying the thought of actually doing something rash and adventurous. It was going to be a good day!

He didn't know Calgary's churches and had no personal connections there. So his strategy was simply to approach the city, get off the highway on the outskirts of town, and start cruising the larger streets and boulevards in search of one of those universally recognizable blue and red signs saying, "The Anglican Church Welcomes You." He was confident this would lead him to a church where, whatever they might do to butcher the liturgy, he could still receive the comfort and nurture of holy communion.

He pulled off the highway as planned, into an expanse of development spreading out from a city skyline that rose up in a little clump of tall buildings, like Oz, to the northwest of him. Beyond the city Father David could catch his first glimpse of the Rockies, their bluish form rising like a painted theatrical backdrop on the western horizon.

His first foray into the city led him smack into the middle of an industrial park, its winding streets and sprawling warehouses confusing his sense of direction. Round and round he went, coming back to the same intersection three times, and each time from a different direction! Finally he found his way out and pointed his car toward an older housing development that seemed to represent an outer ring of the city's core.

Just as he felt he was getting too close to downtown he saw the sign he was looking for and followed its direction down a narrow street to "The Church of the Holy Spirit (Anglican)," an old clapboard church that had recently distinguished its new life from its old with an idiosyncratic addition ballooning out at one end. The new addition conspired only to insult the building's traditional aesthetic, like attaching a clown's nose to a portrait of the Queen.

One entered the church at precisely the juncture where the old met the new, in a lobby that led you to the right into the old church — which Father David could see had been cleared of pews to serve now as the church hall — or to the left into the new worship space.

The service was already loudly in progress, and Father David was met at the door by a designated greeter, a pleasant-looking sixty-ish man with a wide toothless smile, clutching a bundle of pew bulletins that he had rolled up in his hand like a baton. He took a step toward Father David, taking in the clerical collar. His kindly face melted into a compassionate gaze that might otherwise have been reserved for the physically handicapped or for a member of a visible minority.

This was no church like any Father David had ever seen — and he had seen a few. The floor of the main seating area slanted down to the front like a movie theatre. Where the chancel should have been was a stage, overhung with theatrical spotlights and loudspeakers suspended from the ceiling. At stage left was a raised platform for the band, a seven-piece outfit that included a drummer, a bass player, an electric guitarist, a keyboard player surrounded by rising banks of digital sound equipment, and three upfront female vocalists, each clutching a hand-held microphone.

At stage right was a plexiglass pulpit with a small row of chairs set behind it. Three white-robed men — a priest and two assistants maybe — were on their feet, blissfully singing and clapping and swaying to the music, virtually dancing on the spot. Between them and the musicians, in the middle of the stage, but set back closer to the rear wall, was a large plexiglass table, evidently the altar. High above it, on the white plaster wall, the words of the song were being projected from an overhead projector that was fixed in its own space in the third row of seats, just in front of a wide sound board. "God is in this place," the congregation was singing over and over, "and we have been redeemed."

The joint, as they say, was jumping. Not only was the packed house on its feet, hands clapping or raised high above heads, voices shooting for the ceiling with unbridled praise, but some people were actually waving banners and flags as if it were a political rally. Children raced up and down the aisles pulling long streamers behind them.

For a moment Father David was not sure quite what to do. A few of the members of the congregation who were standing closest to the back acknowledged him with their eyes, noting the collar as they did, but they were too caught up in the worship themselves to extend an actual word of welcome to a stranger.

So he moved into an aisle seat in the back pew, the large clapping woman beside him catching him in the corner of her eye but stopping short of making eye contact. When she raised her hands in praise, he had to take a half step back out into the aisle to accommodate her. The song was winding up, and as the musicians extended the last chord, the guitar player strumming, the drummer doing a prolonged roll on his snare, the place dissolved into ejaculatory praise. "Thank you, Jesus!" people shouted. "Praise you, Lord!" others murmured beneath the din. Open palms rose into the air, waving like wheat in the wind.

A voice could now be heard over the sound system. "Oh, Jesus," it moaned plaintively. "We just want to thank you. We just praise your name, Lord. We give you the glory. We give you the glory." As the room began to settle, soothed now by the pastor's voice, he continued to speak aloud to God, in couplets: "We are not worthy, Lord, we are not worthy. But you are worthy, Lord, you are worthy. Of glory and praise, Lord, of glory and praise. Receive our prayer, O Lord, receive our prayer. Amen, amen."

All around Father David the congregation was joining in the amens, some speaking in a babbling flow of sounds that he figured must be glossolalia, speaking in tongues. Slowly they began to take their seats, the large woman beside him falling backward into the pew, her head raised, her eyes closed, still lost in wonder, love, and praise — leaving Father David no option but to wedge himself sideways into the tiny space that remained between her hips and the arm rest at the end of the pew.

The pastor continued to pray, thanking Jesus and asking for the guidance of the Holy Spirit for what he was about to say, asking for faithfulness to God's leading as they now broke open the word, the precious word, the eternal word, the divine word, the word of life. "We are not worthy," he again reminded Jesus, "but you are worthy. Now make us worthy, through your precious blood, make us worthy, Lord, to speak your word."

The pastor's words had a powerful hypnotic effect, Father David found, the repetition of sounds, the coupling of ideas, like poetry, like many of the psalms. It was artful, masterful. And now the pastor stood silently at the pulpit, gripping it with both hands, his face raised, his eyes closed, his breathing washing over the congregation in diminishing waves from the speakers high overhead. Until the room was absolutely still. Not a child called out, not a worshipper stirred. All was ready. He began his sermon.

It was not new, what the pastor had to say. Father David had heard it before, but not from an Anglican pulpit: the demise of the modern church with its shrinking membership and its accommodation to the ways of the world; the lack of moral fibre among its leaders, their faithlessness in the face of the devil's onslaughts; the church's slavish obedience to the tired traditions of the past; its hardening of heart to the new outpouring of God's Spirit.

It was, so far, less a sermon about the good news than about the bad news. But that was the point, Father David knew. Once you have convinced everyone of the problem, then of course you can prescribe the solution — which only the preacher possesses, he and his handful of loyal truth-seeking followers. None of this was shocking to Father David, nor even offensive really. It only bothered him that the sign had directed him to an Anglican church: this was, to all intents and purposes, not an Anglican church.

It hadn't occurred to him to get up and walk out. The pew bulletin promised that this was a service of Holy Communion, and he figured if he waited long enough they would finally get around to it. In the meantime this was sort of like religious entertainment, like television, but better. It was so unrecognizable from anything that he himself did on a Sunday morning that Father David found himself fascinated by it, in the way one is fascinated by an open sore or a sucking mosquito. You can't quite believe you're just sitting there, watching it.

But Father David began to notice something strange happening in the room. People were looking at him, taking sidelong glances. Even the large woman next to him shifted her weight away from him so as better to peer at him from the corner of her eye. He realized, as he looked down to the preacher, that people were just following the preacher's own gaze, which was leading them right back up to Father David. Seated demurely in the back row in his black suit and Roman collar, his shiny shoes and silver cuff links, he was attracting attention to himself, as if perhaps he were a spy sent by the bishop to scope out the place.

Meanwhile the preacher's sermon seemed stuck in a groove, his lilting sentences coming back time and again to the corruption of the church, to its grieving the Holy Spirit. And his eyes kept coming back to Father David, sitting there high at the back of the sacred theatre. More and more people began to pick up the vibe, casting a look over at the dark-clad figure, as if maybe *he* were that faithless church, as if *he* were its corruption, its apostasy.

Father David grew uncomfortable, readjusting himself in the pew. But it was no use. His presence there was quickly becoming untenable. He felt their stares, like scorn. Maybe God was in this place, but not the God that Father David knew, who was not a God of paranoia and of loathing, who was not a God of emotional manipulation. So, slowly, he rose from his seat. The entire room was watching him now. The preacher stopped. Colour rose to Father David's cheeks — he could feel it. He wanted to do something, say something. But instead he simply turned and went out through the door.

The greeter, on the other side, oblivious to the subtler dynamics happening inside the church itself, said to him as he brushed past, "I'm so sorry you have to go. I hope you'll come again. God bless you!" And he flashed him a broad toothless grin. Walking into the sunshine Father David could hear the preacher's voice over the sound system. "People," he was saying, "I think we need to stop and have a moment of prayer."

As Father David drove off, in search of an on-ramp to the highway, it was as if he was outside of himself, checking his own pulse for a reaction. He knew he should be furious, he should be outraged. But he felt ... almost nothing at all. It was all so surreal. It was like a movie, a bad western, where the law man walks into the saloon, sidles up to the bar, and orders a drink. The bartender begins to oblige but the clearing of a throat stops him in his tracks. The room falls silent. The crowd parts and there, at the end of a human corridor, hunched at a poker table, surrounded by dancing girls, a stogy at the corner of his mouth, is the fearsome One-eyed Jack. Now it becomes clear who owns this dust-ridden town. The law man won't be drinkin' here tonight.

Father David shook his head in disbelief. Back at clericus he had been attacked by the liberals; now he had been run out of town by the charismatics. "A plague on both your houses!" he said aloud. *Now* he could feel the anger rising.

He fumbled with his collar, with the tiny studs that held it in place, front and back, ripping it from his neck and throwing it onto the seat beside him. "A goddamned plague on both your houses!" he yelled. And he drove off toward the mountains, clouds gathering in the west beyond the snow-capped peaks.

. . .

It surprised Father David how suddenly the mountains rose up around him. As he left Calgary it still felt as if he were driving toward a painted backdrop stretched across the horizon. But the highway began pitching and rolling as the prairies folded into foothills, the mountains appearing and disappearing as he climbed hills and rounded sweeping curves. Then he rose over the brow of one final hill and found himself descending to the very foot of the mighty Canadian Rockies. They parted to receive him, unimaginable slabs of rock rising on both sides.

As he entered the mountains, passing the turn-offs for Canmore, he wondered if the residents of this town felt a bit claustrophobic or, at the very least, if they were intimidated by their massive mountainous guardians, looking down from all around them. Would it not be like having a team of suma wrestlers to watch over your children as they sleep, but then having to endure them hanging about all day, silent and sullen, menacing in their pure bulk? They're just too big to have in the house.

The toll booths at the entrance to Banff National Park presented him with a decision: was he going to stop in the park, for which he needed a permit, or was he driving through? It was still early afternoon. His destination was Kamloops, a mere four or five hours away, and he didn't see himself pressing on to Vancouver from there, if he arrived by supper time. So why not put in a little time in this picturesque world-famous mountain town? He could arrive in Kamloops after dark, still get a good night's sleep, and then complete the final leg of his journey, all the way to the coast, the next day. So he purchased a day pass and turned off the highway for the town centre.

The place was teeming with tourists. Oversized buses were pulled up in front of the lodges and motels that lined the main street leading into the heart of town. The sidewalks were crowded with clumps of walkers apparently intoxicated by the bracing mountain air, pouring off the edges of the sidewalk and into the path of the slow-moving traffic. Vehicles neither honked nor swerved, but just floated dreamily along under the same euphoric spell as the pedestrians.

The town's visitors fell easily into two groups. The most noticeable were those on packaged tours, the kind that include visits to designated outfitters who specialize in bright outdoor clothing designed to impress the friends at home, but more likely destined to remain in dark stuffy closets back in Osaka or Bonn or Phoenix. This group was just too giddy to be self-conscious in its odd combinations of light summer slacks, street shoes, and colourful down-filled ski jackets, puffing out at the torso and sleeves like the Michelin Man.

The second group consisted of the young and the restless, their fashion statement no less marked than that of the tourists: GAP-inspired drifters in dreadlocks, khaki army pants, thick sweaters, and bandanas. Generally they were not walking. They were loitering in small clutches, gazing out onto the passing world through hooded eyes, holes at the fingers of their wool gloves, dreaming perhaps of the beaches in Morocco or the dope in Amsterdam.

The locals were harder to spot at first, mainly because they looked so, well, normal. In shirtsleeves or sweaters, in sneakers or hiking boots, they strode along with purpose, as people do who are going about their daily business. With practised ease they side-stepped the slow-motion clumps of fashionable colour and the lingering clots of khaki without losing speed, just as one learns to do in the city. They themselves were transplants, of course, opportunists scaling the high slippery slopes of the yen and the mark and the almighty American dollar. But clearly, they were prevailing.

Father David drove slowly with the stop-and-go flow of traffic, crossing the broad stone bridge at the head of the main street, up the winding road that led to the town's most enduring symbol, the tall turreted Banff Springs Hotel. It was like a movie set. People in tuques crossed the road in front of him, skiis slung over their shoulders, even though snow was visible at only the highest altitudes of the surrounding mountains. Was this yet another fashion statement? Or was it the result of a cruel trick played by Canadians on unsuspecting American visitors who had been told they had better take along a French-English dictionary as well?

Father David was not sure how best to enjoy his few hours in this alpine showpiece. Having parked his car along a side street back in town, he joined the moving throng along the main street, feeling vaguely disappointed. He was in the mountains, to be sure, and the clear cold air was rejuvenating. But somehow, walking the pavement in the crush of a slow-moving crowd had not been one of his fantasies of the Rockies.

He turned into a restaurant that featured "Bison Burgers" on a handwritten Bristol-board sign in the window and ordered up the platter, which included a hefty helping of "Buffalo Chips." It arrived with a limp lettuce side salad, thick-cut French fries (being, apparently, the "Buffalo Chips"), and an ordinary-looking burger slopped with a ketchup-mayonnaise sauce so thick that any distinctive flavour in the meat was all but smothered. It could have been a horse burger as far as Father David could tell.

As he left the restaurant, Father David stopped to gaze up at the massive wind-swept peak of Mount Rundle, a deceptively smooth face rising gently to a sudden drop-off, just the sort of jagged precipitous edge that would instil the fear of heights into an otherwise stable person. You could walk right up to that edge, he thought, and his eye followed a possible line of ascent.

He fell into a reverie, allowing himself to imagine the details of a strange scene. A family huddles together at the windswept summit for a group shot, the father, triumphant, setting up his camera on a tripod. "Just a little farther back," he directs them. Nervously glancing behind them, the mother holding her children tightly now, they inch backward. With the timing device on the camera now ticking, dad scrambles to rejoin them, slipping in behind. But just as the shutter clicks he leans back, too close to the edge, and loses his balance. He falls backward into the void, his last sight being the horrified faces of his wife and children as he plummets down, away from them.

Father David shivered. His heart was pounding. He took a deep breath. It was only a daydream, he told himself, only a daydream.

But this was the problem with nature, he thought as his breathing subsided. To really experience it you have to put yourself almost in harm's way — climb the mountain, shoot the rapids, blaze the forest trail. Otherwise you might just as well look at a postcard. Or do what he was doing — stand on a crowded sidewalk outside a greasy spoon, safe in the puffy folds of red and orange Michelin people.

Before he left town he pulled into a gas station. A young man, direct from a sales course perhaps, greeted him with more enthusiasm than a tank of gas really warranted. While the tank was filling the young man initiated a conversation.

"So how do you like the Sprint?" he asked.

Father David was a bit surprised by the question. "It's fine, I guess," he said.

"Does it have enough oomph for the mountains?" the young man asked.

"Oomph? I don't know yet," Father David said, "but I guess I'll be finding out."

"Ya, my mom used to have this car," the kid gushed. "It was great for running around town. But, boy, was it ever slow when she drove through the mountains. It just didn't have the oomph, y'know? But what can you expect from three cylinders?"

Father David took a moment to process this new information. "This car has only three cylinders?" he asked.

"Ya. Didn't you know that?" the young man smiled engagingly, without being derisive.

"No," Father David said, "I didn't."

"Ya, well anyway, it's good on gas," the young man said, winding up. "That'll be fifteen dollars, sir."

Three cylinders, Father David thought. Three cylinders! He had traded in a car that good ole' Al had said he himself wouldn't drive through the mountains — because it was running on only three cylinders! And then Al gave him a car that *has* only three cylinders! He shook his head. Unbelievable!

The sun was sinking low behind the mountains as Father David pulled back onto the highway. It was growing dark, even though it was still only late afternoon. Of course, Father David reasoned, when you're surrounded by such awesome height, you'd likely get only about four or five hours of direct sunlight, even on a good day. You would be living in the twilight of perpetual shadow, not a pleasant prospect. Clouds were spreading across what open sky could still be seen, too high to be threatening but low enough to make the claustrophobic illusion complete. Father David was starting to feel boxed in.

The highway wound alongside the Bow River, the mountains receding for a while to create a broad river valley. But past the exit for Lake Louise — a prospect that didn't tempt Father David, who did not wish to repeat his Banff disappointment — the mountains began closing in again. It had become dark enough that he saw them now as silent shadowed sentinels, their craggy features only faintly visible in the failing light.

How indifferent the mountains were to his passing, he thought, these great hooded Gargantuas, neither blocking his way nor granting his passage, as the thin line of headlights now threaded its way through their lower reaches. Like silent and distant gods, Father David thought. Like a silent and distant God, he thought. Like God ....

His mind fell silent at this sudden revelation. Like God.

Father David had always imagined God to be somewhat remote, aloof even. That was why he preferred the soaring ceilings of continental cathedrals and their provincial imitations here in the New World. They inspired a sense of awe under that vast weight of God's grandeur. This had been a comforting image for Father David, conforming to his own experience of God. He had not shared in the folksy familiarity with which God was approached by the sixties' generation. Nor could he claim the "personal relationship with Jesus" touted by the evangelicals, nor the ecstatic spiritual highs of the charismatics. God, in his experience, was not unlike his own father — austere, formal, loving of course, but with high expectations. But all that was before he had entered into the faceless gaze of these unyielding mountains.

This new austerity — the austerity of the dark rock formations that now rose up around him on every side — this was beyond love, wholly indifferent to suffering, to ecstasy, or to anything as minuscule and insignificant as human thought or feeling. It looked down impassively from remote heights, neither judging nor condoning, but watching nonetheless, ever watching.

These frightening new thoughts pushed their way to the surface slowly and with great force, much as the mountains themselves had been formed, the slow tossing of stratum upon stratum, the weaker buckling beneath the grinding advance of the stronger, until the relentless peaks emerged from the primordial oceans, rising up, releasing fire and heat from the earth's core, from the depths of his soul, a rumbling now so deafening that the ground trembled and the earth shook, until white-hot lava spewed forth, overflowing down mountainsides, flooding the valleys with this new and imponderable reality: God did not care!

Blood rushed to Father David's cheeks and pounded at his temples as he allowed himself to feel the full impact of this thought. God, his God, did not care. The reason that Father David could not feel God leading him one way or another as he had set out on this journey was not that he was misinterpreting God. It was not that he was failing to grasp the divine will. It was that God *had* no will about this, about any of it. God was watching, impassive as the mountains, as Father David himself slipped from the jagged precipice, plummeting backward, downward through an endless darkness. God was allowing all of this to happen, leaving him alone in the universe, abandoned in his fall through space, to be crushed, flattened, smashed into a million pieces, lost to the void. This was "God's will"?!

Father David's anger rose unchecked to the surface. He hated the idea of this God. He railed against it. After he himself had worked so hard to do what he believed God had wanted; after he had chosen consistently the higher path, the greater good, suppressing his own inner desires for the sake of doing God's will; after all this, to think that God merely stood far off, observing everything, but caring no more or no less than if Father David had made other choices, than if he had been reckless and foolish, just as he was being right now. None of it mattered. Because the truth was: God didn't care!

And slowly, from the depths of his rising anger was summoned the one thought Father David had not yet permitted himself to examine. The mental image he feared most rose up now and found its way to him from the darkness. Like a spectral presence, it stood proud and naked before him, mocking and derisive. Its time had come.

It was the image of a woman. She was not alone. Father David turned aside, trying to shake off the familiar contours of her body. But wherever his eyes led, the vision followed. It was Beverley ... and it was Jill ... their bare limbs intertwined.

He shook his head and concentrated on the broken yellow line pulsing before him. But still he watched helplessly as their hands, touching, caressing, moved soundlessly down, down. Tears flooded his eyes, blurring his sight, but the vision was unrelenting. He saw the small of a back, the flow of dark hair. He saw the two bodies moving in rhythm against the whiteness of a vast bed, his bed. He saw one convulse; he heard one cry out. His hand came up to his own mouth; he bit hard into his finger.

He pulled the car roughly over to the side of the road, to a scenic lookout over what was now a dark chasmic void. Hot tears ran down his cheeks as he sobbed openly, convulsively, his two hands gripping the wheel. He gasped for breath, and wailed aloud from a place deep and hidden into the dark indifferent night. Forward and back he rocked, moaning, until there was nothing left.

For a long time Father David sat, depleted, his hands on the wheel, the car gently idling, the warmth from the heater rising up to enfold him. There was no deeper place for him to go. There was no diversionary thought, no stabilizing idea, that would stave off this pain. He had fallen from a great height, and this was the bottom.

He looked out into the darkness. He had no idea where he was. The clouds parted overhead. For a moment a bright moon lit the forested mountain slopes surrounding him. He could summon neither the will nor the energy to move from this spot.

The futility of this journey was clear to him now. Nothing on Vancouver Island was going to change anything. But he had come too far to turn back. Maybe he should just press on — what did it matter? He had already destroyed whatever fragments of his life remained behind. They had been shattered like gravel beneath his spinning wheels, so foolishly desperate was he to leave. His marriage was probably over, he had abandoned his children, his career was in tatters. Why *not* just venture forth into this dark night? His life was already ruined.

Finally he put the car into gear and pulled back onto the highway. He was numb to the hours and to the distance that still separated him from sleep, as he wound down out of the mountains in an almost hypnotic state. Part of him was saying, *What the hell, just let the car go, let it sail right off the highway into the void*. But he heard another voice, that of his mother. Her voice was soft, but strong. *You can salvage this, David,* she was saying. *You are not lost; you are being found.* He could not comprehend what she might mean by these words. But the mere sound of her voice reassured him.

So he pressed on into the night, through deep-cut valleys, alongside moonlit rivers and lakes, following the winding road until the bright lights of Kamloops guided him safely to a hotel. He took the key, found the room, and fell into bed fully clothed. He pulled the covers up tight around him and slipped into a deep and dreamless sleep.

. . .

Father David woke with his shoes on. The bed sheets were tangled round his legs and his shins felt bruised, as if he had been kicked. It was a struggle to focus his mind. He couldn't quite recall at first just where he was, or why. He noted that he was still in his clothes, the black suit and clericals from the day before, a lifetime ago. He noted as well, as if observing someone else, that he was crumpled and dirty.

A hot shower helped, but he could move only heavily, as if in slow motion, like a drunk rolling out the daylight end of an all-night bender. He sat at the edge of the bed, naked, his wet hair dripping into his eyes and down his back.

His mind permitted only the simplest and most immediate of thoughts: Was he hungry? Yes. Would the car need re-fuelling? Yes. How was his money holding out? He reached for his suit jacket and pulled out his wallet. He took out the bills, fanning them like a deck of cards in his hand. Okay. Was he ready to head back onto the highway for the last leg of the journey? He took a deep breath. No. He fell back on the bed, rolling under the covers, pulling them up over his head.

Some time later a knock on the door woke him up. He sat bolt upright, throwing off the covers.

"Housecleaning," he heard, in a heavily accented voice, East Indian, or perhaps Hispanic.

He drew the covers up again. "No," he said too loud, his heart pounding, trying to bring himself round.

"Sorry," he heard the voice say. Someone ambled off down the hallway pushing a cart with squeaky wheels. He heard her knock at the room next door. "Housecleaning."

He'd better do something. Otherwise he could languish in this place, just fold up and die — without even knowing what Kamloops looked like. He could not afford to stop, not yet. He had to press on, put one foot in front of the other.

Father David pulled on his clothes. He gathered up his things and headed out the door. It was not as late as he'd thought, not quite nine-thirty in the morning. He returned the key at the front desk and found his way outside to his car.

It was a cool morning with a high sky, ripples of white clouds strung loosely across it, light blue beyond. He surveyed the land-scape. He was surrounded by a high sierra grassland, dry and barren. There were long ruts traversing an adjacent hillside — cattle tracks? Definitely cowboy country, something he hadn't associated with British Columbia. British Columbia. Ha! He was almost there.

It gave him a small lift to recollect that he was, in fact, still engaged on his great adventure. Something of his excitement was dashed, he knew, by the revelations of the evening before, revelations he was not anxious to recall or revisit. But still, the thought of the open road, the ride on the ferry, and his arrival later in the day at his new home on the coast — this was enough now to keep him moving. He picked up a juice, a coffee, and a toasted bagel from a doughnut shop, gassed up the car, and again found himself pulling onto the highway.

The road climbed steadily southward along the spine of the interior mountain range that would form the alpine route of the Coquihalla Highway. With his three-cylindered flivver struggling to maintain momentum, Father David ground the gas pedal into the floor. The little engine whined shrilly but still she lost speed. Strung-out tractor trailers, loaded-down logging trucks, beat-up camper vans and old sedans, their boats and U-hauls bouncing along behind in tow, all straining to make the steep grade, pulled out and passed him.

The weather was changing. The cloud cover had turned gray and was constant now. There was more snow on the mountaintops here than there had been on the Alberta side. Father David could feel a chill in the air at these higher altitudes.

He passed a sign warning of sudden changes in the weather. Then he glanced ahead to see that, indeed, snow flurries were sweeping the air in front of him. The road was turning slushy, forcing the traffic into a single lane. The car fishtailed as he changed lanes. It wasn't even October.

Then, just as suddenly, the cloud lifted, the snow vanished, and Father David found himself gazing out over the verdant Nicola Valley, cloud shadows chasing one another across the broad valley floor. The highway dropped down the slope, climbed the other side, and then, once again beneath low threatening clouds, he found himself back in an avalanche zone, cannon mounts fixed strategically at the sides of the road, the better to blast some distant snowy peak and control the release of its downward flow.

He turned on the headlights as he coasted through tunnels designed to protect his little tin car should half the mountain decide to give way. There was no question he and all the others — the transport trailers, the camper vans, the sedans — they were all driving at the mercy of earthly forces far too great and too fickle to be harnessed or controlled. He gripped the wheel with both hands. He would be relieved to get through to the other side.

Finally, as the highway wound down into the Fraser River Valley, Father David could see that the mountains were pulling back, rounding off, becoming less severe; they were losing their edge. They were giving way now to something new, something gentler. The clouds had descended with him, forming a low ceiling that rested atop the few peaks that could still be seen around him. The others were lost in the cloud cover itself, out of sight. As the coastal range parted, delivering Father David at last out onto the broad Fraser River delta, it started to rain. The windshield wipers slapped back and forth in the slower of two speeds that the Frog Prince made available to him.

Father David was disappointed with his approach to Vancouver. It was such a romantic city in his mind, yet it yielded little more than wet fields on either side, a gray overhung sky, and a common tree-lined highway racing now toward the city. It was a new landscape for him, a few low mountains still visible to the north. But the billboards, the increasing pace of the traffic, the dull grayness — this all felt sadly familiar to him, like a mild Toronto day in the middle of February.

He stayed on the highway, following the signs for Horseshoe Bay, where he would catch the ferry to Vancouver Island. This led him across bridges, past high-density suburban developments and industrial malls, through the east end of the city. As he approached the Second Narrows Bridge a trio of soft coastal mountains rose up to define the city's natural northern boundary. The sprawling suburban houses, chiselled into solid rock, or sunk in lush vegetation, grew more lavish, more grandiose, as he continued west along the north shore.

The city revealed itself to him in a few stolen glances across Burrard Inlet as the highway swept him along. He recognized the Lions' Gate Bridge from pictures he'd seen, and the rising mound of green representing Stanley Park. A dense cluster of high-rise office towers indicated the city's downtown core and, beyond them, Father David caught his first glimpse of the dark waters of the Strait of Georgia, cold and forbidding under low-hanging cloud.

But it was not until he arrived at Horseshoe Bay that the swirling coastal mists began to work on him. Having just missed a sailing, he parked the Frog Prince near the head of the line-up for the next ferry two hours hence, stepped stiffly out of the car, and walked back toward the main street to find a place to eat.

There was something invigorating about this seaside air. It almost stung his nostrils as he sucked it in. The ocean was pungent at low tide, dead matter rotting in small clumps upon the rocks and sand. The dark forests that rose up sharply along the shore were wet and fungal, a thin fog lifting finger-like through the trees. He could feel the dampness penetrating his clothes, his skin, even through his sweater and coat. He could feel his cheeks colouring, as if pinched to life by the salt spray and cedar mist.

He had prepared himself for spectacular scenery. This is what the coast is known for. But with the low gray clouds precluding any panoramic views, he now felt himself being seduced in their stead by subtler forces. While the mountains of the interior had been dangerous, wind and weather swirling around their distant inscrutability, these seaside forces were dangerous at an altogether different level — at the invasive level of the senses.

It was as if, following his dark night on the mountain, Father David had now descended to the village, to fall into the waiting arms of some new lover, his ears tickled by her soft breezes, his hair licked by her gentle fall of rain, his skin caressed by her ocean mists. He could feel himself yielding, letting go, as if to forbidden fruit. In the context of this new day, with all that had gone before, it was not a bad feeling. Not bad at all.

The ferry itself did not permit much of a view as it chugged through the muffling fog, around the coastal inlets and islands, and out into the open waters of the Strait. Standing outside on the deck, leaning over the cold painted rail, Father David was fascinated by the flotsam swept outward by the wake of the ferry's broad beam: whole logs, stripped clean of bark; streams of seaweed, kelp and wood chips, held loosely together in a greasy slick at the juncture of countervailing currents; bright painted buoys, bobbing jauntily, guiding the boat's passage.

Even as he shivered in the damp chill, he could not bring himself to leave the deck. This was a strange new world indeed, drawing him deeper into itself. Like a jungle, it was not a world that would brook the arrogance of outsiders, being in possession of its own laws, its own hidden truths. Whatever had been his source of confidence back east, the realization was growing within Father David that he had arrived at the very edge of his known world.

Disembarking in Nanaimo, the landscape still obscured through light fog and mist, Father David sought landmarks that would help orient him to his new terrain. But, following the road signs, he was swept along on a highway that looked not so different from parts of southwestern Ontario, green farmland and rolling hillsides with the usual assortment of cows and horses.

It was not until he turned off the exit for the Pacific Rim that the landscape began to change. Like a gentle giant waking from sleep, the island began to rise up and show itself. Soft hillsides straightened into rock faces; lush green forests strode right up alongside the road with their gnarled moss-covered spruce and spreading cedars; gushing streams flowed out from the forests' dark folds.

Cameron Lake suddenly appeared on the right, like a Scottish loch, deep, troubled and forbidding, mountains rising high on each side. The road hugged a narrow shoreline between the water and a wall of rock and forest. Then, leaving the lake, Father David was delivered into a dark grove of towering trees so tall they disappeared altogether into the mists high overhead. He couldn't resist the urge to pull over. This was the renowned Cathedral Grove.

The traffic abated as Father David got out of the car, and along with it died all human sound. He stood perfectly still beneath a canopy of distant foliage, enveloped by a profound and overwhelming silence. There was no wind that Father David could feel but, higher up, the spreading branches of the Douglas firs and red cedars were swaying in a lofty breeze that could not penetrate the forest's dense lower reaches. The grove was well-named, he thought, as he strained to detect even the slightest sound of life. Surely God was in this place! Though perhaps with no less indifference here than in the mountains. But still, there was something ...

Port Alberni was overcast with the same low cloud that had followed him from the mainland. Father David could sense that the day was losing its light. He had to look at his watch, so disoriented had he become to the time of day: approaching five o'clock. He was within reach of the coast now, and his heart thrilled at the thought. The damp smell of cedar and the clinging coastal mists were leading him "home," to a place he had never seen before.

The last leg of his journey led Father David on a winding road deep through the interior of the island, past the long westward arm of Sproat Lake and up into the MacKenzie Mountain Range. Visibility diminished even further in the falling dark, but he could feel the car rising to the occasion, could hear the pumping of its little pistons, the high whine of its tire treads on the wet pavement. He found himself glancing out across sudden drop-offs, the road rising now above the tree-tops, which appeared in his headlights through the mist.

There was no dozing on this stretch of broken road. It rose and fell without warning, now hugging a rocky cliff, now doubling back in a hairpin turn, requiring of Father David the nerve-racking attentiveness of a rally driver. So abundant had been recent rains that waterfalls literally sprung from the rock out onto the open road, causing small-scale flash floods. His little car charged through them, almost with enthusiasm, sending a watery spray high up both sides.

Finally Father David reached a T-junction that pointed right to Tofino and left to Ucluelet. He had utterly lost his bearings in the fog and rain and dark, so now he simply allowed the signs to lead him the rest of the way. Ucluelet presented itself after a short drive up and over hills and through dark forests, the sudden lights of a gas station casting an eerie glow in the night. The town seemed to be sleeping, tossed on a ribbon of roads, lit houses and locked-up businesses appearing and disappearing through the fog like passing beacons of welcome.

Father David followed the directions he had received from Bishop Hovey and pulled up in front of a small green cottage bearing the address of the rectory. A note had been taped to the front door. "KEYS IN KITCHEN," it said. How was he to get in then, he wondered. But he tried the door, which opened, and he stepped into his new home.

Bringing in just what he would need for a night's sleep, he acquainted himself only with the rooms that presented themselves to him immediately off the front hall — an empty living-room, a bathroom, and a large adjacent room which seemed to be the master bedroom. There was a double bed and a long low dresser. He looked through the closet, but there was no bedding. Father David hadn't considered that he would have to provide his own bedding, and he hadn't thought to bring a sleeping bag. But, aching and exhausted now, he got partially undressed and settled down on the wide mattress, his duffel coat for a blanket, his pile of clothes for a pillow.

As he turned off the light and drifted into sleep, a fog horn moaned in the night, warning sailors to keep their distance, but reassuring Father David that he had finally arrived.

# Chapter Three

Father David woke early, his first day in the new world. He pulled on his sweats and went out to stand in his bare feet on the front stoop, drawing his first daylight impressions.

The sun was trying to pierce a wispy layer of gray cloud that was rolling in low overhead. The grass glistened, and a large spreading spruce in the front yard hung heavy with the residue of last night's rainfall. The chilled air hinted of salt spray, but also of smoke trails, a hundred wood-burning stoves bringing the community to life, like morning in a campground.

Father David sucked in the bracing morning air. This should be a day of exploration, he told himself. There were people to contact, arrangements to be made; but all that could wait. He was not yet ready to be, well, Father David. For this brief span — a day, maybe two — he could just be his interior self, extending the solitude that had enveloped him on his cross-country journey.

He turned back into the house. "Partially furnished" was how Bishop Hovey had described it, but that was certainly a stretch. The hallway led back to the kitchen, past a bathroom and a small bedroom, which was carpeted but empty. Off the front entrance was the living-room, bare right down to the hardwood flooring, which echoed his footsteps as he passed through.

The house was actually larger than it appeared from the street. A picture window in the dining-room at the back of the house looked overtop a small grove of cedar and spruce trees and across the dark waters of the outer harbour. On the far side of the inlet the forested shoreline gave way to the slow rise of a low bald mountain. Recent logging had stripped it bare of trees, exposing its face, which was slashed with the scars of old logging roads. Its round summit was ridiculously capped by a tiny white dome, like a sailor's cap, likely some sort of communications tower, that poked its way up into the low ceiling of cloud cover.

A smaller window over the kitchen sink afforded a more Zen-like view of the same vista, permitting only the narrowest glimpse through the trees down to the water where, at this moment, a fishing boat was slowly chugging its way past. Father David could not see the boat in its entirety but watched as it revealed itself to him section by section: the painted wooden bow, stubby and scraped, the small-windowed wheel house with the high thin stabilizing rods drawn up tight against the sides, then the long low rear deck. He could hear the deep-throated throbbing of the boat's engines as it slipped out toward the open Pacific Ocean. It made Father David anxious to get out and see it all.

On the counter lay a set of keys, assorted and unmarked, attached to an oversized paper clip. A chrome-legged kitchen table and some matching leatherette chairs filled the breakfast nook at the other end of the room. Father David pulled open the refrigerator door. The light went on but there was nothing there. He explored the cupboards. They offered a few plastic cups, some old chipped coffee mugs, and a stack of mismatched plates of various sizes, the "unsellables" from the bazaar, no doubt. Down below was an assortment of cast-off pots and pans. A drawer yielded some cutlery. Not much to work with, but it would do.

A narrow set of stairs led from the corner of the kitchen up to an unfinished attic where a large window, opening to the north, offered a panoramic view of the inland mountains, rising mounds of scarred rock and earth from which virtually every tree had been removed. A desolate view, but magnificent nonetheless. There was a basement below the kitchen, with a room at the bottom of the stairs that Father David assumed was the study, a small space with a desk and filing cabinet and some built-in bookshelves. Too bad he wouldn't have books to fill them, he sighed to himself.

He returned to the main floor, pulled on his jeans and a sweater, sneakers and his duffel coat, and left the house to explore the town. On his way out the door he wondered if he should lock up. But there didn't seem to be much point; likely the keys hadn't been used in years.

The next-door neighbour's house was a small white cottage set back from the road beneath some towering cedars. The front curtains parted slightly as Father David passed; he gave a neighbourly wave in the cottage's general direction.

The road rose and fell as it wound back into town, riding the rough contours of the rocky land, permitting occasional glimpses of the harbour but not of the ocean itself which, he knew by the map, lay on the far side of the peninsula. He would find it all in good time. For now the morning air was bracing, the sun was breaking through, and he could feel the blood beginning to flow in his veins.

As he walked, taking in the odd juxtaposition of neat suburban-type homes and lowly moss-covered trailers, he rehearsed to himself the name of the town. It was spelled "Ucluelet," probably a native word. Taken at a glance, pronunciation was a challenge. But breaking it into its constituent parts, Father David found it became easier: U-clue-let. *Ucluelet*, he said aloud, slowly, and then again, faster. That wasn't so bad. You just had to think of it as three separate syllables, not as a single word. He wondered what it meant.

He found his pace picking up as he sauntered along, until he was met by a roving pack of dogs, four or five mongrels of varying shapes and sizes, including one comical low-to-the-ground sausage variety, its short legs padding furiously to keep up with the rest. "Hi there" he called and he put his hand out as if to pat them. The hair bristled on the backs of their necks; they reared back, bearing their teeth, and snarled at him. "Okay, okay," he said, hurrying past. Glancing back, he saw that they had quickly lost interest in him and were trotting off, presumably in search of a garbage can to overturn or a cat to torture.

The road eventually met up with the town's main street at the Ucluelet Hotel, a shabby brown two-storey building with a separate rear entrance to the bar. He turned down toward the water, past the bank and the liquor store, the district offices, and the post office, to the government docks.

Several large fishing vessels were tied up, their names painted boldly on the bows, sounding like pirate ships, evoking the gods of stealth and swagger, names like "Knight Dragon," "Bank Robber," and "Viking Warrior." Clearly, these steel-hulled ocean raiders meant business, big business.

Two fishermen in rubber overalls were mending a vast orange net they had spread across the dock. Father David walked out over the massive creaking planks of the upper dock to take a closer look.

"So, are these trawlers?" he asked the men, looking toward the boats.

"Nope," one answered. "Trawlers are on the East Coast. These here are draggers." He looked up. "You from the East Coast?" he asked Father David.

"No," he said, "Ontario."

The man sniffed, wiped his sleeve across his face, nodded at him, and went back to work.

"So why are they called draggers?" Father David asked.

The man straightened up again. "That's what they do," he said. "They drag the nets."

"Do you drag them across the bottom?" he asked.

"Wherever there's fish," the man answered.

"How do you know?" Father David wondered. "I mean, where the fish are."

The second man nodded toward the wheel house of the Knight Dragon. "Take a look," he said.

The tide was low so the wheelhouse rested at eye level. Inside Father David could see two captain's chairs on metal swivel bases. Spread before them, on a broad dashboard, was an array of — he counted them — eleven different monitors, some as large as television screens, some small like toy computers. The net-mending seemed a quaint anachronism beside the Knight Dragon's steely bulk and this tangle of electronic wizardry. The fish didn't stand much of a chance, he guessed. Father David nodded to the men on the dock as he turned and walked away.

He continued along the waterfront, passing several fish-processing plants, only one of which seemed to be in operation. A small crew of workers in rubber boots and white smocks was hosing out a large vat of mashed fish parts. The pungent odours wafting up from the plant on any other day might have assaulted his senses. But on this day of discovery Father David found it all invigorating. He felt immensely pleased with himself, just being there.

The twisting waterfront road led round to a protected inner harbour, a shallow basin tucked in behind a forested spit of land. The harbour was dominated by a great white ocean-going vessel, anchored permanently in the mud alongshore, a line of colourful flags flapping in the breeze above its polished decks. The Canadian Princess, as she was called, seemed more tourist attraction than working ship. A flotilla of small touring boats was docked alongside her hull, painted up and named as if they were the offspring of the Princess herself: the "Salmon Princess," the "Coho Princess," the "Nootka Princess," and so on.

The rest of the inner harbour was filled by a complex of interconnected floating docks, accommodating smaller craft, the working trollers and the re-fitted house boats. In contrast to the mighty draggers, the names painted on these battered wooden-hulled vessels evoked not the pirate gods of the high seas, but the deities of hearth and homeland, names such as "Nordic Freedom," "The Dori-Louise," and "Devotion."

Every slip was occupied, which made Father David wonder if these small craft were like the family farms back in Ontario, the remnants of a dying culture, where once a man with a boat could make a living for his wife and children, hauling in enough fish in the twilight hours of daybreak to put a roof over their heads, and perhaps send someone off to college.

But not now. Not since the salmon stocks had dropped off. Even in Ontario Father David had read about the restrictive quotas set for the modern-day fisherman, making it harder and harder for the smaller operations to survive. Some were probably selling out, Father David guessed; some were waiting, hoping for the fish to return; others were just walking away. And here was the sad testimony: row upon row of small one- or two-man fishing boats, tied up here in the shadow of the mean fleets of draggers and beneath the cheery flags of the tour operators.

Father David returned home by way of the main road, lined with houses in need of painting and storefronts that were closed and boarded. On his way, he passed a white clapboard church, its high bell tower overlooking the harbour. A hand-painted sign by the front door identified the church as St. Aidan's. This was to be his charge. Soon, he would be once again a parish priest. He didn't even try the door. He was not yet ready for whatever burden of responsibility awaited him inside.

Back at the house, Father David ate a hearty lunch and decided to drive up to Tofino to inspect his other pastoral charge. The map indicated there was only one way to get there, the Pacific Rim Highway. That would lead him alongside the ocean, through the renowned Pacific Rim National Park, to the northern tip of the peninsula and to Clayoquot Sound — another word he would have to work on — which had been the focus of worldwide attention some years ago. Protestors tied themselves to trees and blocked roads to stop the logging of the region's legendary old-growth forests. Their actions led to confrontations with police and to many well-publicized arrests and, eventually, to the collapse of the local logging industry. Father David had read about that too.

As he approached the junction, where the main highway turned back to Port Alberni, Father David pulled over to pick up a hitchhiker. This was something he almost never did, invite a stranger into his car. He did not know why he had done it now, as a young man, long-haired and smelling of wet wool, climbed into the passenger seat, pulling a heavy backpack onto his lap. It must have been something in the air.

"Thanks, man. This is great," the young man said.

"You're welcome," Father David said.

"Cool car! Paint it yourself?"

"No," Father David replied, "it came this way."

The young man nodded appreciatively. They drove along in silence as the road cut through a tall dark forest that possessed the same stately grandeur as Cathedral Grove. But this growth was more dense, more alive, a thick underbrush rising to mingle with the furry vines that hung rope-like from the branches high above, like jungle.

The young man turned to Father David. "I'm Sun," he said.

"I'm sorry?" Father David replied. "You're what?"

"I'm Sun. You know — Sun, Moon, Stars? Sun. That's my name."

"Ah," Father David said, comprehending only in a vague sort of way. Feeling it necessary to reciprocate, he added, "And I'm Father David."

"Father?" the young man asked, puzzled.

"Yes," Father David said, smiling. "You know — Father, Son, Holy Spirit? Father."

"Wow." The young man mulled this over. "I've never heard *that* before. Is that, like, religious or something?"

"Yes, I guess it could be called that," Father David said. "I'm an Anglican priest."

"Hm," the young man said, nodding, but not knowing quite what to do with this information. "Well, I was never allowed to go to church," he said.

"Not allowed?" Father David queried.

"Ya. My mother's Wiccan." He looked at Father David to see if that was registering. It was not. "You know, a witch. She was high priestess of her coven."

"A ... witch," Father David repeated slowly, his eyes widening. "Well. Now *that's* interesting."

"Ya, so we were never allowed to go to church. I think she felt it was, like, the enemy or something? But I don't know. Me, I think we're all, like, on the same path, y'know?"

This was too much for Father David to take in. It was a drop into some other dimension altogether. He had the son of a witch in his car, a seemingly nice, if somewhat naive, young person, sharing with him now his first glimpses of the Pacific Ocean, a suddenly awe-inspiring, almost sacred, sight.

Father David had been disappointed that signs along the way had pointed off the road to various beaches that were not themselves visible from the highway. But on this long descent the road pitched slowly to the right as the trees parted on the left and there it was: a wide expanse of tossing deep blue, stretching as far as the eye could see.

"Wow," Father David said softly, more to himself than to his passenger.

"Some place, eh?" the kid said, watching Father David's reaction to the vista spreading before them.

"Ya. Some place," Father David said, still looking out, entranced, across the open ocean.

"There's some kind of energy here, man," the young man said. "It's, like, cosmic or something, a place of extremes, y'know? Extreme waves — *foosh*," and he brought his hands together and apart like crashing waves. "Extreme mountains," he went on, one hand shooting up to suggest great height. "Extreme green," he said, his hands expanding outward, open-palmed, fingers tickling the air, as if to indicate spreading coastal flora. "Extreme red," he said, one hand folding into a fist, pounding into the other, "like redneck, you know what I mean?" He wasn't really asking. "I mean, this place has everything, man, *every*thing!"

Father David nodded, without really comprehending.

"Hey, you want some extreme shit?" the young man asked.

Father David was startled by the question.

"I got some real extreme shit here," explained this innocent-looking wide-eyed teenager sitting next to him, patting his backpack. "Opium-cured or something. You want to smoke some shit?"

"Ah ... no thanks," Father David replied, trying not to sound out of his depth. "And I'd appreciate it if you didn't, ah, smoke in the car. If you don't mind, that is."

"No, that's cool, man," the kid said, unruffled.

In Tofino the trees parted again, this time to the north, revealing a rising array of thickly treed coastal mountains, what Ucluelet must have looked like before its own mountains were logged down to the bedrock. It was immediately apparent that, while it may have been only a forty-five minute drive from Ucluelet, this was another world altogether, a surrealistic world in which his strange young travelling companion was right at home.

The main street was a tourist's dream come true: unpainted clapboard shops hung with fish nets and glass floats; artists' studios displaying pottery and silver jewellery on shelves visible through paned blown-glass windows; funky coffee shops with outdoor tables and stools fashioned from lacquered tree stumps; and all this nestled against the spectacular backdrop of the forested islands of Clayoquot Sound and the snow-capped inland peaks beyond.

Down along the waterfront, single engine float planes roared across the open waters on their way in or out, vying for runway space with aluminum water taxis and chartered fishing and tour boats. This place was happening.

Father David dropped his young charge outside the Coffee Pod, a corner gathering place painted sea-blue with round bubbled windows and a large open front porch. "This is the *place*, man," the kid said with emphasis as he hopped out of the car. And the young people sitting in khaki clots confirmed it, gazing out upon the weary world through the same hooded eyes as their tribal relatives back in Banff.

It was easy for Father David to find his way to St. Columba's Church. He could see the cedar-shingled steeple several blocks away, and simply followed it down a side street to the tiny red building looking out across the Sound. If ever there was a photogenic frontier church, this most certainly was it.

As he pulled up, a small colourfully clad group of tourists was assembling in front of the church's front doors, posing for a group shot. In a thick German accent one of them asked if Father David would mind taking the picture for them. He took the picture, handed back the camera, and immediately they fell back into a spirited conversation among themselves.

He didn't need to look inside the church just yet. It was enough to be there, to sense its pioneer history and its quaint present-day aesthetic. It must represent a potential gold mine to entrepreneurial developers, Father David guessed. Good thing it had not yet fallen into their hands, to be turned into a restaurant, or a pottery studio, or — who knows! — into the friendly local gathering place of a witches' coven.

. . .

The next day there was no escaping it — Father David would have to make some phone calls announcing his arrival. First he wanted to check in with Beverley and the kids, let them know he was okay. A phone call would have been easiest, of course, but as he picked up the handset, he realized that Paul and Catherine would be at school by now. That would mean speaking with Beverley, which he was not yet ready to do. A quick note would have to suffice, at least for now, he thought, sitting down at the desk in the study and pulling out a writing pad.

He did not want to get into anything too deep, just establish contact, as if he were away at a conference and were writing merely to keep in touch. So he addressed the note to all of them, using the clipped sentences of a man on the fly.

*Dear Bev, Paul & Catherine,*

*Arrived at the Coast the day before yesterday, after a wonderful cross-country drive. Why did we never do this trip as a family? This country is just enormous, it goes on and on. Took me two whole days just to leave Ontario!*

*The car broke down in Saskatchewan but was able to replace it at par with a little Chevy Sprint. You'd like it, I think, Paul. It's been painted lime green, a young person's car, and I am a middle-aged man driving it, which must attract some attention. Though maybe not, out here.*

*This is some place, I can tell you. Haven't seen any whales or eagles yet, though it all feels very wild. The beach is fabulous. Wish I'd thought to bring along the camera.*

*I think of you all and hope you are well. Write me when you can. I'll find out the address and write it on the envelope. I love you all very much.*

*Love, as always,*
*Dad*

Next he thought he ought to check up on his books, left on a porch back in Grenfell, Saskatchewan. He had been surprised to discover, among the few papers and pamphlets on the shelves in the study, a directory for the United Church of Canada. Odd, he thought, for an Anglican rectory to have such a thing. But he turned to it now. The information was organized into lists that were drawn up in about a half-dozen different ways according to whether you were looking for the name of a church, its location, the presbytery to which it belonged, its elected presbytery and conference members and, only then, the name of its clergy.

This was so typical of the United Church, Father David thought, shaking his head — to list everyone else ahead of the clergy! It would never occur to them to list their congregations according to the ordained people who served them. This was clear evidence that clergy in the United Church were not allowed to rise above their station, nor were they permitted to fall into the mistaken assumption that they actually possessed any authority, any power, any place other than as the humble servants of the fickle whims of the congregations they served. He shook his head again at the thought.

But then, as he began thumbing through the directory, it dawned on Father David that he did not actually know the name of the minister of the Grenfell United Church and that, in fact, that particular congregation was easier to find without it. He ran his finger down the list of Saskatchewan congregations.

Grenfell, it appeared, was part of a five-point pastoral charge, but large enough to be its anchor, and therefore the location of the manse. Father David breathed a sigh of relief. His assumption had been a good one; the boxes of books would have fallen into the sympathetic hands of someone likely to understand. He cross-referenced the list of congregations with the list of clergy, but no name connected the two. He decided simply to dial the number listed for the church.

At the other end, after five or six rings, a scratchy tape-recorded message started up, thanking the caller for reaching the Grenfell Pastoral Charge, announcing the times of the Sunday services at each of the five churches, then explaining that there was no resident minister at the moment and therefore no one to take a message; callers were advised *not* to leave one at the sound of the tone. No alternative number was given before the tone sounded and the line went dead.

"No resident minister," Father David repeated aloud to himself. No resident minister! This meant that his books had made it to the right place, but there was no one there to receive them. How long was the vacancy to remain in effect? Through the winter? Through frost-bitten nights and swirling snow? Through the spring rains and thaw? Oh, Lord! He imagined the cardboard cartons, softened gradually by the elements, slowly giving way at the corners, sagging slightly at first, until the weight of the books brought one down upon another, splitting the seams, scattering his precious library across the barren windswept yard, the bindings breaking, the pages ripping, some falling into puddles of prairie mud, others sliding off under the porch, fodder for field mice.

*Got to find the number of the presbytery office,* he thought to himself. But just as he was reaching again for the phone, it rang, startling him. Picking it up would be his first official act as priest-in-charge of his new church. He took a deep breath and pulled the receiver from its cradle — but what was the name of this parish again? Frantically he ransacked his memory. He couldn't remember. "Hello?" he said meekly after a long pause.

"Is this the reverend?" It was a young male voice.

"Ah, yes," Father David stammered.

The caller paused. "Well, is it or isn't it?" he demanded.

"Yes. Yes, it is," Father David said with forced conviction. "I'm Father David Corcoran."

"Father?" the voice asked. "Have I reached the Catholic church? Is this the Catholic church? I wanted the Protestant church."

"No, this is the Anglican church," he said. "But I go by 'Father.'"

"Okay, whatever," the man said. "We need you to do a funeral service for us. My dad's died, and we're planning a service for Friday at one o'clock at the Rec Hall. Can you do it?"

"Um, I think so," Father David said. "But why the Rec Hall? Why not at the church?"

"We don't go to church." The answer was unapologetic, simply a matter of information.

Father David's professional integrity was pricked. Too often the church was pressed into service for the needs of a secular society, needs that were spiritual, to be sure, but having little to do with what the church had to offer. Weddings, for instance, where young unchurched couples wanted the quaint atmosphere offered by country churches, or perhaps the pageantry afforded by the long aisles of big city churches, but not the actual religious ceremony that went with it. It was hypocrisy when the church allowed itself to be used in such a way.

"Maybe I should meet with you and with the other members of the family first," he suggested as an interim step.

"What do you mean?" the man asked.

"Well, we should talk it through first, that's all," he said, struggling to take control.

The man put his hand over the phone. Father David could hear him addressing others in the room. "He wants to meet with us. The minister! Do we want to meet with him?" He came back on the line. "No, that's okay. You can just do the service."

"Oh," Father David was thrown off. "But we really should talk about what's going to happen."

"Well, I don't know what there is to talk about. It's going to be real simple," the man said. "We're decorating the hall, some people are doing some food, Bryan's going to say some things, maybe Tammy too, we don't know, and we wanted you to, like — what's it called? — like, MC the service."

"MC the service?" Father David repeated. "But you'll want some readings, surely, and some prayers. Will the casket be present?"

"The what?" the man said.

"The, ah ... coffin," Father David tried. "I'm asking if there will there be a committal."

"I don't know about those things," the voice said. "Just keep it simple. My father was a simple man. So, is that it?"

"Um, well, I'd still like to meet with the family, if that's okay," Father David said, as he felt the reins slipping through his hands.

"No, that's okay, don't worry," the man said. "So, thanks. What was your name again?"

"David Corcoran. Father David Corcoran."

"Okay. Well, thanks, man. We appreciate it," and he hung up.

Father David put the phone down. He sat for a moment, trying to understand this odd arrangement. He permitted himself a wry smile. "Toto," he said to the empty room, "I don't think we're in Kansas anymore."

He reached for his wallet and pulled out the scrap of paper Bishop Hovey had given him. If he'd already agreed to do his first funeral — if indeed that's what it was! — he figured he had better be in touch with his new bishop. He dialled the number for the bishop's office down in Victoria. "Bishop Douglas Long, please," he told the receptionist. "Father David Corcoran," he replied when she asked if she could tell the bishop who was calling.

After a long pause Bishop Long came on the phone.

"Sorry," the bishop said, explaining the delay, "but I had to think for a moment who 'Father David Corcoran' was. Do you always go by 'Father'?"

"Yes, I do," Father David said firmly.

The bishop welcomed him to the Coast, hoping that this time would provide some healing for him so that his family situation could resolve itself. Father David thanked him for his concern, but it made him uncomfortable, and he wondered just how much he knew. Had Beverley already spoken with Bishop Hovey back in Ontario, revealing more than was necessary? He certainly hoped not!

Bishop Long was explaining that the task of this interim ministry was simply to keep the wheels greased. That meant maintaining the schedule of worship services, visiting the sick, as well as anyone else who needed special care, but otherwise just keeping the place going until a new minister was chosen in the spring.

Father David wondered to himself why any Anglican bishop would call an ordained priest a "minister" rather than a "priest." This bishop must be pretty Low Church, he thought, which was not what he had heard about him.

The main thing, the bishop was saying, was to not make any changes. If there were things that needed attention, the new minister could deal with that; he himself was just to leave everything as it was while providing a basic ministry. "Don't work too hard, David," he said, "Father, I mean." Then he added, "So do you really want to be called 'Father'?"

"Yes, I do, Bishop," he said, "unless that presents a problem."

"Not for me personally," the bishop said. "But it might raise more than a few eyebrows at presbytery."

"Presbytery?" Father David asked. "I don't understand. Do you mean at clericus?"

"No, presbytery," the bishop repeated. "Didn't Bishop Hovey tell you? Tofino and Ucluelet isn't your typical Anglican parish.

It's a shared ministry of the Anglican and United Churches. So you're not just there as the Anglican priest. You're also the United Church minister. You didn't know that?"

Father David fell back in his chair. "No, I didn't," he said feebly.

"So you see, calling yourself 'Father' would be a bit of a stretch for our United Church brethren. As well as for some of the Anglican folks there, for that matter," he added. "I'm sorry Jim didn't tell you this. Though perhaps I didn't make it clear enough myself. Anyway, I hope this isn't problematic for you."

"Well ..." Father David wasn't sure just what to say. It *was* problematic for him. But what was he to do? "So do they not have the Eucharist every week?" he asked.

"I don't know what their routine is right now, to be honest, but it's likely Eucharist every other week, something like that, with a United Church service — basically a preaching service — alternately. In any case, I should reiterate, David, that you're not to change anything. You're doing me a great favour by coming all the way out here to take this ministry; but not if I have to pick up the pieces after you're gone. Are we understood?"

"Yes, of course, Bishop," he answered. Bishop Long launched into some details about the payment of David's stipend, about a few upcoming diocesan events, and about the process that had begun in the parish to choose a new minister, more than likely a United Church person, the last incumbent having been an Anglican. But David couldn't get past the sudden stripping of his priestly rank and title. *Hi, I'm David,* he rehearsed in his mind, standing before his new congregation. *I'm your new 'minister'! But, hey folks, you can just call me Dave, or why not Davey?* He could feel his pulse pounding in the veins of his temples.

"So I hope everything goes well," the bishop was saying. "If you have any problems or questions, just call me."

With effort, David managed to remain courteous and respectful as he thanked him, said good-bye, and hung up. He sat in the chair, unable to move, gazing down at the United Church directory open before him. *Shit!* he said to himself. But why not? What else did he have to lose?

The words of that old hymn emerged again out of nowhere, rising up as if to mock him:

*Forbid it, Lord, that I should boast,*
*save in the cross of Christ, my God;*
*All the vain things that charm me most,*
*I sacrifice them to his blood.*

There could be no doubt about it now: he was not in Kansas anymore!

. . .

The next day David called the phone number of a churchwarden, Len Olson from Tofino. Len told him that they tended to keep things pretty simple, that both churches followed the same weekly pattern in their worship, and that this Sunday would be a United Church service in both places. David should be in touch with someone named Mimi, a school teacher in Ucluelet, who would help him prepare the pew bulletin. The rest, Len told him, was pretty much up to him. "Just do whatever it is you do," he said. "You're the minister."

*Yes, I guess so*, David thought to himself, appreciating a whole new meaning to the word "fatherless." *I'm the "minister."*

There would be time to prepare for Sunday, a task he considered now with dread. So David turned his attention instead to the funeral he had agreed to "MC" the following day.

Just what did this mean, he wondered — "MC" the service! Clearly these were unchurched people who probably didn't have a clue themselves what they were asking him to do. That meant he could probably just do what he usually did, a traditional Anglican service. This would certainly place him back in his comfort zone.

But somehow this did not feel like a safe place for doing what he usually did. Not only were these people strange to him, but he was starting to feel a bit strange to himself. For one thing, he was no longer "Father David," an Anglican priest; now he was "Reverend Corcoran," a United Church minister, a generic pastor of an all-purpose Protestant church. And just how is one such as this supposed to "MC" a funeral? He had no clue.

He decided to write out an order of service for himself, based on the Anglican funeral liturgy, but leaving lots of room for dropping or adding things as necessary. For instance, he would be prepared to do a committal if the casket were present, but also just to conclude with a blessing if it were not. And he would do the usual readings, or some of them anyway, if it appeared there was the opportunity. But he really didn't know what to expect; he had to be prepared for whatever presented itself.

What presented itself, when the time came the next day, was certainly not anything David could have imagined. The Rec Hall itself was a large wooden structure set at the edge of a playing field, a former sea plane base from the war years, when Canadian forces had occupied this part of the coast in defence against a possible Japanese invasion. Ucluelet, a deep and protected harbour, had served as the base for both seaplanes and ocean-going vessels. Now this building was the town's only gathering place.

David drove the lime-green Frog Prince into the muddy potholed parking lot, squeezing himself in among the rough lines of pumped-up pick-up trucks, the Dodge Rams, and the F-250s, some with heavy-duty raised suspensions and fat oversized tires, the cabs so high they seemed to sneer down at David as he stood beside them, more monster than machine, and menacing with all that implied muscle.

But entering the hall itself, David found himself walking into a re-created forest wonderland of tree trunks and green cedar boughs, chain saws and work boots propped up against the foliage, hard hats and lanterns displayed amid the wet greenery. On the far side, the "forest" gave way to symbols of the sea — huge nets draped across wooden planks and laid out across the flooring; colourful styrofoam floats of yellow, white, and orange; and smaller cork floats, chipped and faded, scattered on the netting and around the room. The place was like a natural museum.

The hall was large. A small sea of folding chairs had been set out in rows in the middle of the room. But it had been expertly brought under control by these life-sized re-creations of the working life of the deceased. From the front of the room a sound system was blasting out country and western music. A portable podium had been fashioned from a common music stand, cedar boughs tied lengthways up the base. Tall candelabra, rented perhaps from a florist, intertwined with flowers and ferns, stood on either side of the podium. No casket was evident.

As was his custom, David wore his clericals — he would not have thought of doing otherwise — but he felt immediately the distance this created between himself and the people. This was not exactly a white shirt and necktie crowd. Some women wore skirts, there were a few sports jackets, but the congregation more typically had turned out in jeans and work boots, in plaid shirts and wind breakers.

There was no turning back now. So he took a deep breath and ventured into the room. But an odd thing happened. At his approach the crowd parted before him, like the parting of the

Red Sea, the troubled waters rearing back on either side as he walked through on dry land. He was trying not to be conspicuous, but his black suit and Roman collar pretty well ruled that out. And it was evident that, unlike at the Westview Nursing Home, his appearance did not exactly fill the room with hope and consolation. He tried to make eye contact, but as he entered people's line of vision, they jerked their heads away reflexively, some almost wrenching their necks.

He made his way to the front of the room where a small knot of young adults were engaged in intense discussion. He approached, caught their attention, and introduced himself. They stopped talking and looked him over. It was an awkward pause. Finally, one stepped forward. Marty, a wiry long-haired man of about twenty-five, introduced himself as the one who had called him. He did not extend his hand.

"So we were just wondering when people should speak," he said, " — at the beginning, or at the end? What usually happens?"

"Well, I don't know what usually happens *here*," he said, keeping things tentative for the moment. "But ordinarily you would have the readings first, then the homily — or, in this case, the eulogy, I guess — and then the prayers." They were still studying him. "So, if you like, I could start things off with some readings and then call upon the people who will be speaking."

They looked at one another, nodding their approval. "Okay, that sounds good," Marty said.

"Forgive me," David said, "but I don't know your father's name,"

"Stan," came the reply from several people at once.

"And which of you are members of his family?" David asked, feeling out the extent of his pastoral role.

Marty made the introductions, which included his three older brothers — beefy guys, unlike Marty himself, who must have been the brains rather than the brawn of the family — one of their wives, several girlfriends, and a couple of cousins. There were no adults older than perhaps thirty. Each one in turn met his gaze, some offering a hand or nod, and then turned away.

"Well, it's certainly a magnificent display, a great tribute to him," David offered, gesturing to the room. They were nodding. "Was he a lumberjack?"

They smiled to one another. "A *logger*," Marty corrected him. "A *faller* actually."

"But he also fished," one of the brothers offered.

"Until he sunk his boat," another brother added, everyone smirking at a familiar unspoken story.

"And how did he die?" David asked.

This drew blank stares. Some looked at the floor. "Booze," the daughter-in-law said finally in a gravelly voice, a lit cigarette held between her fingers, mascara generously applied but slowly losing its grip beneath her swollen eyes. The others nodded.

The group fell silent. Marty finally looked at David. "Thank you, Father," he said. "We appreciate your doing this."

"Well, thank you for asking me," David replied. "But you can just call me ... David. Just David. That's my name."

Marty extended his hand. "I'm Marty," he told him again.

"I know," David replied, smiling. "So, is it time to get started?"

He took his place at the microphone, assuming a leadership role that seemed otherwise to be absent from the proceedings. He asked for everyone's attention. People shuffled into the rows of chairs and the room grew silent.

David introduced himself as the "minister" from St. Aidan's Church, inwardly chafing at the new bridle but keeping his mind trained on the job at hand. He said that, while he himself had never known Stan, having been in the community precisely four days, he was privileged to preside at this memorial service for him, especially seeing all the work that had gone into decorating the hall for this occasion. He noted a few nods throughout the gathered assembly. Clearly, he said, Stan was well loved. A few more nods, some people dabbing at moist eyes.

The purpose of this service, he ventured to say, was twofold: first, it was an opportunity to give thanks to God for Stan's life, for the friendship and love he had shared during his time with us on earth; second, it was the occasion for letting him go, for commending his soul to a loving God, from whom Stan had come, and to whom he was now returning.

Uncharacteristically, David then concluded his remarks by expressing his hope that the service he had planned would be appropriate and that the assembled group would allow him to lead them through some readings and prayers that placed Stan's death in its proper context, that is, within the larger canvas of God's eternal love for all his children. There were more nods, people granting him the permission he was seeking.

He launched into the introductory scripture readings that open the funeral rite. He then read a portion of Psalm 139, with its comforting verse: "If I take the wings of the morning and dwell in the uttermost parts of the sea, even there your hand will lead me and your right hand hold me fast." The opening prayer followed, asking that we may go forward eagerly to meet our loved ones, where "every tear will be wiped away"; then the longer readings, including one from Ezekiel, the prophet likening the people to a cedar in Lebanon, "with fair branches and forest shade, and of great height, its top among the clouds." At length he invited those to come forward who were to speak personally about Stan.

Two speakers approached the podium in turn. The first was Tammy, a hard-mouthed middle-aged woman with deep-cut lines at the corners of her eyes whose relationship with Stan was not made clear. She unfolded a crumpled sheet of foolscap, taking her time to smooth it out on the flat surface of the music stand, preparing herself. It was a poem she had written herself, in rhyming quatrains:

*Dear Daddy, we're crying and everyone's sad.*
*We're missing our lover, our buddy, our dad.*
*You were the best friend that we ever had,*
*And you wouldn't want us to be feeling so bad.*

Put a few guitar chords behind it, David thought, and you'd have a country and western song right there. As literature, the poem was a masterpiece of doggerel. But it was strangely affecting, Tammy's voice trembling as she forced herself to read the lines aloud over the sound system. People in the congregation were struggling to contain their emotions.

The poem turned out to be quite an epic, recounting adventures in Stan's life, of which there had been many, praising him for single-handedly raising his four sons, for being a friend to all of *their* friends, for being a good lover with a heart of gold, and generous to a fault to any in need. A chord was being struck, all right, as the room began dissolving in sobs. But this only seemed to give Tammy strength as she straightened herself, gearing up for the last verse:

*Dear Daddy, we miss you as if you weren't here,*
*But we know you are listening, and that you are near.*
*You've left us with memories that will always be dear,*
*As you call out from heaven, "Hey! Got any beer?"*

The room roared its approval, breaking into wild applause, whooping and calling out as if Tammy herself were some C&W icon, finishing her set at the local tavern. She held her head high now, tears glistening at the corners of her eyes, her nostrils flaring as she walked away from the podium. She had done her man proud.

The second speaker was Bryan, a large balding man with enormous forearms. He was shaking visibly and his voice broke into high squeaky realms as he spoke of having worked with Stan both in the bush and on the open waters. He had to stop frequently, sniffing loudly, wiping his sleeve under his nose. He was trying to hold it together. The room fell silent out of respect. He soldiered on.

No one was a better buddy than Stan, he said. He was there for you, in the good times, and in the bad. Bryan looked up at the ceiling, holding onto the podium with both hands, trying to compose himself. Whatever Stan did, he said, he did it one hundred and ten per cent, no holding back — that was how he worked, that was how he played, and that was how he drank. A loud whoop went up again from the congregation, rough bearded men raising imaginary pints to the deceased.

"I'm going to miss you, buddy," Bryan stammered, breaking down. "I love you, man." And he quit the podium. Hands reached out from the crowd to comfort him as he walked up the aisle to his seat.

The room wept openly now, men choking in their tears, women wailing loudly, people falling on one another's shoulders, grief heaped upon grief, feeding on itself — *getting out of hand*, David suddenly realized! *Do something!* he told himself.

He strode up to the podium, wrapping one hand around the microphone, raising the other to get the room's attention. "FOLKS," his voice boomed with authority over the loudspeakers, breaking in on the rising din. "We have a job to do here today. And we're not done until *it's* done." *Lord!* he thought, *who do I think I am?* But something more substantial than formal biddings and prayers was being called for here, and he felt a rush of adrenalin as he seized the moment, following instincts he didn't even know he had, hurtling himself out into the void, unassisted by book or collar, bidding the storm to cease, calming the wind and waves with outstretched hand.

"We came here today to give thanks to God for Stan's life. Well, we've done that." The room fell silent. "Now it's time to say our good-byes. So now I'm going to ask you all to stand." And obediently they stood, holding on to one another, looking up at David.

David launched into the prayer of commendation, his voice strong and sure:

*Into your hands, O merciful Saviour, we commend your servant, Stan. Acknowledge, we pray, a sheep of your own fold, a lamb of your own flock, a sinner of your own redeeming. Receive him into the arms of your mercy, into the blessed rest of everlasting peace, and into the glorious company of the saints in light. Amen.*

"Amen," the room repeated as one.

David then concluded with a blessing, his hand rising instinctively to make the form of the cross in the air before him. A few members of the congregation followed suit, crossing themselves. He paused for a moment, looking out into the crowd. They were like children, their faces turned upward, waiting for him to tell them what would happen next. "God bless you all," he said. "This concludes our service."

As he turned to walk away from the podium, loud recorded

music burst from the loudspeakers, filling the hall with a cutting guitar lick that led into a Country & Western song, with its raunchy chorus:

> *I can't wait to get up in the mornin'*
> *And do it all over again.*
> *I'm a hard livin,' hard workin' man.*

The service was over, the dark spell broken. Beer caps were being pried loose. The party was underway.

Stan's boys and their small entourage surrounded David, shaking his hands, thanking him. "You nailed it, man!" someone said. "That's just what the old man would have wanted." Marty shook David's hand, pressing into the other two crisp one-hundred dollar bills. "We really appreciate it, Father," he said.

As David walked out to his car he himself didn't know whether Stan was a saint or a sinner. He had referred to him as a "sheep of your own fold," a "lamb of your own flock"; but he didn't even know if the man was a Christian. Still, if the love of one's friends has anything to do with it, Stan had been well commended to God in heaven that day. David felt relieved that his job was done.

And also, that it had begun.

. . .

Sunday morning David rose early, showered and shaved, and tried to prepare himself to meet his new congregations. But he found he was nervous, which was not like him, this being his professional turf, after all, and worship being what he did best. If he were the new rector, and not just the interim minister, it would have been easier — he would have known what to expect. There would have been a parish profile, he would have been interviewed by the parish leaders, he would have known what his "job" was supposed to be. But in this new situation there were just so many unknowns.

His confidence might have been bolstered by the funeral on Friday, which he considered a success, at least pastorally: he had risen to the occasion; he had made a good impression on the local community; he had even broken through some of his own stuffiness. He was not displeased with this. But as liturgy, the service had left much to be desired — maudlin undignified eulogies, the absence of a proper homily, hence no real mention of the resurrection and, to cap it off, a Country and Western song for a recessional hymn. Clearly, it was not his best work.

But there was something else that conspired to undermine his confidence, something even more deeply disconcerting to him. Since arriving at the Coast, David had been making an unsettling personal discovery: he was no longer able to pray.

For years, ever since college, David had begun each day saying the morning office from the *Book of Common Prayer*. He was religious in this daily observance, in every sense of the word. He used a low prayer stool, a gift from a monk at an Anglican monastery in upstate New York. He offered the prayers and canticles not simply by rote, in order to get through them, but with real devotion. Most days the recitation of the service brought him a feeling of closeness with his God, even on days when he was tired or sick or distracted; he simply allowed the printed words to carry him along, which they did unfailingly.

But it had been almost two weeks now since he had been able to say his prayers — morning, evening, or anything in between. While on the road, he hadn't even tried, everything being in such flux and turmoil. But each morning since he had arrived on the Coast, he had taken his prayer stool upstairs to the attic;

he had placed it on an old ring rug in front of the window overlooking the inlet; he had knelt down, prayer book in hand, fanning the well-worn pages until he arrived at the starting place; he had found a comfortable position, calmed his breathing, cleared his mind; but then ... nothing. He could not open his mouth. He could not focus his thoughts. He just could not bring himself to do it.

Each day he sat for the allotted time, twenty minutes, and sometimes longer. Gazing out the window, he observed the harbour's deep troubled waters, swirling in confusion with the changing of the tide. Raising his eyes, he surveyed Mount Ozzard, the ravaged mountain that rose from the far side of the inlet, and he meditated upon its scarred face. But looking inward, upon his own interior landscape, he saw nothing: only a dark yawning emptiness.

This bothered David. But he viewed it with a strange detachment, as if he were hearing the confession of a stranger, as if something were unfolding before him over which he had no control. Nor could he find a ready explanation for what was happening to him; he was not angry at God, for instance. It was more that there was simply nothing to say, a void having opened up where once God had been.

So it was with enormous effort that, early Saturday morning, David had made himself a cup of coffee and descended slowly to the study to start preparing the Sunday services.

He pulled the files containing the Sunday bulletins from previous years. They were laid out reasonably well, giving him a pretty good idea of what a United Church service looked like. As he scanned a bulletin insert that contained the hymns for the week, reprinted, he was alarmed to pick up several glaring misspellings. The beautiful hymn, "Take Up Thy Cross," with its consoling lines, "His strength shall bear thy spirit up, and brace thy heart, and nerve thine arm," was here rendered, "His strength shall *beat* thy spirit up...." Well, yes, he thought. This was just about how it felt — God's strength, beating his spirit up.

He was surprised to see that United Church worship did in fact have some sort of structure to it. He had always assumed that a United Church service would be like a folksy quilt, the kind raffled off at church bazaars, a colourful collection of hymns and readings and prayers all jumbled together, with a sermon thrown in somewhere for good measure. He had imagined United Church congregations singing campfire songs and breaking into small discussion groups, anything to keep the people interested, the preacher in his place and, above all, the service from becoming too predictable, too — shudder to think of it — liturgical.

But the bulletins he leafed through now revealed something far more intentional than he might have thought. In most cases there was a definite gathering rite, with a call to worship, an opening hymn, and what he would refer to as a collect for the day. The readings were presented in an orderly fashion, from Old Testament through to Gospel, reflecting the same lectionary with which any Anglican would be familiar. The sermon was followed by intercessory prayers, just like in his own church and, in some cases, by a prayer of confession. The adjustment, David realized, was not going to be that great: these were not foreigners after all.

So he poured over the readings for the coming Sunday, noting the various themes as he went. He hunted for hymns that would underline these themes from the three or four hymnals he found in the study. He chose prayers that would advance the themes and, where none could be found, he wrote his own, a freedom he had never explored as solely an Anglican priest. He typed up a draft of the service on the old Corona that was the study's only piece of office equipment, gathered up his hymnals, and found his way to Mimi's house a few blocks away.

Mimi greeted him at the kitchen door. She was diminutive, thirty-something, with short-cropped hair and lively eyes. Her greeting was effusive as she ushered him in, inviting him to join her at the kitchen table, offering him a coffee. She was single, it became clear, had lived in Ucluelet since her student-teaching days, over ten years ago, and was currently teaching third grade at the local elementary school. She was a live wire who was in constant motion, talking fast, gesturing with both hands, moving in short spurts, like a mouse, about the small space of her tiny kitchen, the constant flow of skittish energy being fuelled, David guessed, by a constant supply of coffee.

She was curious about him, wanting to know where he had come from, how long he would be staying, whether the "manse" provided for his needs. She nodded and smiled encouragingly as he answered. The one thing she did not ask about was his marital status. So David volunteered the information himself, saying this was a sort of working sabbatical for him and that his wife and children might come out to join him at the end of his time there. This was not something he had thought about before, but it suddenly struck him as not too bad an idea at that.

This served to stem the flow of Mimi's personal questions as she took an abrupt change in tack, feigning interest in the draft order of service David had brought along. She bent in close as he spread it open on the table before them. When he glanced up, he found her face very near, her large green eyes looking directly into his. She did not look away. He smiled politely, sat back in his chair, and asked what it was, exactly, that she did at the church.

Mimi's job — her "ministry," she called it — was to prepare the Sunday bulletin according to whatever form of service they were doing that week, pulling it up on her computer, and changing the details — the readings and the hymns — that were provided by the minister. Every week she printed off, as well, a bulletin insert containing the words to all the hymns being used. The two congregations used so many different hymnals and song books, plus an assortment of gospel choruses, that there was no way to have all this music in the pews. That's why the songs were reprinted in the insert each week, she explained.

David asked about copyright. Mimi looked at him, nodding and smiling, but drawing a blank. Did they have permission to be printing off all these hymns, he asked her. She didn't know what he was talking about. Why would they need permission, she asked. Who would know anyway? He decided to let it drop. And he decided not to raise the other question either, the one about her spelling.

The first Sunday service, held at nine a.m., was at St. Columba's in Tofino. The church, inside, was dark and inviting. In the tiny entrance hall a table displayed some items for sale: the ubiquitous church plates, mugs, and teaspoons one encounters in churches all across the country; postcards and note paper bearing a photograph of the church on a sunny day, surrounded by rhododendrons and the hanging branches of a large willow; and a curious book, a collection of short stories written by a former incumbent. Sad, David thought, that some clerics felt driven to distinguish themselves in this way. What was wrong with the simple honour of humble priestly service?

Inside the church, up in the sanctuary, a small older woman was standing on her toes, arranging flowers in large vases on the altar, her back to the new minister. He cleared his throat as he started down the short aisle, but she did not seem to hear him. "Good morning," he said. But she continued working away, undisturbed.

Finally, as he stepped up into the sanctuary just behind her, she spun around and let out a little squeal of surprise. She was deaf as a stone. When she spoke it was a garble of unconnected vowels and consonants too loud for the confined space. She seemed to be explaining to him who she was. He put out his hand as if to say it was all right, she didn't have to explain anything. But this seemed only to confuse her. She turned back to the flowers, visibly agitated.

David went behind the curtain that served as an entrance to the tiny vestry, an alcove with room enough only for a built-in desk, a chair, and a couple of coat hooks on the opposite wall. He tried to robe in the cramped space, contorting his body so as not to stick his elbow or his backside out through the curtain into the chancel area. That would not be the best way of introducing himself, he thought.

David waited to hear music, or some other sign that the congregation was assembled and ready. He didn't want to peak out through the curtains — that would look too ridiculous — so he stood, wedged in the tiny space, looking at his watch. Finally, in the absence of any audible signs of gathering, he decided it was time to go forth and face his new congregation. He parted the curtains and stepped out. All six of them looked up at him from their places in the well-worn pews, five older women and one scruffy-looking young man who seemed to have just wandered in, perhaps drunk, or high. There was no organist. Mysteriously, the flower lady had vanished.

"The Lord be with you," David greeted them.

Only one elderly voice responded, "And with thy spirit." Okay, so she was the Anglican. This was going to be uphill.

"Might I just inquire," he said, "where the organist is this morning?"

"Don't you play?" a woman asked. "All our other ministers have played themselves."

"Or their wives," another added.

"I see," David said, his mind racing ahead to figure out his options. He *could* play himself. He had taken piano lessons throughout his childhood and was still a pretty good sight-reader. But he didn't want to be the organist. It detracted from his role as presider. Yet, in this instance ...

He looked in the bulletin for the opening hymn — "Awake, my soul, and with the sun." Yes, he supposed he was up to playing this one. So he introduced himself, saying he was sure they would be able to figure things out as they went along. They looked at him without surprise, as if that's precisely what they *always* did, week by week — figure things out as they went along.

So David sat down at the organ, a dated two-manual parlour model with a whole bank of percussion sounds and rhythms, from Rhumba to Swing, from which he kept his distance. He found a few of the more conventional stops — flute, violin, and bass — and launched into the last two lines of the verse, by way of introduction. His was the only voice he could hear over the crackling rumble of the organ's speakers, singing the verses as Mimi had reprinted them:

*Awake, my soul, and with the sun*
*Thy daily stage of duty run;*
*Shake off dull sloth, and joyful rise*
*To pay thy mirming sacrifice.*

Thy "mirming" sacrifice? David sighed inwardly. Morning! *Morning* sacrifice! But, yes, he had to admit this was a sort of "mirming" sacrifice, their voices scarcely rising to the rafters, let alone to the heavens.

St. Aidan's, back in Ucluelet, was a bit more promising. Someone was already seated at the piano as he entered the bright sun-lit church overlooking the harbour. There was a larger congregation assembled here, relatively speaking: there were seven, including Mimi; eight, including himself; nine, including the rotund middle-aged man at the piano. He seemed to be trying to pick his way through a gospel chorus. David nodded a greeting to him as he approached. The man stopped mid-note and turned to shake David's hand. He said his name was Ernest. He seemed a bit simple.

"Are you playing for the service, Ernest?" David asked him, hopefully.

"If you like," he answered him.

"Yes, that would be grand," David said. "Thank you."

But as the service began, and David announced the first hymn, Ernest spoke right out. "I don't know that one," he said.

"Oh," David said. "Well, is there something else you could lead us in, to help us get started?"

"I can't read music," Ernest answered.

"All right then," David said, "is there something we all know that you could play?"

Mimi was sitting in the second pew. "Play 'Shine, Jesus, Shine' Ernie," she said. "That's a nice one."

"Thank you, Mimi," David said. "Okay, Ernest, lead away."

And Ernest leaned into a plodding chord-based rendition of what ought to have been a lively song. Everyone seemed to know it. Mimi raised her hands slightly in a gesture of praise. The others sang along politely.

David had prepared a homily concerned with God's act of creation, the beauty of the earth, and our responsibility to care for it. Half way through, it began to dawn on him that the people here might interpret his comments as an unqualified endorsement of the environmentalist movement. And these hearty folks looked like they just might come out on the other end of that particular issue.

But as his mind briefly wandered to consider how he might avoid causing offence, a sudden sound from down in the harbour shattered his thoughts. It was a loud barking, resounding across the inlet. The windows on the north face of the church looked out over the harbour and from his place at the chancel step David could see quite distinctly that something was thrashing about in the water. A dark form suddenly thrust itself out, like a harbour seal, but larger.

David couldn't help interrupting himself. "Forgive me," he said, "but what *is* that?"

The congregation, jolted into sudden attentiveness, followed his gaze. They smiled. "That's just a sea lion," someone said.

"A sea lion?" David asked, incredulous. "Really?"

"You'll get used to that," they said, smiling up at him, enjoying the rare moment of spontaneity.

"Thank you," he said to them. "A sea lion. Well, what do you know! Thank you."

Later, David's energies were depleted as he pulled the car up to the rectory. He did not feel very satisfied with his performance that morning. He had tried his best — and hadn't done too badly for someone working outside his usual comfort zone. He had to give himself at least a little credit.

But the young visitor up at St. Columba's had got up and walked out just as David was starting his sermon. St. Aidan's had been somewhat more responsive, but there was scant evidence of anything resembling Anglicanism. The gospel choruses and songs led by Ernest, pounding away on the piano, certainly put some life into the service, but it did not feel like "liturgy," at least as David understood the term.

And at both churches he had found that the professional distance required of the good liturgist was hard to maintain. He looked out and saw these small clutches of morning worshippers, content enough just to be there, asking nothing of him except that he lead them through the time-worn rituals in his own way, whatever that was. Decades of "revolving door clergy," coming and going, two or three years at a time, had drained from them any expectations they might have had for any particular style of worship. They were happy just to be there.

And oddly, he had to admit, so was he.

The curtains moved in the window of the cottage next door as David gathered up his robes and books from the car. His arms full, he could only give a friendly smile in the direction of his strange unseen neighbour.

. . .

David wasn't sure if he got a day off with this new job, but no one seemed too concerned about his punching a clock. So on Monday he finished his morning "sit" up in the attic and decided he might just walk into town for a newspaper. There was no television in the rectory, which was all right with him, but he did miss his morning paper.

He found his way to Murray's, a large convenience store on Peninsula Road, the town's main thoroughfare. It had a promising magazine rack with all the weekly community papers from around the Island, from Port Alberni and Nanaimo, and most of the dailies from Victoria and Vancouver. What David was looking for, though, was the *Globe & Mail*. Not only was it "Canada's National Newspaper" but, more important, it was a familiar friend from his home town.

By the time he arrived at the store it was just after eight a.m. All they had left were the tattered remains of the weekend papers. The bus, he was told, wouldn't be getting in for another half- hour. That was okay with David, who did not have plans for the day anyway. So he drove the Frog Prince a couple of doors down to the Peninsula Restaurant for a coffee, parking in front of its street-side picture window.

"The Pen," as it was called locally, proved to be the morning gathering place for the town's elders, older guys in jeans and wind-breakers, lounging in booths or huddled around tables, cups of coffee coddled in their hands, telling stories, laughing easily. Several at one booth looked up as David entered, taking an interest in him as he made his way to a table by the window. When he looked over in their direction, they returned to their talk.

He watched the lazy traffic making its way up and down the street, no one in a hurry, everyone taking the day as it came, just as he was doing. He finished his coffee, paid at the counter and, seeing the table of old guys looking at him again, nodded and smiled. One, whose arm was draped over the back of the padded bench seat, motioned with his hand for David to approach. He was being granted an audience. David walked over to them.

"That was a nice service you done for Stan," the old guy said, the others nodding.

"Thank you," David returned. "It was an honour to have been asked to do it, especially being new and everything."

"So which church are you?" another said.

David pointed up the street. "St. Aidan's," he said.

They nodded.

David lingered for a moment, but that seemed to be the end of the interview.

"So," David said, "I guess I'll see you around."

Their good-byes were offered by way of nods and hand ges- tures. David knew as he walked away that, after he was gone, they would pronounce their judgement on him. He hoped he had made a good impression. Just as he reached the door he heard one of them say, "Nice car!" They all chuckled.

He returned to Murray's, picked up a paper from the fresh bundle that the bus driver was just then dropping onto the floor in front of the magazine rack, paid at the cash, and made his way home. There was something about this pace of life he could get used to.

David was just inside the front door of the rectory when the phone rang. He strode quickly down the hall and picked it up. "Hello?"

"Hello, David." The voice at the other end was instantly recognizable.

"Hello, Bev," he said. Then he froze, holding his breath. He waited for her to speak. It was bold for him to have called her by her shortened nickname, but it had been instinctive; it just came out that way. He hoped this would not have set the wrong tone.

Both were silent for a moment.

"So, were you going to call us?" she asked him at last. "We thought you were going to call us."

"I *was*," David said, trying not to sound defensive. "I wrote you a letter. I guess you haven't received it yet."

"But you said you were going to call," Beverley said. "It's important, David. It's important to the kids."

"I'm sorry," he said.

Beverley let out a sigh. She clicked her tongue. "No, *I'm* sorry," she said. "I didn't want to do this. I didn't want to start off like this. We were worried, that's all. I had to call Bishop Hovey at his home to get your number."

"I'm sorry," David said again. Neither one spoke for another moment.

"So, how is it going anyway?" Beverley asked. "What's it like?"

"It's okay," David said. "The drive was fantastic. We should ... well, you know, we could ... take it sometime, maybe. As a family."

Beverley did not respond. Again they fell silent.

"You're all right then?" she said finally.

"Ya, I'm okay."

"Do you want to talk to the kids?" Beverley said.

"Are they home?" David asked.

"It's a professional development day," she said. "Here's Catherine."

Catherine's voice bounced onto the line. "Dad?"

"Hi, sweetie!" he said. "It's great to hear your voice. How are you? Is everything okay there?"

"We miss you," she said. "I got an A on my French lab last week."

"That's great, Catherine," David said, knowing he would be lucky now to squeeze in even a few words. He leaned against the doorway, smiling, as a rush of details poured forth about her life at school, about her tiff with Odessa, her best friend, about her try-outs for the basketball team. When the words finally ran out she grew suddenly silent.

"So, are you okay, Dad?" she asked him.

"Yes, I'm okay," he said. "But I'm missing you all."

"So why did you do this, Dad?" she asked. "Why did you go away?"

"I don't know if I could explain it," he said, honestly. "It just seems to be something I needed to do." He left it there for the moment. It sounded like she might be crying. "But it's okay, sweetie," he reassured her. "Really. We're still a family, and when I come back we'll all be together again. Okay?"

Catherine sniffed into the phone. "Okay. Here's Paul," she said. "I love you, Daddy."

"I love you too, Catherine."

Paul came on the line, his voice deeper and more resonant than David had remembered it.

"Hi, son," David said, surprised by his sudden retreat behind such a formal greeting, a greeting that might have come from his own father. "How are you?"

"Okay," Paul answered him, also stiffly. "How's the car doing?"

"I just wrote you about that," David answered him. "I had to give it up in Saskatchewan. A blown head gasket or something. But I got this little Sprint. It's painted green. You'd like it."

"Dad!" Paul chided his father. "A Sprint has only three cylinders! You don't want a three cylinder car!"

"You're absolutely right," David said, "I don't. But I didn't know at the time that it had only three cylinders. I think I sort of got taken advantage of."

"Dad!" Paul chided him again.

David asked Paul about his classes, about plans for his upcoming birthday, and then about the youth group retreat coming up the following weekend.

"I don't know if I'm going," Paul said.

"But why wouldn't you?" David asked him. "You'd have a great time. And they'd miss you."

"Ya, but we haven't gone to church the last two Sundays," Paul explained. "Mum feels too awkward. And I guess I do too. Like, what are we supposed to say if people ask about you? So I don't know. It feels weird."

"Oh, Paul," David said. "Don't stay home on my account. It'd be so much fun."

Paul didn't answer.

"Well, I guess we'd better go then," David said. "Is Mum still there? Can I talk with her?"

"No, she's gone," Paul said. Then, after a pause, he added, "She's pretty upset, y'know, Dad."

David didn't know what to say. No words presented themselves to him. He clung to the receiver as he gazed out through the kitchen window to the mountain beyond, scarred and naked to the elements. He began choking up. He put his hand over the mouthpiece, blinking away the tears.

"Dad?" Paul was asking. "Dad, are you still there?"

"Ya, I'm still here, Paul," David said, steadying his voice. He took a deep breath. "So, you guys are okay?"

"Ya, we're okay," Paul said. "When are you coming home?"

"Well, I've got this job to do here," David said, trying to sound positive. "But I'll be home after that." Then suddenly he was struck with an idea. He added, "Hey, Paul?"

"Yes?"

"How would you like to come out and join me?"

"Join you? How could I do that?"

"When's your spring break this year?"

"Middle of March, I guess," Paul answered, sounding interested.

"Well, I'm here until Easter," David said, thinking out loud. "And Easter comes early this year. If it coincides with your spring break why don't we fly you down and you and I could spend my last week here together. Then we could drive back."

"Fly *up*, you mean," Paul corrected him. "You're at the forty-ninth parallel, Dad. We're below the forty-fourth. You're farther north than we are."

"Right," David said, getting excited, "I guess I am. But you'd love this place, Paul. We could do some whale-watching. Did you know that twenty-two thousand gray whales make their migration past here in the spring? Twenty-two thousand! They have quite a celebration, with parades and I don't know what all. But I'd love to show you this place! Think about it. Speak to your mum. We can talk about it later."

"The whales?" Paul asked.

"Yes, what about them?" David asked.

"The whales have a parade?" Paul asked dryly.

David laughed. "It's so good to talk to you, Paul!"

They said their good-byes. David could feel seeds of hope being planted. Just think — Paul, joining him for a father-and-son week! And then driving back together! It could be wonderful, not to say also enormously healing. He wished they could be doing it right now, spring seemed such a long way off. David wondered if Paul would still be as interested in joining him after five more months had gone by.

Which led David to begin wondering about how they would handle the Christmas holidays. He wouldn't try to go back, he knew, and they couldn't afford to fly the family out. He guessed they'd be separated over Christmas. He sighed. There was so much about this trip he hadn't thought through!

But that was a dark hole he didn't need to jump into right now. It was enough that there was this new possibility, this bright spot on the horizon, this visit from his son. There would be time enough to figure things out as they went along, one day at a time, one foot in front of the other. That's how to get through this thing, he said to himself, whatever it was he was doing.

He put on his coat and went out again, waving cheerily at the cottage next door, without waiting to see if the curtains moved. He took the Frog Prince to the far side of the peninsula. He was ready to explore its wide beaches and its windswept headlands. He was ready to fix his gaze upon the vast Pacific Ocean.

# Chapter Four

As the days passed, it was becoming clear to David that the weather was taking a turn for the worse. The low cloud banks that had been gathering on the horizon were now moving inland, cloaking the town in a gray mist by day and muffled rainfall by night, the fog horn droning its sombre warning in the wet darkness. Winter was coming, and with it the winter rains and storms that bring over twelve feet of rain each year to this part of the world, though David was told it could easily be more. The town was battening down the hatches, preparing for the coming onslaught.

But the darkening days and weeks gradually fell into a rhythm, which suited David just fine, a man of routine. In the mornings he would have his meditative "sit" in the attic, then walk into town for a newspaper, sometimes taking it into the Pen, where he would order toast and coffee and, if the day was particularly gloomy, a slab of home-made pie as well. He was sure to give a friendly nod to the old guys, who returned the gesture. He would return home by way of the post office. Mid-morning, the mail was still in the process of being sorted. But this meant that he could come again in the afternoon, and thus provide another anchor for his day.

The post office clerk's name was Denise. He had learned in his first conversation with her that she was a single mother of four children, that she had lived here all her life, that she had seen a lot of ministers come and go, and that Tuesday was bingo night at the Army, Navy, and Air Force Veteran's Hall. He should come by some evening, she told him, and get to know some people. Her chattiness made him feel welcome, and he was grateful for it.

Back at the rectory he would sort through the mail, quickly casting aside the ubiquitous flyers and solicitations. Eagerly he tore open anything resembling personal correspondence, though that was rare. By then he was ready to get down to work planning his sermon and working up the order of service for the coming Sunday.

He found the task of worship preparation more challenging here than in a conventional Anglican parish. No longer could he simply rely on the Prayer Book to tell him what to do. Especially on United Church Sundays, he had to build the service from the ground up, using the week's appointed scripture readings as a foundation. But the task satisfied him, and it was often with an artist's sense of pride that he delivered his latest creation to Mimi's door, along with more helpful suggestions for the layout of the bulletin than she could possibly execute.

For his afternoon rounds, David split his days between Ucluelet and Tofino. In Ucluelet he made home visits to some of the older members, and to others referred to him by parishioners. That's how he got to know Maisie. Her husband, Norm, had died shortly before David arrived. But the bitterness she harboured was not about his passing, his health having been in decline for years. Her special wrath was reserved for the "tree-huggers" who had caused the stress which, in turn, had contributed to his dying at only fifty-nine.

Norm "drove truck," as they said, for a logging company. It was a good job, and Norm was good at it. He was bringing a load of logs down the mountain the day the protestors set up camp at the bridge. No one had told him. He rounded the last turn, one hundred and fifty tons of downward momentum carrying him home. There, spread before him, was a small city of tents, women with babes in arms tramping through the mud. He couldn't stop; there was nowhere to turn. He pulled long and loud on the horn and headed straight for the bridge. What else could he do?

As he sped across the bridge, his breaks smoking, he saw in his side-view mirrors people flying out from both sides of his passing rig. It was a miracle he hadn't killed someone. Maisie said his hands shook for days. Then he read about himself in the papers, how a logging truck had tried to mow down a camp of peaceful protestors. He quit the next day, and never worked again.

In Tofino, David acquainted himself with the small ten-bed hospital. There he met Ruth, a nurse who was also a strident environmentalist. She had come to join in the fight against the logging of old growth forests in Clayoquot Sound. But she so fell in love with the natural beauty and vitality of the place that she never got away again.

There were seldom patients to visit, so David would stand at the nurses' station and visit with Ruth. If the world were seen as a single organism, she explained to him, then we would no more rape the earth than we would our own mothers. It gives us life; we should walk respectfully, reverently.

It turned out that Ruth had been on the bridge that day when Norm's rig had come barrelling through. She was one of those who were sent flying in its wake, one of those Norm had seen through his side-view mirrors. She had landed on a pile of rocks, breaking her arm, something the reporters picked up on for their stories. It was a small price to pay, she said, to save the forests.

When he felt he had done his visiting for the afternoon, David would go for long walks. On Ucluelet days, this meant clambering over the rocky headlands on the rugged ocean side of the peninsula. David would kneel down and peer into the deep clear tidal pools to watch the tiny hermit crabs scuttling and scurrying about their busy days. He would prod the tentacles of the green and red sea anemones, and marvel at the reflexes of these deceptively flower-like carnivores who, sensing danger, fold in on themselves, closing up tight, like a bell pepper. Somewhere near here, he had been told, in the deeper channels, octopus abandoned their young so they would learn the ways of the tide and grow to claim their place on the food chain. David steadied himself on rocky ledges to catch a glimpse of them swimming about in the dark waters, though he figured that fall was likely not the season of their infancy.

On Tofino days, he would stroll the misty beaches in the park, stooping to inspect whatever the tide had left behind that day. He examined the scallop shells and miniature conches, pocketing as mementoes the more unusual specimens. The smooth sculpted driftwood was like some sort of natural Rorschach test, this one a woman's thigh, this one a jester's hat. He pocketed the woman's thigh.

On each expedition David was awakened to a childlike sense of wonder; every new discovery surprised and delighted him. He bought himself a rubberized raincoat with a hood for his afternoon walks, his wool duffel coat being of little use in this wet climate. He also purchased a pair of black rubber boots — "wellies," he had called them in his childhood; "fisherman's Oxfords" the salesclerk had called them in the tiny nook that served as the clothing department at the Co-op.

One day, as he was eating his lunch at the kitchen table, David heard what sounded like the barking of dogs down in the harbour, the sharp distinctive sounds echoing across the inlet. But by now he knew better. Hoping this might be his first chance to observe a sea lion up close, he jumped into his boots, thrust his arms into the sleeves of his slicker, and dashed across the back yard and down to the refuelling docks at the waterfront.

Running out onto the high planked dock, he found himself staring down upon not one sea lion, but an entire family. Eight or ten California sea lions, identifiable by their dark colouring and their protrusive foreheads, were frolicking around the hull of a large dragger that was refuelling at the floating dock. Rolling about in the frigid waters, they were performing for their supper, or for their hopes of supper, their dark shimmering eyes fixed constantly on the boat.

David could not suppress a broad grin as he leaned over the wooden railing, his hands thrust deep into his pockets, his collar turned up against the cold. This was the sort of sight that might merit only a glance as you passed the concrete water tanks at the zoo, on the way to the gorillas. But this was not a zoo; this was the real thing. And he was being granted the incredible opportunity of standing in this spot, of witnessing this scene, a scene to which no camera could ever do justice. His was the irreplaceable thrill of *being there*.

The stiff wind blowing up the inlet from the open ocean was doing its best to dissuade him from lingering, sending shivers across the surface of his skin and bringing water to his eyes. So, yielding to his discomfort, he took a deep satisfying breath and turned to leave.

But now a new wonder offered itself to David. Above him, two bald eagles hung in the air overhead, riding the incoming southeaster, their magnificent wings spread wide, the wingspans measuring easily the full height of his own body. They were so close to him he could hear the wind rustling through their flight feathers. Unconcerned with his presence, they were neither hunting nor hurrying but, like the sea lions, appeared simply to be enjoying the moment: they were playing! Forgetting the damp and the cold, David stood gaping on the dock beneath them, transfixed by the sight of these proud mythical creatures borne aloft so effortlessly by the steady invisible hand of the wind.

Was he really allowed to be here, David asked himself, to witness all this? He felt intoxicated by the natural drama unfolding around him every day. It made him want to see more, to experience everything. He began to venture farther and farther out on the rocky outcrops, edging closer to the slippery interface of sea and shore, to feel on his face the spray of the pounding waves and the power of the rising wind.

David's mornings, then, were taken up with pleasant industry; his afternoons were filled with wonder. It was the evenings that proved difficult. With darkness descending now by suppertime, David faced the falling of night as if it were an encircling gloom. The events of the past weeks crept out from the shadows and followed him through the empty house, demanding some sort of accounting, which he was unable to give. Without television, something he never thought he would miss, he wandered aimlessly from room to vacant room, searching for something to engage him.

It was in the evenings that David would write his letters home. He wrote his mother and his sister. He wrote individual letters to Paul and to Catherine and, of course, to Beverley, struggling to make their separation come off sounding normal, as if he were merely away on retreat, soon to return, bearing in his arms gifts for all. He and Beverley were not addressing the real issues, and he knew it. They were keeping their hailing frequencies open, that was all.

Later in the evenings, he would read, the sad remnants of his library offering him only the driest of provisions. One night he turned in desperation to several old binders he had discovered in a cupboard in the study. David blew the dust from the covers and began flipping through the pages, which contained the minutes of meetings, the financial reports, and the membership lists that constituted the official records of the Long Beach Pastoral Charge from the days before the Anglican and United congregations joined into one. Absently turning a blue-lined page dating back to the 1960s, some yellowed newspaper clippings fell out.

The clippings concerned a United Church minister — David's predecessor by some thirty-five years — who, a few weeks before he was to leave the Coast to begin doctoral studies at Oxford, headed out for a three-day excursion by boat from Ucluelet to Vargas Island, in Clayoquot Sound, for some beach combing. He never made it. His empty boat was found soon enough, all the equipment and motors in proper order; but it was four months before his body washed ashore, his red life-jacket still secured around his bloated remains.

David was intrigued. He searched back through the minutes for some clue as to who this man was. But unlike the rectors of Anglican parishes, who often have a dominant role in church meetings, this minister was mentioned only in passing. It was reported that he opened a meeting with a reading from scripture; that he made some suggestions for a new purchase; that he closed a meeting with prayer.

In the pages that followed the clippings — after his death, in other words — he was mentioned only twice in the official record, and both times indirectly. One was a line item saying that the church had agreed to buy the ditto machine back from his widow. The other was a motion, several weeks later, granting her three months of her husband's salary. The motion passed.

So this is what it is like to be dead and gone, David thought

— a transfer of ownership, a pay-out of funds. But otherwise forgotten. He thought of his own congregation back in Ontario. How were they getting on, he wondered. Did they miss him? Did they talk about him? Did they even think of him now, a month later? Or were they smitten by the interim priest who, in all likelihood, was already dismantling all that he, David, had been trying so obsessively to establish?

David removed the newspaper clippings from the binder and pinned them to the bulletin board above the desk. For the brief time he was here, he would remember this man; it was the least he could do.

Reluctantly, David began picking up cheap paperback novels from the racks near the check-out counters at the Co-op, the popular pulp of airport authors, writing to advance a quick plot, not to deepen understanding. But they did serve to divert his attention, to keep the shadows at bay, and he came to count on the predictable antics of the cardboard characters to lead him into weariness and, finally, into sleep.

Of course, Sunday had always been the big day of the week for David: everything pointed to Sunday, and his work week did not end until Sunday ended. But here, Sunday seemed strangely understated. People's expectations were low. His congregations seemed content merely with his showing up. Over time, this had an effect on David, and his own expectations began dropping a few notches. One would be hard-pressed to call it "laid back" exactly, but David's officiating style was changing as he settled into his new role; as he was getting to know his people, and they were getting to know him.

Up in Tofino, they seemed actually to be enjoying the sight of their earnest new minister in his flowing robes, gliding in behind the organ to lead the hymns, then sliding out again to take his place at the lectern or the altar. In Ucluelet, the musical repertoire suffered from Ernie's technical limitations, the congregation singing far more gospel choruses and campfire ditties than proper hymns. But at least they were singing, and David along with them.

David couldn't help feeling that his preaching was suffering from the dearth of scholarly resources he had at his disposal. He found himself speaking more from personal observation than from official church positions or established theological dogmas. When he referred to situations that he encountered here on the Coast — the brokenness of the native communities, the contentious confusion about logging rights, the new fishing restrictions that were fast destroying a way of life — he did so with the care and respect of someone who was aware he did not really know what he was talking about, someone who was asking questions rather than offering answers.

He wished he could show them the stuff he was really made of as a preacher, quoting entire passages in Greek, referring to the Early Christian Fathers with their strange exotic names — like Tertullian, Origen, Clement of Alexandria — or using impressive scholarly terms like 'eschatological' and 'anthropomorphic.'

But this new simpler approach had its own rewards. He found that now, whenever he cast a glance out across the faces of his tiny congregations, they were actually looking back at him; they were paying attention. It was becoming more a conversation and less a monologue.

This was confirmed by the remarks they would make later in the week as they passed him in an aisle at the Co-op or waited in line behind him at the post office. One day a complete stranger stopped him on the street in Tofino to say she had heard that he preached a good sermon on Sunday. About whales or something, she thought. He himself couldn't remember preaching about whales. But then, when you start preaching more or less extemporaneously, you can no longer be altogether sure just what you've said, after it's done.

So he accepted the compliment with gratitude, the first real compliment he could remember receiving in years, and his first *ever* hearsay compliment. Someone, at last, seemed to be listening.

. . .

From day to day, David could not help but grow troubled by the movement of the curtains next door, parting slightly each time he went to or from the rectory. He never saw anyone, but someone was in there, watching him. This bothered him, to be watched. But even more troubling was the thought that they had nothing better to do with their time than to sit by that window all day long as the world went by.

Pulling up at the rectory one day after an afternoon of pastoral visiting and seaside exploration, David once again saw the curtains part in the front window of the little white cottage next door. This is ridiculous, he thought. He got out of the car, walked over, and knocked on the door.

An old man appeared in the doorway. He wore overalls and a thick wool sweater, moth-eaten and soot-smeared.

"Hi," David said. "I'm Father David ... no, sorry, that's just David, David Corcoran. I'm staying at the rectory next door for a while, so I thought I should just come on over and introduce myself to you."

The old man studied David through small dark eyes that peered out from deep-set hollows. There was nothing to him, just leathered skin stretched across bone, and several days' growth of stubble on his face. He had once been a big man, David guessed, from his long bent frame.

"I guess you'd better come in then," he said to David, turning back into the house, which opened directly into the kitchen, a table and chair pulled up tight to the window.

"No, no, that's not necessary," David said. "I just wanted to meet you, and to let you know who it is that's been coming and going every day next door."

The old man turned around and looked at him again. He said nothing.

"So I didn't catch your name," David said.

"I didn't tell you my name," the old man replied.

"Right," David replied, chastened. He waited for his neighbour to speak.

"It's Cecil," he said, finally. "What's yours again?"

"David. David Corcoran. I'm the new ... *minister* at St. Aidan's. At least for a few months." David felt that an actual conversation with Cecil might require more energy than he had to give. "I'll have you over for coffee some day," he offered, "but I should go now. So take care."

David was aware of Cecil watching him from the door as he made his way back to the rectory.

In the city David had his hair cut every three weeks, usually on a Friday, and he saw no reason to break that pattern now. So one Friday he got out the slim paperback booklet that served as the area's phone book and searched for the hair salons. There were only two listed. One was "Lucille's Hair Boutique and Submarine Sandwiches" in Ucluelet. The mental picture this evoked — of meatball sandwiches and airborne clumps of hair — brought on an involuntary gagging reflex. So David called the other listing, "Randy Hair Design," even though it was up in Tofino. A male voice answered and said that, yes, he had an opening that afternoon.

Just before three o'clock David showed up at Randy's, which was in the back of a curio shop, itself tucked in behind the Coffee Pod. One certainly had to know where to look. David stepped over the legs of the young drifters who lounged outside on the porch, their dogs and guitars strewn about nearby.

As he entered the shop, Randy himself came out from behind the partition separating the sales area from the salon area in behind. He was tall and good-looking, his blonde hair carefully sculpted, close-cropped on the sides, longer on top, swept over to one side. Randy introduced himself, greeting his new customer in a breezy style that assumed familiarity. "Cher's Greatest Hits" was playing on a CD player. He invited David to take a seat for a few minutes.

Randy returned to the back, picking up his conversation with another client. "No ... God!" he was saying, "we saw her in Vancouver. She was FABulous! I mean, the outfits! She's so outrageous. She had this one hairpiece? It had to be at least three feet high. Everyone just went crazy. Do you want me take a little more off the sides?"

When it was his turn, David slipped into the hair-washing chair. Randy tipped it so that David's head tilted backward into the basin, and he began massaging shampoo into David's scalp, the warm water hissing as it ran past his ears.

"So, where are you from?" Randy asked in a sing-song voice designed to lead directly to personal revelatory conversation, like pillow talk.

"Toronto," David answered.

"Toronto," Randy repeated. "I lived there for precisely one winter. Couldn't *wait* to leave. Then I spent four years in Vancouver. But even *that* was too much for *me*. That's just me, I guess. I'm not much of a city person. Are you staying here in Tofino?"

"No," David answered. "I'm down in Ucluelet."

"On holiday?" Randy asked.

"Not really," David said, the suds running back down his head into the sink, chased by the tiny jet streams of rinse water.

"Doing some work here then?"

"Yes, in a way," David said, "but just for six months."

"So ... what do you do?" Randy pressed on, sitting David up and leading him over to the hair-cutting chair.

"Well, actually, I'm a priest, an Anglican priest." He let that hang for a moment before adding, "but I'm acting as the United Church minister as well. I'm doing an interim ministry at St. Aidan's in Ucluelet and St. Columba's here in Tofino."

"St. Columba's?" Randy exclaimed with interest. "Oh, I just a*dore* that little church. I've always meant to look inside. So you can tell I'm not much of a church-goer myself."

David saw that Randy was inspecting his new customer in the mirror. David glanced in the mirror himself, curious to see what Randy was seeing. What he discovered, looking back at himself, was a clean-shaven middle-aged man with unimaginatively short-cropped hair, pleasant enough, a little jowly, but with something in his eyes, something fleeting, a secret perhaps.

"So ... you're a minister ... from Toronto," Randy was saying. "Well, *that's* interesting!"

"Yes," David continued, feeling encouraged. "But I have to admit everything feels quite different out here than in Ontario. I don't know what it is, exactly."

"I'm sure that's true," Randy said, nodding sympathetically.

Randy was still studying David in the mirror. "Married?" he asked him, beginning to make little snips here and there with the shears.

"Yes," David replied.

"Hmm. Children?"

"Two."

"Boys or girls?"

"Both."

"How old?"

"Thirteen and fifteen — well, soon to be sixteen."

"And they're here with you?"

David shook his head.

"Hmm," Randy said again, trying to put the pieces together. "So what would bring you way out here, on your own?" he asked him. "Why didn't your family come with you?"

David swallowed hard. "I think I just needed a break," he said, trying to maintain his equilibrium while the ground fell away beneath him. "I don't really know what to say. It's just one of those things." He stole a glance at Randy in the mirror. He was saying too much. "I'm sorry," he said, "I guess that doesn't make much sense."

"No, no," Randy reassured him, "that's okay. We all need to get away sometimes. And this is certainly the place to get away *to*." Randy kept snipping as he went on. "Did you know we get almost a million visitors here each year?" he asked David.

David opened his eyes wide in response, fearing that any words would reveal a tremor in his voice.

"It's true," Randy said. "People come here from all over, from the States, a lot from Germany, and from all across Canada too. They come not just because our dollar is low. They come because this is a very special place, a very ... spiritual place. Some say it has healing properties. Do you know about *feng shui*?"

David shook his head.

"It's Chinese," Randy went on. "It means 'wind and water,' something like that, and has to do with the earth's energy. Well, this place has *tons* of it. Or so I'm told." He patted David on the shoulder. "No, you're going to *love* it here! It'll be good for you. You'll see."

Odd, David thought, that he should be sharing himself so readily with a total stranger. But perhaps this was the advantage of being strangers. After all, for centuries this *had* been the secret of the confessional. Randy was like a priest in his booth, just out of sight, an anonymous but encouraging voice, saying, *What else, my son?* In time, David felt, he just might be inclined to tell him.

. . .

After weeks of David's persistent inquiries about how decisions were supposed to be made, a meeting was finally called of the church council, bringing together the elected officials from the two congregations. It was to be an evening meeting, held at St. Aidan's in Ucluelet.

When the time came, David put on his clerical collar, gathered up the files he thought he might need, donned his duffel coat, and opened the front door, ready to go. There, standing on the stoop, was Cecil. It was not clear whether he had tried the doorbell, or whether he had even intended to. He was standing before the open door as if perhaps he had been about to do something but then forgot what it was, and was just waiting for the thought to return.

It so startled David that he stepped back, dropping his files, scattering papers across the floor of the front hall. "Oh, hi," he stammered. "I didn't know you were there." Cecil watched in silence as David stooped to gather up the papers and stuff them back into the file folders.

"So," David said, "I was just on my way to a meeting at the church."

Cecil looked at him without responding. Then he said, "I'll tell you how to get to the blowhole."

"The blowhole?" David asked him, trying to hide his rising annoyance at this unexpected intrusion. "What's the blowhole?"

"Where the tide surges up a narrow cut in the rock. The spray shoots out like the blowhole of a whale. But it's tricky getting to. I'll tell you how you can find it."

"Okay," David said, trying to sound interested as he fussed with his files and papers, sorting what went where.

"Just take the old logging road from the highway outside of town, down near Mill Stream. It's on Indian land. There's a concrete abutment there now, painted yellow. But you take that road and stay to your left when you get to the fork. Then you've got to find the trail. I don't know if I can tell you how to find the trail. You just keep heading toward the sound of the water."

David waited respectfully, in case there was more. Cecil seemed to be finished. David bounced the file folders in his arms, as if they might be getting heavy. "Well, I appreciate that," David said. "I do. Thank you very much."

David waited another respectful moment. "Well, I'd better be going. Take care now," he concluded.

Cecil turned and David watched him make his way home, walking stiff and bow-legged across the uneven ground.

Down in the church basement, a circle of wooden stacking chairs was set up around a couple of tables. More than a month had gone by already, and David was anxious to start laying out his plans for his ministry in their midst.

David carried with him into this ministry, as he had into each of the two parishes he had served as rector, the advice his father had once given him: Be sure to make your mark wherever you go, and make it early. He knew that six months was not a lot of time to begin with, and that now only five remained. He knew as well that Bishop Long had told him not to change anything. He chose to interpret this as meaning he could not change anything that *now existed*. But he *could* suggest *adding* a few things. Surely, this would not be seen as meddlesome, but rather as earnestness — a parish priest (or *minister,* as the case may be) simply doing what was in the best interests of his parish.

In the East it was customary for the rector to chair parish meetings, so as the small group gathered, David assumed the role of host, welcoming each one as they made their way down the stairs. Len was the first to arrive, a fifty-ish man with a receding buzz cut and intense blue eyes. David had not yet seen him in church. A successful tour operator in Tofino, Len was all business, and appeared a little peeved to have to be spending the evening this way.

Len brought regrets from someone named Marina, whom David had not yet met. She was St. Columba's' treasurer, a yoga instructor and Reike practitioner, and she would not be coming tonight, he explained, because she had some meeting with the Clayoquot Sound Players, a theatrical troupe that performed dramas in the streets and in the schools, mostly around environmental themes of respecting Mother Earth and saving the forests. Len rolled his eyes.

Accompanying Len was Marilyn, the other churchwarden from St. Columba's. David had not met her yet either. She was a large open-faced woman in her seventies who ran a successful B & B, which she closed in the off-season so she could travel. She was heading to Tucson, Arizona, in a few weeks, she said, to be with her son and his family. Then she would be off on a cruise through the Panama Canal. They would not be seeing much of her over the next few months, she told them without apology.

St. Aidan's was represented by Ken, also a stranger to David, a laid-off fish plant worker with dirt under his fingernails and several days' stubble on his face. He fidgeted like a man in need of a cigarette. Grace was St. Aidan's' other churchwarden, though she also acted as treasurer. Here, at last, was someone David recognized from Sunday morning. She was easily in her eighties, if not her nineties. She wore a print dress overlayed with a bright ski jacket. Her sturdy shoes rose to her shins, like hiking boots. Angling her way sideways down the narrow staircase, feeling out each new step with her foot before lowering her weight, she looked round the room, saw David, and gave him a proud motherly smile.

Mimi was there as well, as church secretary, which meant that she would be taking the minutes. She too smiled at David as she took her place at the table, a smile that seemed to imply a deeper level of personal friendship than he himself felt existed between them.

David was getting ready to formally welcome everyone and start the meeting. So it caught him off guard when Len suddenly took charge, calling the meeting to order. Apparently Len did not think it necessary to welcome anyone or even to acknowledge David, since everyone had now met him, and he launched into the business at hand without so much as an opening prayer. David readjusted his position on the hard wooden chair so that he leaned forward, looking attentive; but the wind was gone from his sails. He was not used to being an outsider to church business. Though for the moment it appeared that he had no choice.

Finances were down at St. Columba's, Len reported on behalf of Marina, as was attendance, since the last minister left three months ago. But the good news was that expenses were down too, there being no salary to worry about now. The diocese had agreed to pay the expenses of the "interim minister" — meaning David, of course, but not naming him — with the presbytery throwing something in as well. But that was between the two denominational judicatories, he said. There would be no direct expense for them, which was a good thing.

Grace reported similar statistics for St. Aidan's in a lilting Welsh accent, passing around copies of her report, each one labouriously handwritten. It appeared to David that things were not looking very good for either congregation. But this merely prepared the ground for the helpful ideas he was intending to bring to the table.

Conversation wandered for a bit then, touching on the general downward trend in the local economy. Ken said there were rumours of yet another fish plant closure. Len, sounding like a man in the know, countered that he'd heard that a Korean outfit was looking at buying up one of those plants. Ken lowered his eyes as his news was superseded by Len's.

Of the two communities, Tofino was the more prosperous, its burgeoning tourist trade more than making up for the recent downturn in the traditional resource-based economy. It was Ucluelet that was suffering, a town of fishers and loggers that David sometimes heard referred to as the "working town," a description that not only irked those in Tofino, with its implication that tourism was not real work, but also belied the reality that few residents of Ucluelet were actually at work.

David could feel the tension between the two communities as the church leaders continued to talk around the table, moving on to the coordination of dates for the two churches' upcoming bazaars. He felt invisible, a stranger from the East parachuted in without any consultation with the parish, whose salary they didn't have to pay, whose life they didn't care to know about, and who would be gone again in a few months anyway.

Suddenly it appeared that Len was wrapping things up. David jumped in, asking if he might have a few minutes on the agenda to talk about some of his plans for his time among them. They looked a little surprised but agreed, turning now to look at him — all but Len, who picked up his papers, shuffling them on the table in front of him, then layed them down again. He was ready to go.

Well, for one thing, David said, he was concerned that communion was not being offered every week, though of course he understood that this was not the United Church custom. He wondered if he might offer an early morning communion service each week at St. Aidan's, for those who missed their weekly communion.

They looked at each other. They guessed that would be okay. He shouldn't expect many to attend though. They'd never had an early morning service. What time was he thinking? Seven-thirty, he told them. Some shook their heads. That would be pretty early. But it was up to him … whatever.

David then wanted to know about the native communities in the area. Was there any back-and-forth between the reserves and the towns? Why weren't there any native people on the parish list, for instance? Was there any way of bringing the two communities together, of honouring their diverse histories and traditions?

There was silence for a moment, as the church council members looked at one another, as if perhaps David were inviting them to join him for a stroll out across an open mine field. No, Marilyn offered at last, there probably wasn't a way of bringing the two communities together.

David appeared confused. Marilyn tried to explain herself. She knew a lot of the native people from the reserves up around Tofino, from Ahousaht and from across the sound at Opitsaht, and from Hesquaht, up at Hot Springs Cove. Good people, most of them, she said. But you get them together in a group, as in these land claim negotiations, and they could be quite cagey.

You never knew what they were really thinking. The others nodded.

A fish farm had its nets cut again last week, Ken said, leaving unspoken the implication that natives were to blame. And while whites couldn't fish the Coho, the natives could fish whatever the hell they wanted, he went on. Then they cooked it on the beach for all to see. It wasn't fair, he said. It was causing bad blood between them.

Mimi spoke up, attempting to soften any wrong impressions David might be getting. It wasn't that there was any prejudice, she said. It was more that there were lots of reasons for distrust between whites and natives. And now this whole land claims business had opened up.

"Well, I think they're lovely people," Grace said with warmth. "And they've had such a hard time of it. And such beautiful children!"

Okay, David realized, this was an issue on which he might not be able to make any immediate headway. He decided to move on.

Next, he wondered if the churches were doing anything for the displaced loggers and laid-off fish plant workers. He was thinking of a food bank, or a clothing depot, something like that.

No, the Lions' Club gave out hampers at Christmas, Len said, and people drove into Port Alberni if they needed social services. Ken dropped his head, looking down at his hands. Well, would they mind if he explored the possibilities anyway, David asked them. No, they guessed that was all right, they said, if he wanted.

And speaking of Christmas, David pushed on, he didn't know what their plans were for the Christmas services. What usually happened?

An early Christmas Eve service up at Tofino, they told him, and a midnight service in Ucluelet.

And those would be communion services, of course, he said, nodding in anticipation of their agreement. No, they said, it was always a carol service, a candlelight carol service.

Oh, David replied, taken aback. But wasn't communion expected at Christmas — even in the United Church?

No, they assured him, it wasn't. They pretty much did what they wanted here anyway.

David considered this. He knew he was not supposed to change anything. But he also knew that, even in the United Church, communion was the norm at the church's feasts and festivals, at Christmas and Easter at the very least.

Well, he said, he was pretty sure both denominations would want them to offer communion at Christmas. So he wondered if they might allow him to move the carol service ahead to the previous Sunday evening and make the Christmas Eve service at each church a Eucharist.

"A what?" Len asked.

"A Eucharist," David repeated, "a service of Holy Communion."

No one spoke for a few moments. Only Len held David's gaze, drumming his fingers on the table. He looked annoyed.

He should do whatever the hell he wanted, Len said finally. But he should be warned: no one would come. The Sunday before Christmas was when the Pacific Rim Arts Society sponsored an annual performance of Handel's *Messiah*. He couldn't expect to compete with that. Even Tofino people would be driving down to Ucluelet to see it. It was a big deal here.

The meeting ended soon afterward. David took Grace's arm and helped her climb the stairs leading up to the back of the church. It was very nice to have him there, she told him as they negotiated the top steps. She hoped he might even stay a while; they had had so many clergy come and go over the years. They even had a woman once. Divorced, she was, but they had all liked her anyway.

He was surprised to see that Grace had driven herself to the meeting in a large modern pick-up truck. He helped her climb up into the cab. She patted his hand as he let go.

Mimi was suddenly at his elbow as he closed the door to Grace's truck. "I think communion on Christmas Eve would be lovely," she said.

"Thank you, Mimi," he said. She smiled up at him. "Well, good night," he said.

He turned back to the church. Ken was coming through the doorway. "You know the definition of an expert?" he asked David. David didn't. "A guy from Toronto with a briefcase," Ken snickered. David permitted himself a small obliging smile, though there was no doubt that he himself was supposed to be that guy.

He said goodnight and made his way home, uncertain as to what the meeting had actually accomplished. It was like a hollow ritual, something they did out of habit, comparing hard luck stories, but seeking no way through the difficulties. He was sure he would be able to help them out. He even felt a slight rise of excitement as he considered the new challenges that lay before him. It did seem that they were giving him a pretty broad reach to carry the two congregations forward. It was an opportunity to make his mark, just as his father had said.

. . .

David found that, after the fact, he was growing intrigued by Cecil's tip about the blowhole. Had Cecil been aware how David had been spending his late afternoons, searching out the shoreline? Or was this something he told every new minister? Whatever the case, it opened up a whole new avenue for exploration.

So one afternoon, when his visits in Ucluelet were done, David decided to search out the blowhole for himself. With Cecil's vague instructions in mind, like a tattered pirate's map, he headed up the highway in the Frog Prince. As he neared Mill Stream, a tiny cluster of houses and properties on the outskirts of town, his attention was caught by two bright yellow concrete abutments, just as Cecil had described. David pulled over and parked the car at the side of road.

The abutments blocked motor entry to what appeared to be little more than a parting in the roadside brush. But it led him onto a gravel roadbed that was overgrown with slender alders and low cedar saplings. The surrounding forest was young, and he guessed that he was on an old logging road. The area had likely been logged some years ago and then left to "green up," as the loggers called it.

David started out like a bold explorer, trusting that it would become clear what Cecil had meant when he told him to stay left when he got to the fork. He listened for the pounding of the ocean. But the rustling of the leaves overhead and the steady padding of his own footfalls were the only sounds that came to his ears. As the trail narrowed and he pressed deeper into the heart of the new growth, he could feel the beating of his heart. He could not help wondering if, through the dense foliage, he was being watched. There were cougars in the area, after all. And bears. This served only to heighten his sense of adventure, but he glanced back over his shoulder, just in case.

The thrill of doing something potentially dangerous felt new to him. It was something he should have been able to recall from the distant days of his childhood; but he could not. He wondered now if he had ever really learned to play as a child. Had he ever allowed his imagination to run away with him? Had he ever inhabited the imaginary worlds of childhood, where every new turn in the path presented the possibility of pirates, or Indians, or perhaps a dragon to slay? It was a shameful admission for someone now in his forties, but the racing of his pulse as he plunged deeper into the woods was a novel experience for him. How much had he missed, growing up so quickly in that silent and serious household? Is this what his mother had meant, he asked himself now, about his being her "little man?"

His excitement mounted as he ducked beneath some low-hanging branches and emerged at a sudden turn in the trail. But the sight before him as he rounded the bend caused his breathing to stop and his body to freeze in its tracks. A large pile of dung marred the path directly ahead of him. Beyond it was another. He approached cautiously and knelt down for a closer look. He was by no stretch a woodsman, and the thought of his trying to identify a wild animal by its dung was laughable. But he himself was not laughing as he probed the pile with a twig. Blackberries. That could mean only one thing: bears!

David rose slowly and looked around. The dung did not seem to be warm; it might be too late in the season for bears to be up and about. Still, the fact that bears used this trail at all was not a comforting thought.

He tried to recall the conventional wisdom on what to do if you meet a bear in the wild. Don't climb a tree, he thought, because bears can climb. Or was that cougars? Were you supposed to roll up into a ball and play dead, or were you supposed to run? He seemed to remember hearing that, if you did run, you should go downhill because a bear's smaller front legs would slow him on a downward slope. Or were you supposed to make yourself appear tall and threatening, because bears have poor eyesight? He thought he could recall that you should make some noise to alert a bear of your presence, like wearing a hiking bell attached to your hat, or whistling while you walked. And always carry a can of bear repellant.

What was that old joke about bears? "How can you tell a bear from its droppings? A black bear's will have roots and berries. A grizzly's will have hiking bells and bear repellants." But he didn't think there were grizzlies on the Island. Or were there? Oh, God! He didn't know anything!

As he began his retreat, he chose the opposite tack to noise-making. Taking care not to snap any dry twigs underfoot, he stole swiftly back along the narrow path to the safety of the Frog Prince. He considered himself lucky. He had made it out in one piece. But he felt a hint of satisfaction as well. This brush with danger seemed to him like a rite of passage, a retracing of his steps to manhood. There was a smile on his face as he drove home.

Over the next few weeks, David got to work on the goals he set for himself at the church council meeting. He began making inquiries about setting up a food bank, testing out whether this might be a feasible project for the church. He made an appointment to see Murray, the mayor.

David was surprised how professional the mayor appeared. His office was neat and orderly, as was Murray himself, his desk clear of clutter. Plaques and black-framed degrees decorated the wall, along with a bookcase that contained more bound documents than David presently possessed in his own collection.

It made him realize that he had brought with him certain prejudices, certain stereotypes about coastal people, and most of them were not flattering. The mayor of a town like Ucluelet, for instance, should be an auto mechanic or a back hoe operator, with a bad haircut and blackened hands, not a university-educated businessman like Murray. But the tables were turned now as he sat opposite Murray's wide desk. It was David who was feeling the lesser of the two men.

"I don't know, Reverend," Murray was saying. "People here are pretty proud. I'm not sure anyone would come to your food bank. And then, if they did, you might get taken advantage of. I mean, how would you know if someone was really in need, or whether they were just looking for a free hand-out?" He looked directly at David as he spoke. "So I don't know," he said again.

David wished he had prepared himself better. He wished he had done some research, put something on paper, something more than an idea in his head, however well intended it was.

"Do you think perhaps a focus group might help then?" he asked Murray. "I could call together some people who would know — social workers, health care people, the police .... " He couldn't think who else to include.

"Union representatives for the fish plant workers, the health and welfare committee on the reserve ..." Murray added, filling in the blanks David was leaving. "Sure, you could do that."

"Well, maybe that's the best way forward then," David concluded. "I'll meet with some of these people and see where we should go from there."

Murray seemed to be stifling a grin. "Well, where *you* go from there," he corrected him. "The town isn't on board with this yet."

David felt like he was being humoured. What was that definition of an expert again? At least he hadn't brought a briefcase. He would have to prove himself to these people. But that was okay; he could do that.

He rose and shook Murray's hand, thanking him for his time. "I'll get back to you, if I may, with what I find out."

"Okay, you do that," Murray said as he saw him to the door. With the groundwork now being laid for the church's outreach to the town's material needs, David turned his attention to the church's outreach to its spiritual needs. He began envisioning the Christmas services.

In the parlance of the church growth experts, he was conceiving the traditional service of lessons and carols as a "seeker service," designed specifically to attract newcomers. As he saw it, the evening service on the Sunday before Christmas could be quite beautiful, the church aglow in candlelight, fresh cedar boughs decorating the window ledges, brightened with red bows, and small Christmas trees positioned in the sanctuary, strung with tiny flickering bulbs. It had the potential for making a deep impression on unchurched folks, perhaps even enticing them to venture into the church for one of the regular Sunday morning services.

They would sing a standard repertoire of familiar Christmas carols, interspersed with the traditional readings, telling the story of the Saviour's birth. He would not preach, allowing the readings to do the work for him. Instead, perhaps he could find someone who played a flute or a harp, and they could do solo arrangements of seasonal Canadian folk songs. There wouldn't be snow, he guessed, but still it could be a carol service to remember, a way for him to make his mark. He bounced on the balls of his feet with anticipation.

When David next saw the curtains move at Cecil's, he was feeling the self-confidence of a man with a plan and decided to go right over and report on his first foray into the woods in search of the blowhole.

"Bears," he said solemnly to Cecil, when he had been invited in to take a seat at the kitchen table. "There was clear evidence of bears on the trail."

Cecil was at the stove heating up a battered aluminum coffee pot. He did not seem to be taking an interest. David brushed some toast crumbs from the table into the palm of his hand, but was then unsure what he should do with them. Placing them in a little pile at the table's edge, and rubbing his palms together over top of it, he went on.

"I came across two piles of bear dung. They had berries in them, so that's how I knew." He felt proud of his discovery, as if it might be some sort of initiation rite into West Coast living. "Are there grizzlies on the island?" he asked Cecil.

"Grizzlies? Nope," he said.

David nodded, relieved.

"So did you find it?" Cecil asked him.

"What?"

"The blowhole," Cecil said.

"Well, no," David answered. Perhaps Cecil had not understood. "I turned back. There were bears on the trail...."

"Bah!" Cecil cut in. "They wouldn'ta hurt ya. Too stupid." He smiled the first smile David had seen on his weathered face. The skin folded up at the corners of his mouth and his eyes shone. An empty gap appeared where his two front teeth should have been.

"So, what is it you're supposed to do, Cecil," he asked, "if you see a bear?"

"You go your way, and you let him go his," Cecil said. "He's not looking for trouble."

David marvelled at the nonchalance. Was this West Coast bravado? Just let a bear go its way. Right.

"Okay, so what about, say, a cougar?" he asked him. "What do you do if you see something like a cougar?"

Cecil was filling two mugs with a thick black liquid David

supposed was coffee. He stopped and put the pot down, thinking of something, remembering. Then he picked it up again, finished pouring and brought the mugs to the table. He didn't offer David any cream or sugar.

"Now cougars is another matter," Cecil said. "If you see a cougar, it's likely because it wants to be seen. Which means it's already too late."

Too late?" David asked.

"Too late," Cecil repeated. "You're supper."

David shivered. "So ... what do you do?" he asked.

"Shoot it," Cecil answered without a moment's hesitation.

"Shoot it," David repeated.

"These here modern fellas say, you see a cougar, you tranquillize it, you cage it, you move it off somewhere, up-island or something. Well, that's bullshit. You see a cougar, you shoot it. Cougars don't belong where people are. Nowheres near."

"Or maybe it's *us* who don't belong where *cougars* are," David offered, the idea of a city person, which didn't seem to be worthy of a response from Cecil.

Cecil sat down at the table. "A kid went missing up in Ahousaht one year. I was with the party that went lookin' for 'im." Cecil's small eyes squinted. He seemed to be following the scene again from inside his head. "And I was the lucky one," he said. "I was the one that found 'im. Or what was left of 'im. Which wasn't much. He'd been dragged off by a cougar." He looked over at David. "You see a cougar," he said, "you shoot it."

Against his will, David found himself imagining the remains of a child torn apart by a cougar. A small rib cage, some bones, some flesh. Cecil had seen this for himself.

"But bears," Cecil was saying. "Don't let *them* stop you. You want to see the blowhole, you gotta walk down that road."

David nodded as he reached for his mug. Grasping it in both hands, he sipped at the black liquid. It burnt his tongue, any flavour having long since been boiled away, replaced now by nothing more than the bitterness of yesterday's reheated coffee grounds. He swallowed hard, wiping his sleeve across his mouth.

. . .

As the weeks passed, the constant cloud turned to constant rain. Sometimes it fell in a steady drizzle, sometimes in driving sheets. David found himself increasingly housebound, walking restlessly from room to room.

If he had even one comfortable chair in which to lounge with a good book, he might not have felt quite so claustrophobic. But as to furnished rooms, there was the kitchen, with its chrome-legged table and chairs; the study had only the desk, with its hard wooden desk chair, the bare bookshelves only deepening his sense of abandonment; and there was the bedroom, where he could sit on the bed with his back propped against the wall, the weight of his body slowing pushing the bed out, requiring him every so often to get up and shove it back into place.

David found himself spending more and more time up in the attic, seated cross-legged before the large window with its disparaging view of the naked mountains. Above him beat the unbroken patter of rain on the roof. A single light bulb dangled from the rafters, casting a dull glow on a small stack of books and letters. If the phone rang down in the kitchen, he would not have been able to reach it in time. But the phone rarely rang.

Living alone, David came to count on his morning trip to the post office, partly because of Denise and her daily news concerning the goings-on about town, but mostly because of the mail itself, and its promise of contact with someone who cared. His own letters took forever to get out from this corner of the world, so they often crossed those that were on their way to him, especially those from his family, making for disjointed conversation at best. But it was still better than the phone.

Sunday afternoons, he would call home. Paul and Catherine were always glad to hear from him, but each passing week took him farther from their daily lives, and them farther from his. Beverley, on the phone, was distant, tentative, cautious, which was so unlike her. The distance he had put between them, and the sudden and impulsive way in which he left, had made him a stranger to her now. Their conversations were strained as a result, almost making matters worse.

So David counted on the mail. The small stack Denise handed him meant for a daily dose of disappointment, of course, as he tossed aside the unsolicited flyers and sorted through the church-related bills. But from time to time a handwritten envelope would fall from the pile. It would bear a familiar name or address in the upper corner, and his own name and address written prominently in the centre, a testimony to his not being forgotten.

One day, such an envelope arrived, identifying the sender as "J. Blanchard." Without recognizing the name, David tore it open as soon as he got in the door. He unfolded the enclosed letter and began reading it as he walked down the hall into the kitchen. He was half-way through the first paragraph when Jill's voice suddenly emerged through the handwriting. He sat down at the kitchen table. Taking a deep breath, he started again.

*My dear David,*

*How can I begin to express my sorrow and regret for what has come between us all? If only you could know how much*

*Beverley and the kids miss you, and how much grief I bear
myself for what has now been lost by all of us!*

*What happened between Bev and me was a horrible mis-
take, though it felt so innocent at the time. I will not take the
full blame for this — complete honesty is now more important
than ever if we are to work this through — but still, you must
know how deeply I regret that my confused feelings and my
thoughtless actions have driven a wedge between the two
people I love most in all the world. That our friendship is over
I have no doubt. But that you and Bev should be split up by
this would be unthinkable to me, and would be the worst
possible consequence of my mistake.*

*I ask you to find it in your heart to forgive me. Despite all
my doubts, I believe that God is, if nothing else, gracious and
forgiving. But even if this is too great a thing to ask, I beg you
not to hold anything against Bev, who still loves you very
much. The break-up of your marriage would be too great a
burden for me to bear.*

*With deep affection, and regret, Jill.*

David placed the letter on the kitchen table, and looked out across
the harbour. A rusted dragger was making its slow way out to
sea. His emotions rose to the surface, his throat constricting, his
eyes filling with tears. He had never allowed himself to think of
this separation in the full light of its possible consequences, that
it might represent the actual loss of his marriage. Even now he
could not bring himself to think of it. Yet there it was on the
page, the prophecy, the warning. It could happen. Perhaps
Beverley herself was talking this way; perhaps that had been the
occasion for Jill's letter.

He folded the letter back into the envelope and rose heavily from the chair. He ascended the stairs to the attic, allowing his body to collapse, cross-legged, to the floor. He stared out through the steady drizzle across the dark turbulent waters to the battered face of Mount Ozzard, its summit lost in a low ceiling of cloud. The world was closing in. David's chest heaved as he breathed, and his eyes burned in their sockets.

There were things he could do, he knew. He could give this whole thing up as a bad job, go down right now, pack up the car, and head for home. He could pick up the phone and confess his love and his regret to Beverley, breaking through this stultifying stalemate. But something was preventing him, something undone, or perhaps started, but not yet finished. He could not go back, not yet. It was not time. But never had he more fully comprehended the danger of this journey, and the full burden of his own responsibility in what had happened. His mother had been right. This was not about him and Beverley, not anymore. It was now only about him.

His next hair cut brought these thoughts within speaking distance, though he knew he was not yet ready to let them out. Still, when Randy asked him, "So ... how's it going?" there was so much David wanted to say.

"Okay," was all he could muster at first.

David decided to go with something safe, so he talked about his ministry, about his love for the church and its traditions. The conversation took an inward turn only when he shared with Randy his disappointment that so few of his parishioners actually went to church, that so few seemed to share his, his ... he couldn't think of the right word.

"Passion?" Randy offered.

"I wasn't thinking of, well, of that word," David said.

"But that's what you're describing," Randy replied. "You feel passionate about your work. Like I feel passionate about mine."

Passion. It had never occurred to him that's what it was. He had been accused of a lot of things — of stuffiness, of conservatism, of emotional constipation (someone had actually said that to him once) — but never of passion. It was an utterly new thought.

"You know what it means, don't you?" David asked Randy. "It's from the Latin, *passio*, having to do with 'suffering'; which is why we call Christ's death his 'passion.' God's love was expressed through his suffering."

Randy hadn't known that, but thought that it sounded about right. He himself had been in a lot of pretty passionate relationships, he said, that had meant nothing in the end but a lot of suffering. For the moment he was happy to be "uninvolved." But he knew it was only a matter of time. "I mean," he continued, "unless you really want to live alone, most of us need companionship, don't we. We're just not always prepared to suffer for it."

"Right," David heard himself saying. "That's right."

It was an interesting idea, and David found himself returning to it often in the days and weeks that followed. He did feel passionate about his work, and was willing to suffer for it. This was probably the root of much of his frustration with other clergy, that so few seemed genuinely committed to their calling, passionately committed to it, as he was — though it was still startling to think of himself in this way.

It was when he considered the more personal dimensions of passion, the relational dimensions, that he had trouble identifying it in himself. He loved his children, he knew that. But he wondered how much suffering he had endured for their sakes. Beverley bore most of the suffering, in the literal sense of having borne them, of course, but also in the sense of being closest to their daily needs, to their own daily sufferings. David himself always had his ministry to attend to, always had some pressing circumstances that took him away from his family. Had his children been missing out on his own sacrifice of time and attention? Not that parenthood was only about suffering. But it was *at least* about suffering, if you truly loved your children.

He knew he loved Beverley too. But theirs had always been an easy relationship for him. They rarely fought, they rarely even sparked, so compatible were their natures, so balanced their daily lives. They understood one another instinctively; there was no question of that. But had they *suffered* for one another? What suffering had Beverley been enduring, he wondered, unknown to him, suffering that eventually found its outlet in this ... thing ... with Jill?

But, even more important, how much had *he* been prepared to suffer for *her*? Their marriage, to him, had been all about gain, not loss. He was so well supported by Beverley and by their stable life together, that he could not recall ever having really suffered for her, or for the sake of their marriage. This bothered him now.

As he pondered these questions, the words to the familiar old hymn returned, playing in his head:

*See, from his head, his hands, his feet,*
*sorrow and love flow mingled down;*
*did e'er such love and sorrow meet,*
*or thorns compose so rich a crown*

"Sorrow and love," he repeated aloud. This seemed close to the heart of some great mystery. Must love — necessarily — bring sorrow? David mused. Are the two inseparable? If one suffers, is it because one has loved? And if one loves, must one suffer?

Jesus suffered. He suffered the loss of everything, not only his life, but his mission too. And why? Because God so *loved* the world, scripture said. But in suffering such a loss, he gained the kingdom. "For whoever would save his life will lose it," Jesus had said, "and whoever loses his life for my sake will find it."

David shook his head. In the end he had to admit that he really didn't know what he was talking about; this was all such strange new territory for him. It was, for the moment, an interesting *idea*. But what did it really mean in his life? He didn't have a clue.

. . .

As the dark days of December closed in upon the Coast, they brought damning evidence that winter here had only just begun. The winds howled through the trees at night, hard rain beating against the windows. Every so often the lights flickered, sometimes dimming to half their strength, a phenomenon called "brown-outs," David learned, which was often preliminary to the power going out altogether. He learned to keep dry matches and emergency candles at the ready.

The dreary emptiness of the house and the ominous shadows of the late afternoon eventually drove David out into the elements. He wrapped himself in his slicker, pulled his boots up over thick wool socks, cinched the drawstring of his hood tight around his chin, and ventured out to the rocky headlands. Roiling waves, tossed up by an angry sea, carried by a momentum begun hundreds of miles out, rolled in at towering heights, some twenty and thirty feet between trough and crest, dwarfing the lighthouse at Amphitrite Point, hurling themselves into the battered rock with such force that the ground shook beneath David's feet.

David leaned into the wind, barely able to see through the narrow slits of his eyes. The drenching spray sought its way inside his clothing through every unprotected seam, every unguarded opening. The slicker did not breathe, and sweat ran down David's back. He tried to make himself remember how this felt, rehearsing how he would later recall this moment, and then the next — how he might describe it to others back home. But he came to suspect that the task was futile. These were sensations only the body could retain, long after the mind gave up trying. The violent physicality of this place left the mind numb, unable to fathom such brute force. It was the body, reverberating with each earth-shattering blow of a wave, pummelled by the steady force of the mighty wind — it was the body that understood; it was the body that would remember.

David's mornings were now taken up with planning the Christmas carol service. He had had no luck getting a soloist since all the available musicians had a role in the town's performance of Handel's *Messiah*. As he explained his plans for decorating the church, the few women who made up the tiny chancel guild readily agreed to help, especially since what he was asking was pretty much what they did each year for Christmas anyway. But he couldn't count on their being present at the service itself, they informed him — all of them had some duty to perform for the *Messiah*, selling tickets or working the bake table.

The possibility of low attendance at the service began to weigh heavily on him, especially as, week after week, he set up for his early Sunday morning communion service at St. Aidan's — to which no one came at all. He would sit at the prayer desk in his robes, gazing out across the harbour, glancing every few minutes at his watch, waiting for a congregation that never materialized. When a half-hour had passed, he would rise slowly, return the communion set to its appointed place, pack up his robes in his small suitcase, and head out for the service up in Tofino.

Still, David pressed on, drawing up a list of well-known carols and having Mimi type them up in booklet form. He found it difficult to get anyone to commit to being readers for the service, so he asked Mimi, who was only too pleased to help him out. She would do all the readings, Ernie would play the carols on the piano, he himself would read the Gospel — "In the beginning was the Word ..." — and lead in the prayers.

David developed a concept for publicity posters, which Mimi cheerfully made up on her computer, and he went around both towns tacking them up on bulletin boards at the post office and the Co-op, on telephone poles, and in store windows.

Then, finally, the great day arrived, the Fourth Sunday of Advent, the Sunday before Christmas. He promoted the evening service of lessons and carols once again at both morning services, expressing his hope that everyone from the two churches would come out to greet the newcomers he hoped would be attracted to the service. At the door people shook his hand and solemnly wished him well, as one might shake the hand of a sea captain who was about to go down with his ship.

At seven o'clock, David moved around the church, lighting the candles he had placed in the windows. He plugged in the strings of Christmas tree lights and the tiny bulbs flickered, just as he had envisaged it. At seven-fifteen Mimi arrived, bringing her hand up to her mouth to stifle a small gasp of delight at the sight of the decorated church. It looked so lovely, she said. He walked down the aisle to greet her, the sleeves of his surplus billowing out at his sides. He turned at the end of the aisle to take it in himself. He had to admit, it looked pretty nice.

With all now in readiness, he put the tape in the cassette

player to set the mood, a recording of the King's College Choir singing "Christmas Carols Ancient and Modern." He waited for Ernie to come and take his place at the piano. By seven-twenty-five David was growing concerned. Ernie wasn't there. Neither was there a congregation. Still, he smiled reassuringly at Mimi, who had taken her place in the front pew. This is what they called "island time," wasn't it, he asked her. She smiled encouragingly up at him.

At seven-thirty David and Mimi were still the only two in the candle-lit church, though people could be heard passing on the street outside. But no one was turning in. David didn't know what to do. He grew flustered before his congregation of one, Mimi, all dressed up in festive Christmas colours and seated demurely before him.

Finally, ten minutes after the service was to have begun, he walked down to where Mimi was sitting and slumped into the pew beside her, his arms dropping between his knees. "They're not coming, are they," he said.

She looked down at her hands. She shook her head.

"They told me this would happen," he said. "But I thought I could attract at least a few. I mean, with all this work. A few would have been enough."

She looked over at him, her eyes brimming with sympathy. She placed her hand on top of his. "It's okay," she said. "They like you, you know. But this is the night of the *Messiah*. It's a tradition. It was just too much for you to compete with."

He gazed around at the lovely little church, sparkling with festive light. "You can still use all this for Christmas Eve," she said.

For a moment neither of them spoke, sharing in this intimate moment of realization, each wringing their own meaning from it. Mimi didn't actually seem too sad. She squeezed his hand.

"Do you want to go to the *Messiah*?" she said. "There's still time."

Well, why not, he thought. It had something to do with joining them, if he couldn't beat them. He nodded his consent to Mimi, rising wearily to his feet. He climbed out of his robes while she extinguished the candles and unplugged the lights. She placed her hand through the crook of his arm as they left the church and headed up the street for the high school. Parked cars lined the streets on both sides.

They purchased their tickets — he paid for hers — from Grace who, seated at a card table inside the door, winked at the couple as if she were a favourite aunt. They squeezed through the crowded room to take their place, standing against the back wall along with the other latecomers. David recognized half his parish, as well as half the town. He realized he didn't really care if he was seen by them here. And, evidently, neither did Mimi.

The musicians began taking their places on the risers. He pressed his back into the cold painted cinder block wall and cursed himself. What a fool he had been! What arrogant pride to set himself up in competition with this! Just who did he think he was?! A line from that old familiar hymn came back to him: "And pour contempt on all my pride." Indeed!

He closed his eyes and clenched his fists and felt, with surprise, Mimi's small hand still locked in his arm. He glanced down at her in the dark. She was looking out on the room, radiant, pleased with herself.

The orchestra, smartly turned out in black pants or skirts and white shirts or blouses, took a few minutes to tune, sounding almost like the real thing. It seemed to be made up of anyone who could play an instrument, no matter what it was, so long as it could be adapted to the simplified musical score. There were high school students, their jaws working furiously on huge wads of gum, for whom this was likely a course requirement; there were several long-haired middle-aged folky types on mandolins and guitars; there were seniors, their clarinets and violas dusted off and sparkling under the stage lights; there were children with violins and flutes, peering out into the audience to catch a glimpse of mom or dad. The glow of anticipation was evident, luminous on the scrubbed faces of this unlikely assemblage of musicians.

The whole scene was really quite remarkable and helped for a moment to lift David's flagging spirits. He knew he would be feeling badly for days, resigning himself to the humiliation brought on by his own stupidity. But for the next hour or so, perhaps he could pass something of his burden over to these people, to this community that was becoming his home away from home. Perhaps here in the dark for this brief time, *they* could now minister to *him*.

Gazing upon the scene unfolding before him — the nervous musicians fidgeting beneath the rented theatrical lights, straightening their music and adjusting their positions on the moulded plastic stacking chairs — he did not notice her at first. It was not until the lights had dimmed and Mr. Abernathy, the band teacher, and the four paid soloists strode onto centre stage. It was not until all was in readiness, and the room fell silent, and Mr. A. raised his baton.

Then, out of nowhere, there she was, seated at the end of the cello section, closest to the audience. She was the picture of composed refinement, her elegant frame leaning forward, taut with intelligent alertness, her long black skirt flowing to the floor, her arms, in a crisp white blouse, poised in playing position. Her straight dark hair was tied back by a velvet ribbon, revealing in silhouette the profile of a princess — no, of an angel.

David was not breathing when the string section launched into its spirited introductory passage, their errant squeaks and squawks failing to diminish the dignified entrance of the tenor soloist. Mimi glanced up at her minister, triumph fairly radiating from her face.

The tenor stood, a broad full-faced man, to prophesy the coming of the Lord. The printed program said he was a carpenter by trade, a soloist in Nanaimo's First Presbyterian Church who had once sung with the University of Victoria chorus. He sang through a wide unrepressed smile, clearly pleased with his charge and responsibility, announcing to the people that "Ev'ry valley shall be exalted, and ev'ry mountain and hill made low"; but even more so, "the crooked straight, and the rough places plain." His jowls verily shook with the good news.

His message thus delivered, the tenor sat down, pleased with himself indeed, and the chorus carried the hopeful theme forward: "And the glory of the Lord shall be revealed," they sang, almost as one.

But, for David, God's glory was already being revealed before him, and she was stealing his heart away moment by moment. He couldn't stop looking at the *Messiah*'s cellist. She was a vision of such exquisite loveliness there in the soft edge of the spotlight. Earnest, focused, intent on the task at hand, she embodied everything he himself endeavoured, but failed, to be. He hadn't even known he had been searching, but suddenly, in this unexpected place, here she was — an angel of mercy, *his* angel.

The alto now rose to join the chorus, a fierce dark-haired beauty, a swimming coach in her day to day life, the program said. Her face wore an expression so intense that her eyes almost crossed, a look so severe as to make even the most timid swimmers cast themselves into the deep end. When she bid the messenger of Zion to "get thee up into the high mountain," one had no illusions that he would be up and gone forthwith.

The alto sat down, breathing hard, passing the heavy mantle to the chorus, who picked up the pace to announce that "unto us a Child is born, unto us a Son is given." Something of the alto's determination was caught by the choristers, who performed their duty as if the fulfilment of this magnificent prophecy rested upon their shoulders alone, indeed, as if it hung on their every word.

The soprano rose now to entreat the daughters of Jerusalem to rejoice at the coming of their king. She seemed too small for the job, fair-haired and fair-skinned, a part-time music teacher and a mother of twins, barely into her thirties. Yet with a serene confidence quite beyond her years, her voice swept up suddenly and unexpectedly to fill the room with the joyful tidings.

And David felt it in his own heart, this good news, this wonderful possibility of new beginnings. The cellist could feel it too, he was certain, though she remained professionally restrained, intent only on the work before her, swaying gently, almost imperceptibly, with the rise and fall of the musical cadences.

David found himself outside of time, barely contained by the confines of the hot crowded room, oblivious to the discomfort of standing, his back pressed against the hard cold wall, oblivious to Mimi as her hand slipped down his arm to take hold of his. His rapt attention was undivided, caught up in the wondrous spectacle of sight and sound unfolding before him, and of the radiant apparition of this most heavenly creature seated, bent slightly forward, at the head of the cello section, a beatific vision if ever there was one.

The musical tone darkened as the alto stepped forward again, this time to tell how the *Messiah* "was despised and rejected of men, a man of sorrows, and acquainted with grief." She seemed genuinely upset, as if reporting something she herself had witnessed, her face folding into a nasty sneer as she recalled for the room how, "He gave his back to the smiters, and his cheeks to them that plucked off the hair." She became so indignant, re-counting how "He hid not His face from shame and spitting," that spit sprayed forth from her own mouth, causing people in the first rows to pull out hankies and wipe their faces.

The bass soloist had been silent far too long, waiting his turn, his tall frame sprawled awkwardly in the hard chair, his bearded face looking down to the floor in front of him as if he too were upset, perhaps even suicidal. He taught classical studies at a com-munity college up in Campbell River, something that in itself could be a cause for despondency, Homer not being a name closely associated with plumbing or with communication technology.

But now at last the bass soloist stood, nostrils flaring, ready to expose the conundrum of the human condition: "Why do the nations so furiously rage together," he demanded of the dark-ened room, "why do the people imagine a vain thing?"

The people sat bolt upright as the string section sawed away to underscore the complaint of the bass soloist, his eyes aglow with passion, his body taut and poised right at the edge of the stage. Why? he was demanding. Why do the nations so furiously rage together? Why do the people imagine a vain thing? The people gathered here didn't seem to have an answer for him, but their upturned faces likely constituted more rivetted attention than he ever received in his classrooms, posing these same questions.

The chorus rose up now to lead the way forward: "Let us break their bonds asunder, and cast away their yokes from us." One might have wondered if, for these people, certain environ-mentalists and government officials were included among the unholy lot whose bonds had to be broken, whose yokes were to be cast away. The chorus sang with such conviction that this seemed more than possible.

Then, suddenly, the orchestra and chorus were surging together toward the evening's finale, the "Hallelujah Chorus." The room rose to its feet in elated recognition. The brass players now had their moment in the spotlight, some actually managing to hit the correct notes. The chorus held nothing back, the young and the old swaying together. The strings, inspired surely by their angelic cellist, cast aside all abandon for the rising crescendo of God's praise, their bows lifting and falling with unbridled passion, if not always with precision.

At the final Hallelujah, the singers now leaning forward precipitously on the risers, the timpanist pounding away, the string players throwing their tousled hair out of their faces, the room roared its approval, breaking into wild applause and raucous shouts of "Bravo!" and "Encore!" The din in the room was deafening, an orgasm of emotional release.

David found himself one with the moment, clapping wildly, calling out with the mob, "Bravo! Bravo!" The fevered pitch rose higher still as the four soloists each stepped forward to take a bow, especially the bass as he raised his head high and peered triumphantly down his nose at them. Mr. A. acknowledged the orchestra and chorus with a sweep of his hand, the orchestra rising to receive the ovation, smiling openly, basking in the triumphal moment, David's angel herself blushing with unrestrained pleasure.

"Magnificent!" David exclaimed to Mimi as they flowed with the crowd out into the cool night. "Simply magnificent!"

"I'm so glad you enjoyed it," she said, looking up at him tenderly, sliding her arm through his.

"Such, such ... passion!" he said, trying out his new word. "I'm amazed! And I've heard Handel's *Messiah* before, I can tell you. But never like this."

David smiled. Mimi beamed.

"And you must tell me," David said, "*who* was that ... angelic ... cellist?"

Mimi looked up at him, mildly alarmed. "What's a cellist?" she asked, smiling crookedly.

David looked down, and suddenly woke from his dream. He felt her arm locked in his. He saw her upturned face, searching his eyes anxiously now. He removed her hand from his arm and held it.

"Oh, dear," he said. "Have I done something wrong here? Have I been giving you the wrong impression?"

She retrieved her hand and looked away. When she looked up at him again there were tears in her eyes. "I'm sorry," she said. "I've just made a fool of myself, haven't I!"

"No, no," he tried to reassure her, "not at all. I'm the one who's been a fool. You have been perfectly, well, you have been very kind."

She smiled, but it was a smile of resigned recognition. She had stood in these shoes before; she had heard these words, or words very much like them.

"Well ... good night, David," she said. "I'm glad you're all right with the way things turned out." She rose up on her toes and kissed him on the cheek.

"Good night, Mimi," he said, and he watched her disappear into the dispersing crowd.

# Chapter Five

Almost any given thing about David's Christmas on the Coast would have been enough to drive him to despair. First there was the weather, which continued foul, each new day bringing only a wearisome variation on a dark and stormy theme. Either there were high winds, or there was pelting rain, or there were high winds *and* pelting rain. David felt he had no choice but to curtail his daily excursions along the shoreline: access to the rocky headlands had become too dangerous; even the beaches were closed off to the public, massive tree-trunk driftwood pitching and tossing about in the surf like matchsticks.

Still, with cabin fever setting in, David decided one day to mount a new assault on the blowhole. He suited up from head to toe in his rubber rain gear, parked the Frog Prince on the shoulder of the highway, and started out. His oversized rain pants squeaked as he trudged up the old road. He reached the turn in the trail where the bear droppings had been, but they were long since washed away by the small river that now flowed down the centre of the track. So he pushed on, his wellies splish-splashing through the run-off. Sparse new growth lined the trail, opening the forest ceiling to the steady drizzle that spilled from the low overhead clouds.

David let the gravel roadbed lead him forward. The trees receded as he traversed a broad meadow. Then, up ahead, a tall stand of un-logged old growth forest gave way to the open sky beyond, indicating the meeting of land and sea. He was getting close. But the road did not lead him to the sea. It brought him instead to the edge of the old forest, its underbrush an impenetrable brier of matted thorns.

The road now forked before him, to the left and to the right, just as Cecil had said. Towering above the fork was an immense silver cedar, long dead, its bare pointed branches reaching skyward like battle lances. Two lesser cedars nearby had also died, their roots rotting, and they had fallen into the upturned arms of this one stalwart guardian, who was as stoic in its solitariness as an ancient helmeted knight, standing tall and proud, even in death, bearing up the hulks of his comrades who had fallen in battle.

Cecil had said to stay left, and certainly the main path veered in that direction. But the trail was immediately swamped by a spreading rain-fed reservoir, too broad and deep for David to cross. So he doubled back and tried the path on the right. It seemed to lead, promisingly, in the direction of the ocean. But then the trail quickly grew in on itself, choked by the low bent branches of a thicket, reduced to little more than a deer run, too small for a grown man to negotiate easily. With the wind howling in the trees above him, and the rain now falling in sheets, David decided this was enough for today. He turned and headed for home.

Thwarted in his attempts to reach the wilder portions of the coastline, David resigned himself to an alternative plan: until the weather let up, he would content himself with a daily drive over to the lighthouse at Amphitrite Point, at the southerly tip of the peninsula. There he could stand like a tourist on the public walkway and gaze out upon the roaring seas. So day after day, buffeted about by the stiff winds, he stood alone against the winter storms as if being chastened. The mean gusts tore at his clothing; the driving rain beat down upon his shoulders; and the waves lashed out at the rocky headland, releasing hopeful billows of sea foam that rose playfully on swirling columns of air, only to be caught in the jet stream of the gale-force winds, and blasted apart.

Returning to the rectory, he would dry himself off and tour the house, turning on all the lights to dispel the gloom. He prepared paltry meals for himself in his Spartan kitchen, re-heating rice from the day before, adding a stir-fry concoction of beef strips and vegetables, but without spices or sauce that would have raised it from the level of prison food.

Then there were the Christmas cards and packages, arriving just under the wire, no one in the East appreciating the long circuitous route taken by mail sent to this part of the world. It was hard to get into any mood even remotely approaching the "holiday spirit." He felt so far removed — an entire continent away — from the people who knew and loved him.

A card from Beverley, announcing the coming arrival of a package of Christmas presents from the family, dealt him a particularly low blow. The generic seasonal card she had chosen wished him a "Joy-filled Holiday Season," an odd and somewhat perverse sentiment, he thought, given the circumstances. But it got worse.

In the enclosed note Beverley confessed that it had been difficult doing the Christmas shopping this year, that Christmas itself already felt pretty much like a bust. She had even been tempted not to buy him a present, she said, though not out of spite. It was more because she could not imagine his life any more. She had no idea what he was doing, where he was living, who the people were who populated his days. What do you give someone you love but don't know anymore, she asked.

He had sent her a pair of locally handcrafted silver earrings, each one etched with an eagle's head. But he wondered now if that had been a mistake. Why would she want to wear something from this journey of his, a journey she did not share, a journey, most likely, that she deeply resented? These were symbols of *his* life, not hers. He imagined Christmas morning, her taking the earrings up to her room, away from Paul and Catherine, and silently dropping them into the bathroom waste basket.

The Christmas Eve services might have lit a little glow in David's heart, both churches magnificently decked out with cedar boughs and the dark green holly that grows so abundantly in that fecund climate. But with his recent loss of anything resembling conventional faith, his sermon preparation kept hitting the bottom of the well, and returning empty. A baby born in a small Judean town two thousand years ago — just what did this have to do with us, he wondered. Ordinarily he would have preached something about God being with us — Emmanuel, and all that. But God's presence had not been making itself known to him too clearly of late, so it would have been a stretch for him to go there.

And then there were the services themselves. Having offered the service of lessons and carols the previous Sunday evening — even though there had been no takers — David stuck with his plan of celebrating holy communion on Christmas Eve. But the word had not got out, or perhaps had not been taken seriously to begin with, for both churches were filled mainly with strangers fully expecting an hour or so of their favourite sing-along carols. David's words of welcome at the beginning of each service, inviting all baptized Christians to come forward when the time came to receive communion — a generous offer, David felt, considering the religious diversity of these communities — only served to set people off. A buzz ran through the congregations. What? This wasn't the carol service? What's communion? What's he talking about?

The people belted out their beloved carols with vigour, but the traditional readings and prayers were met with cold stares and stony silence, especially the long prayer of consecration. People were waiting for the next hymn, but waiting too long, judging by the looks on their faces. Some left before communion. Others chose to wait and greet the new minister at the door to express, without much delicacy, their disappointment in this year's service. Some asked him how long he was staying, the corollary clear enough, but left unsaid.

Back at the rectory, well past midnight, David consoled himself with a glass of scotch. Bishop Hovey's strange gift had accompanied David right across the country, tucked into the bottom of his suitcase. When he unpacked, the bottle had been stashed at the back of the cupboard over the fridge, a cupboard that was otherwise bare. Out of sight, the bottle of sixteen-year-old Laphroig had remained also out of mind. But in the aftermath of last Sunday evening's fiasco, and now after the Christmas Eve disaster, David remembered the bottle of whiskey and reached for its cold comfort.

He stripped away the seal and pulled the cork. Instantly the room filled with the astringent scent of Scottish peat and seaweed. He wasn't sure if maybe the whiskey had gone bad. He poured a couple of inches into a tall glass. Raising it to his nose, he couldn't bring himself to take a sip. He plopped two ice cubes into the glass, added a third, and a fourth, and then passed the glass under the tap to add some water. Even then, the taste was frightful. The whiskey burned the back of his throat going down. The aftertaste was even worse. But the kick was almost instantaneous. Sitting alone at the kitchen table, calling to mind entire pews of dark disappointed faces, he took another sip, and another, and another, until the glass was empty. Then, his head spinning, a buzzing in his fingers and toes, he tottered off to bed.

David awoke to the pounding of rain against the window — such a cheery Christmassy sound! It was still dark, but he sensed that it was already day. His eyes were sore, his throat parched. He was glad, at least, that he had agreed not to do a Christmas Day service. He was about to roll over and go back to sleep when the telephone rang in the kitchen. He fumbled for his bath robe and stumbled down the hall, picking up the phone on its third ring.

"Merry Christmas, Dad!" came the gleeful greeting.

"Merry Christmas, Catherine," he said, his voice low and unfamiliar, like a growl.

"It's Christmas, Dad!" she said, as if he might not have got it.

"I know, I know," he said. "I just woke up. What time is it?"

"It's almost nine o'clock," she said. "Mom wouldn't let us call before now."

"Right," he said. He quickly calculated the time difference and realized it was only six in the morning. He rubbed his face with his free hand, trying to raise himself to their time zone.

"Thanks for the sweater," she gushed. "It's really cool! No one here has one like it! Did the Indians make it?"

"I'm so glad you like it," he said, deeply massaging his eye sockets. "I don't know if it was made by local people, or what. But I'm glad you like it." He stifled a yawn.

"Did you get our presents?" she asked him.

"Um, not yet. I mean, I got them, but I haven't opened them yet. Do you want to hang on and I'll go get them? I could open them right now, while you're all on the phone."

"Hi, Dad." Paul's voice broke in from an extension. He sounded more man than boy.

"Hi, Paul. Merry Christmas!"

"Merry Christmas, Dad. Thanks for the books. They're great. They're all about your part of the Coast, aren't they? They look really interesting."

"Dad's going to open his presents while we're on the phone," Catherine interjected. "Okay, Dad," she went on, "we'll wait while you go get them."

"All right," he said, "just hang on."

He went to the living-room, where he had placed his small pile of presents on the floor before the cold empty fireplace. He picked out the ones bearing his family's names and brought them back to the kitchen. Standing by the counter in his bare feet, he pulled out a bright yellow package from Catherine. She had used several layers of boxes and wrapping, the size of the gift shrinking as he removed each new layer. Such tricks were her stock and trade. When finally he got to it, he unwrapped a CD entitled "Cool 3 — A Collection of Chart-topping Pop."

He picked up the phone. "Wow, Catherine, this is really neat! I'm sure I won't know a single song on here ... but I guess that's the point, isn't it?"

Catherine giggled. "Now you can be the coolest old guy on the Left Coast," she said. "That's what people here call it when I tell them where you are. They say it's such a cool place to be; so I thought you should at least have some music to go with it."

"I love it," he said. "Thank you, Catherine. Now I'm going to go over and open Paul's gift."

He put the receiver down and began to unwrap a small present. The paper was festooned with festive green frogs in Santa Claus hats and Christmas ties, like tipsy workers at an office party. It was hilarious, and raised a thin smile to David's dry lips. Inside were two gifts, wrapped separately in tissue paper. One was a tie, a fun design featuring frogs, some sitting, some swimming, some leaping. The other was a key chain, a squatting frog with a crown on its head holding the small chain links in his mouth.

"This is great, Paul," David said into the phone.

"In honour of the Frog Prince, of course," Paul explained.

"I got it, I got it," David chuckled. "Thank you, Paul. Is your mom there?"

"Ya, she's right here," Paul said.

David could hear Beverley covering the mouthpiece, telling Catherine to get off the other phone. "Merry Christmas, David," she said.

"Merry Christmas, Bev," he said. "I sure wish I was there with you all. I'm really missing you." It just came out. He hadn't intended to open things up, not right away, and not like that. But there it was.

"We miss you too," she said. She asked him how he was. He found himself beginning to choke up as he answered that things were going okay. He struggled to regain his composure. She asked how the Christmas services had gone, safer territory. "Pretty disastrous, actually," he said, but he didn't want to go into it.

"Thanks for the earrings," she said. "They're beautiful."

"You think so?" he asked.

"Yes," she said.

"I'm glad you like them. I'll go get your present now." He reached for the one remaining gift, wrapped in a tasteful paper with a Dickensian Christmas montage, quite formal for Beverley. Tearing away the wrapping, David found himself holding a book in hard cover. "Lost and Found," it was entitled, with the subtitle, "Learning to Wait Upon the Lord." He turned it over in his hand. He did not recognize the author, but the subject was right on the money.

"This looks excellent," he said. "Thank you, Bev."

They were both silent for a moment. He could hear the faint conversations of other Christmas callers on other telephone lines, distant and jumbled, ghostly echoes spiralling down long cross-country corridors.

"The thing I want to know, David," she broke in, "the thing I need to know, is: Are you finding what you're looking for?"

"I don't know yet," he said. "I wish I did. Sometimes I wonder what I'm doing here. Other times, it feels like there is something happening, though I can't explain what it is. So ... I don't know."

"Are you coming back?" she asked him, straight out. Not, *When* are you coming back, which might have been a guarded euphemism, but going instead right to the heart of the issue. It was so like her, and he remembered for a moment why he loved her.

David had no reason to think he wasn't coming back, no cause for seeing this as the beginning of a permanent separation. It certainly did not feel like he was building a new life for himself here. As far as he was concerned, his intentions of returning at the end of the six months remained unchanged. Yet he found himself stalling. When finally he answered her that, yes, of course he was coming back, too much time had elapsed. It no longer sounded convincing, not even to him.

After he hung up the phone, David climbed the stairs to the attic and sat down on his prayer mat. Gazing out across the black harbour, he let his mind wander off to the exposed face of Mount Ozzard, somewhere out there through the driving rain. For all the recent joys and revelations on this, his journey of discovery, he still felt utterly lost. Some Christmas day this was turning out to be!

Later David made his pilgrimage to the lighthouse, paying homage to the unforgiving winds and ruthless sea. When he returned home, battered and blown, he began rummaging through the kitchen cupboards, searching for something to prepare for his Christmas dinner, something with which to salvage the day. But a knock came at the door. It was Cecil, standing on the porch, an old oiled work coat protecting his thin body from the rain, but his head dripping wet.

"Hello, Cecil," he said with weariness. "Merry Christmas to you."

"I'm cooking up some duck," the old man said without expression. "You want to come over?"

David didn't have the energy to think up an excuse. "Sure," he said. "I'll just finish off a few things here, and I'll be right there."

David didn't want to go to Cecil's. It felt like work to him, and he found himself resenting his willing compliance on this, his day off, and Christmas day to boot. He chided himself for not having made plans, as he began looking about for something to take as a gift. He picked up a bottle of white wine, a present from Paula and Harv. This'll do, he thought, and he slipped it back into its gift bag.

Cecil was already carving the bird when David knocked on the door and let himself in. There were so many competing odours that hit him as he stepped into the cottage, many of them pungent, few of them pleasant, that it was hard to discern precisely the aroma of the roast duck.

Two places were set at the table. David placed the bottle of wine on the counter. Cecil acknowledged the gift with his eyes but said nothing. David asked Cecil where he kept his wine glasses — a foolish question. Or glasses of any kind, he quickly added. Cecil motioned with his jaw to the cupboard over the sink from which David drew down two mis-matched plastic tumblers. He opened the wine with the cork screw he had brought, half filled both glasses, and took his place at the table.

Cecil served up the duck, along with lumpy mashed potatoes and dripping slices of mushy ripened tomatoes. David helped himself to a dinner roll and, while Cecil's back was turned, cut off a few small spots of blue mould that were forming on its underside. His appetite was waning.

David should have been grateful for Cecil's hospitality, he knew. This was a lot of work for the old man. But he was not grateful. He did not want to be here. He just wanted to be home, if only he could be certain of where that was.

"You better say something," Cecil said, as he sat down. So David said a quick grace, tucked a paper napkin into his belt, took a deep breath, and began slicing into the hunk of dead duck piled on his plate. As he took his first forkful and bit down, something cracked in his mouth, and a sudden pain shot up through his cheek.

"Shot this duck myself," Cecil was saying. "Might still be some shot in 'er," he said, glancing over at David's grimacing face. "Ya got some, did ya?"

David reached into his mouth, sifted through the wad of un-masticated duck, and extracted a tiny lead ball, along with a splinter of tooth. He placed both at the side of his plate, his eyes closed against tears of rising rage. He held on to the edge of the table with both hands, his tongue exploring the sharp cutting edge of his broken tooth. It was all he could do not to get up and leave. But he had been too well trained for that. So he forced himself to remain, to do the honourable thing, the polite thing, to carry on.

"So y'see," Cecil began, "the thing about the blowhole —"

"I know, I know," David snapped back, surprising himself. "It's at the top of my list of New Year's resolutions." Cecil eyed his guest across the table. They finished the meal in silence.

When they had risen from the table and cleared their plates, the old man motioned for David to follow him. David was unable to find the words to properly excuse himself, so he allowed Cecil to lead him to the rear of the cottage, to a stuffy wood-panelled living-room with a large picture window overlooking the harbour. There, on a TV table in the middle of the room was a bottle of brandy, two brandy snifters, and two fat cigars.

David smiled in spite of himself. Bless him, he thought. Cecil had planned this out. What sort of pathetic ingrate was he, to have resented the old man's hospitality? What a wretch indeed!

Cecil motioned toward the chair by the window, which opened out onto the black night. David caught his reflection in the glass. It did not look good. He was overdressed for the occasion, as usual, in grey flannel dress pants and the new pullover sweater his mother had sent him for Christmas, as if he had just walked out of a Sears catalogue. In Cecil's smelly ramshackle cabin it only made David feel foolish.

But that was not the main problem. Something else was wrong with this picture. David's hair was tussled and, even in the dark reflection, he could see that his eyes were swollen and red. He was not a picture of health and happiness. Reflexively, his tongue reached round to explore the sharp edge of his newly broken tooth.

All of this, or any of it — the swirling winter weather, the disastrous Christmas services, the lonely distance he had placed between himself and his family, the gruff hospitality of a total stranger — this might have sent David into a spiralling blue funk. But in truth, he was being saved from despair by a single ray of light, a celestial image that shone before him now through the gloom like a guiding presence. It was the image of a cellist, caught in the soft edges of a spotlight, her dark hair tied back by a velvet ribbon, elegantly poised to play, serenely attentive to the task before her, unearthly in her solemn beauty.

. . .

David had never known feelings like this before. A weight pressed itself into his chest, like a fist; a vague panicky confusion ruled in his head, preventing the flow of one clear thought to another; and a dull longing gnawed at him constantly, like a festering toothache. He walked from room to room in the rectory, trying to focus on the tasks before him, on his preparations for the upcoming Sunday services, on his correspondence, anything. But at every turn he saw before him the aristocratic profile of the *Messiah's* cellist.

The image exerted a powerful obsessive hold on him. It swept him up and carried him along on a current so strong he could not get his bearings. His head was being spun round, his body tossed from eddy to whirling eddy, his feet dangling helplessly beneath him, unable to touch bottom.

She was, of course, more fantasy than reality. He knew this. She was to him no more than a fleeting image, a wishful projection of his own desire. But still, he could not keep himself from imagining the touch of her soft skin, her fingers intertwining with his beneath the glow of candlelight, the velvet ribbon that held her hair drifting down across her bare back, falling to the floor. And as these visions rose up from the depths of his secret longing, he had to remind himself to breathe, or suddenly find himself gasping as if in a waking apnea.

He might have permitted this, or at least forgiven it, because he knew it was all so much rhapsodic invention, borne of his loneliness. But he knew also that the woman was real, that somewhere she existed in the flesh, and that this meant there was the possibility, however remote, that they might meet, perhaps at the post office, perhaps down an aisle at the Co-op, and that, meeting, she might well turn out to be the very fulfilment of the fantasies he projected onto her. It could happen. The thought both terrified and excited him. And as long as that possibility existed, try as he might, he could not put her out of his mind.

As David thought of Beverley in the light of this disturbing development, he had to admit that he could not remember a time when he had not loved her. But neither could he remember ever having fallen *in* love with her. Theirs had been a fated soulful meeting, like the reunion of siblings separated at birth. They had loved one another from the start, their courtship more the resolution of longing than longing itself. In no time they were engaged to be married and settling into the predictable patterns that would order their life together. But this — this was different.

So it was that David was lost in a guilty reverie when, on Boxing Day, the phone rang. It was Bishop Long calling from Victoria, asking David's forgiveness for bothering him on his day off. But the bishop and his wife had decided to take a few days off themselves and had arranged to rent a cabin up near Tofino. He was wondering if David might be free the next day, on Saturday evening, and they could take him out to dinner. There would be nothing official about the visit — the bishop was not offering to take the Sunday services, or even attend church for that matter.

But it would provide an opportunity for him to meet David and to learn how things were going in the parish.

David readily agreed, the thought of ecclesiastical company a great relief to him. They would come by and pick him up at six, if in the meantime he could make reservations at a local restaurant of his choosing. There was only one decent restaurant open in town during the off-season. The Penn and the several drinking establishments seemed too homey — and some downright grotty — for a visiting bishop. So David contacted the Kingfisher, down on Ucluelet's waterfront, and reserved a table for three.

He spent the next day cleaning house, mopping the empty expanse of hardwood floor, polishing fixtures in the bathroom and kitchen. He walked into town and bought a bottle of good sherry and three small wine glasses that were part of some promotion at the liquor store. He purchased a set of woven table cloths, took one from the set and placed it in the middle of kitchen table, along with a lit candle and the sherry glasses.

Bishop Long had been ordained in the 1960s, and David was not surprised to see that he still had something of the air of revolutionary fervour about him, though the bishop was now into his early sixties and soon to retire. It was in the trimmed goatee that looked more beatnik than modern chic; it was in the intense blue eyes that pierced the obfuscation that others brought to social issues, issues that, in Bishop Long's mind, were perfectly clear — all anyone had to do was follow the trajectories of logic that shot out like laser beams from a passion for justice and a preferential option for the poor, and the answers were self-evident.

Mrs. Long seemed less certain, but far more personable. A medical doctor, her successful geriatric practice was credited with having paid for many of her husband's causes and campaigns. What she thought of them — or of him, for that matter — was demurely locked away behind a pleasant smile that looked out on the world with calm equanimity.

Sitting around the kitchen table, David found himself looking to Mrs. Long for solace when the bishop, answering his own question about how things were going in the fishing industry, launched into a lecture about the government travesty that protected the interests of large foreign fishing fleets while sinking an entire way of life here among Canada's coastal fishing communities. Mrs. Long simply returned David's glance with a friendly smile. Her message to him, if there was a message intended, seemed to be: Relax — this is the way things are going to go for the evening.

The bishop was on his third sherry and still holding forth when Mrs. Long touched his arm, interrupting him, to suggest that it was time for them to be heading out to the restaurant.

They were greeted at the door of the Kingfisher by a young attractive hostess. She was French Canadian, judging by her accent, a waif no more than twenty, like so many who hitchhiked across the country and ended up at the Coast to take whatever work offered itself for a season, maybe two. She took their coats and led them to a window table overlooking the harbour. The restaurant was mostly empty — there were only two other tables of diners.

David and his hosts settled at their table and gazed out through their reflections in the glass toward the government docks which were lit by high overhead amber spotlights, like a movie set. Mrs. Long thought she detected movement down on the dock and they all strained to make out whether the small animal dashing about in the shadows was an otter, or perhaps a mink. David was of no help, for he had never seen either. He turned to survey the room as the bishop and his wife continued to point and peer out into the darkness.

The three occupied tables were all by the window, one behind David, the other across from an empty table in front of him. He did not want to crane his neck to scope out the diners behind his back, though he could detect their American accents. The table in front of him consisted of a couple with their backs to him and — oh my God! — it was her. It was the cellist, the angel of his dreams, sitting facing him, directly in his line of vision.

She was everything he had remembered her being. She was dressed in a tight black long-sleeved top, like a dancer or an opera singer, her hair tied back as it had been at the concert, her slender arms resting on the table, silver bangles at her wrists. Though the thought had never crossed his mind, he now saw that the fingers of her left hand were devoid of rings. He had never even considered the possibility that she might be married, or that she might be otherwise attached, that he might have been lusting after another man's wife or girlfriend. In his fantasy life he had simply taken for granted her availability for him, and for him alone. But now, there she was, in the flesh, as lovely as he had been imagining, composed, self-assured, her dark eyes sparkling in the glow of the table's flickering oil lamp.

David reminded himself to breathe out, just as he had learned at a clergy workshop on stress, organized by Barbara, his regional dean, back home. When you are feeling stress, remember to breathe out, they had learned; the rest will follow. But it was a struggle. He could feel his body going into panic mode, tightening up, his face draining of colour.

He was surprised, as he tried to return his attention to the bishop and his wife, to realize that they were talking to him, telling him a story. It was about their early years up the Sunshine Coast. He nodded, as if he had been listening all along, but caught only a few passing phrases, something about a native community, something about a chapel. Maybe it was about their wedding. David couldn't tell.

He glanced back. The cellist was receiving a drink from the young hostess, a red aperitif, on the rocks, with a twist of lemon which she expertly squeezed and dropped into her glass. She was stirring the drink with the plastic stir stick, her head slightly cocked, watching the juice from the lemon disperse through the wine.

David dropped his gaze and nodded in the bishop's direction, as if considering the deep implications of whatever it was he had been saying. When he glanced back, he caught the cellist's eye. They both smiled, a noncommital smile, yet friendly, neighbourly. The bishop's wife caught the exchange.

"Parishioner?" she asked.

"No," David replied quickly. "She plays in the local orchestra." The bishop swung around to see. The cellist, finding herself suddenly the focus of attention, graciously acknowledged the whole table with a smile.

Now *her* table companions turned around to see what they were missing. They smiled too, and the bishop and his wife nodded and smiled back.

The American tourists behind David, sensing something was going on of a social nature, now spoke across to the bishop and his wife. "So where you folks from?"

David dropped his head. *Stop it*, he wanted to say. *Stop it, all of you! You're wrecking everything.* But he brought his gaze back to his hosts, letting them do the talking. He was determined to train all his attention on them for the rest of the evening. He could not afford to be caught with his guard down. For the sake of whatever tenuous link had now been forged between him and the cellist, he had to discipline himself, to foreswear any furtive glances, any lingering looks.

The conversation with the American couple flourished for a few minutes, everyone in the room learning that they were from Washington State, a retired salesman and his wife who had lost their eldest son in a car accident a year ago and were taking their Christmas holidays on the road this year in their motor home. But they had found the road from Port Alberni disconcerting, in need of some serious repair, in their opinion, widening being just one of the problems, leading them to wonder about the tax structure here and how much public money gets directed to such things, and whether this was the best a socialist government could do — they had heard that British Columbia was socialist.

With a sharp glance, Mrs. Long succeeded in restraining her husband from rising to the bait, and soon enough they turned their attention back to David. He decided he had better become proactive and take charge of the conversation himself. This would help focus his attention on the people at hand and distract him from looking over to the cellist. At the same time, he would be projecting a desirable image of himself over in her direction, appearing as a man in possession of himself, an interesting man, perhaps even intriguing.

So he launched into a series of self-deprecating anecdotes from his early weeks on the Coast, confessing his surprise to find that he was now a United Church minister, explaining the challenges of learning a new flexibility in his priestly role. He entertained them with the story of Stan's funeral, elaborating the extent to which he had saved the event from a descent into maudlin sentimentalism. He shared with them tales of his discoveries along the broken coastline. But all the time, while engaging the bishop and his wife in animated conversation, he had only one thought, and that was of the cellist. He hoped she was catching a glimpse of his fine performance.

When it was time to leave, with great self-discipline David avoided looking over in the cellist's direction and managed to leave the restaurant without so much as a backward glance. He was proud of himself for this display of self-control.

But as the bishop's car pulled away, David could not resist one backward glance from the dark safety of the back seat. The cellist and her companions were also rising to leave. Had David and his hosts held back for even a few moments, they all might have left the restaurant together: he might have introduced himself; he might have complimented her performance at last week's concert as he helped her with her coat; they might have exchanged names, saying how nice it was to meet one another; and all under the benign eye of the bishop and his wife, all sanctioned in the name of good pastoral style, of extending the church's influence, of making a mark in the wider community. But the opportunity was lost.

The next day was the First Sunday after Christmas. As usual, David met his small flock at the door after the service. No one at either church ventured to make any comment about last Sunday's failed carol service, nor about the disastrous Christmas Eve services. They greeted him with general seasonal pleasantries employed to keep the real issues at bay, shaking his hand as they took their leave.

But in Ucluelet, Grace lingered after the others had gone. As she took David's hand, she looked him in the eye. Suppressing a coy smile, she inquired how he had enjoyed last Sunday's concert. She almost winked. She was thinking of

Mimi, no doubt, who was conspicuously absent from church that morning.

David began rolling out a polite report when, suddenly, it seized him that this was his chance.

"Actually, the whole thing was quite beyond anything I could have anticipated," he told her. "It was just marvellous. What a wonderful collection of musicians. They were excellent!" He was gushing now. "And from both communities, I believe."

"Oh, yes," Grace said proudly, "though not the soloists."

"Right," he said, "not the soloists. But the section heads? Were they local too?"

"I'm sorry," she said, "I'm not sure what you mean."

"I mean the lead players in each instrumental section," he explained, closing in on his real purpose. "Like the, ah, lead player in the cello section, for instance, a woman with dark hair, I seem to recall. Would she be local too?"

Grace thought for a moment, then her eyes lit up. "Oh, you mean Daphne," she said, "Daphne Hart. Oh yes, she's local. She's the vet, you know. She runs the kennel out in Mill Stream, on the way out of town. Trains dogs too, I believe. Oh yes, she's local. They all are. We're very proud of our local talent. I'm so glad you enjoyed it!"

Daphne. Daphne Hart. David sighed. Now she had a name, a mythic name even. She would be in the phone book. She would have an address, a phone number. She was real, and she was local. This was almost too much for David as his fingers fumbled to remove his robes back in the vestry. He had no plan, he had no goal, just this beguiling new possibility rising before him.

A small diminishing voice in his head told him to stop it, to put an end to this right now, that this was all a silly game, a stupid schoolboy crush, nothing more, and that he'd better just pull himself together. But it was too late. Some other part of him had already bolted from the barn and was, even now, galloping across the open field.

. . .

David was now in a constant state of excitement. He was in possession of the most powerful knowledge available to humankind, the knowledge of a name. That name was Daphne, and he rehearsed it over and over in his head. He let it roll off his lips, soft as spring seedlings borne on petals lighter than air, carried on the gentlest breeze: *Daphne*, his heart sang out.

David tried to anchor himself by focussing his thoughts and energies on his ministry. But since the Christmas debacle, he had lost the will to engage in anything novel. In truth, he wanted nothing more now than to do his job, to lead in worship for the few who turned out on Sunday, to visit the sick, and not to climb too far out on any limbs.

There was solace in this for David. His people were quietly, if sporadically, faithful; their habits of church-going had sustained them for many a year before he ever arrived. They were not asking him to be clever, or to be innovative, or to evoke from them any enthusiasm in their weekly offering of worship. They were asking him simply to be with them, to speak openly and simply from the scriptures, to break bread in their midst, to choose songs they could sing along with, to say prayers on their behalf.

He found that, when he attended to these simple tasks, everyone was happy, himself included. It was a ministry of "presence," a description David had once regarded with condescension as a euphemism for a ministry of doing nothing at all. But he was discovering that, as he let go of his grand schemes and plans, and gave himself to the daily tasks of ministry, he was granted a deeper peace and a greater pleasure than he had known before in ministry.

But this new simplicity did nothing to engage that part of him now so distracted by love and lust. It left him with too much time on his hands, too much time to think. He found that the essentials of his job, if begun on Monday morning, could be completed by Wednesday afternoon, when he took the details of the Sunday services over to Mimi. Without other commitments making claims on his time, that left three days to wander the house, pick up the mail, make his daily drive to the lighthouse, open a book, put it down, gaze out the window of the attic beneath the steady rhythm of the falling rain, all the time picturing Daphne's face, whispering the sound of her name. Clearly, he needed something else to do.

So he began accepting invitations to attend the meetings of his deanery and presbytery. He had been putting these off, trading on the fact that he was only the interim minister and not likely to have any contribution to make to the ongoing administration of his local Anglican and United Church judicatories. But now, the thought of driving across the island to meet his ministerial colleagues provided welcome relief from the foul weather and the isolation, and from his obsessive thoughts of Daphne.

The Frog Prince rose and fell along the mist-shrouded ribbon of road that led inland to the next meeting of the local Anglican clericus. "Local" had a different meaning here than it had back in Toronto, where no one was more than ten minutes away from any one else. Here, his closest neighbour, in Port Alberni, was an hour and a half's drive away through some of the most beautiful — and dangerous — terrain imaginable. He chugged up to Sutton's Pass and coasted down the other side to where the road opened up alongside Sproat Lake. Magnificent views and hair-raising drop-offs met him at every turn. It was exhilarating, but David had to keep his mind focused to stay on the road.

The meeting was in Parksville, another half-hour's drive beyond Port Alberni, on the island's gentle leeward side. David sang hymns and songs to himself as he wound along the wet roadway through Cathedral Grove, along the shores of Cameron Lake, and by the farms and hamlets that began dotting the countryside. He was happy to be coming in from the wilds.

His clergy counterparts seemed pleased to meet him as they arrived and gathered round the coffee urn. He had evidently aroused some curiosity within the deanery, his name appearing in the bishop's letter unattached to a face or to a theological predisposition.

In the opening rounds of conversation he became aware that they were trying to place him, to find his slot in the ecclesiastical order of things. What divinity school had he attended? What were some of his goals in his present ministry? What had the Lord been doing lately in his life? Each answer spoke greater volumes than he could ever have intended, as they listened to his vocabulary and watched his body language. Was he liberal? Was he conservative? Was he middle of the road? Would he support or challenge their own causes and predilections? Would he add or subtract to the numbers in their cliques and factions?

More formally, as the meeting was called to order, their conversation revealed that, while they seemed to know one another well, familiarity had not made them any more tolerant of each other's well-established theological stances and positions. There were tensions running through this group. The evangelicals were suspicious of the liberals; the liberals were dismissive of the evangelicals; while the charismatics floated blithely along, the Spirit raising them up and beyond the realm of any earthly din.

The one thing round which they all could rally was the subject of money — specifically, Bishop Long's new equalization policy, a way of flattening the range of clergy stipends, raising minimums and placing a ceiling on maximums. Shocking, they called it. Arbitrary! High-handed! Just who did he think he was to mess with clergy salaries?

As they broke for lunch, David found himself looking around the room and identifying the very people he had left behind in his Ontario deanery. The names and faces had changed, of course, but everything else remained the same. He sighed.

The meeting of presbytery in Nanaimo several weeks later proved far more instructive. It was a gathering of both clergy and lay people from United Church congregations up and down Vancouver Island, everything north of the Malahat, Victoria's northern mountain guardian. There were seniors from the wealthy retirement communities that gazed across the Strait of Georgia to the mainland, with its ready access to medical facilities and opera series; there were trades people from the isolated logging towns and fishing villages up-island; there was a healthy youth contingent, some with nose rings and dyed hair; there were young mothers, their pre-school children enrolled in presbytery's professionally run day care.

David looked forward to seeing Christian social democracy in action. Unlike the notoriously cautious Anglicans, United Church members never shied away from controversy. Whatever the dilemma of the day — the building of a resource-based economy, the just resolution of the scarred legacy of residential schools, the protesting of old growth logging — there were so many issues for a socially conscious church to address.

This was the peculiar genius of the United Church, David had to admit, hot social issues being hotly debated in the feisty spirit of democratic egalitarianism. If the Anglican Church could once have been described as the Tory Party at prayer, was the United Church the New Democratic Party at work? He was eager to find out.

David registered along with the others, attaching a bold name tag to his lapel that announced cheerily, "Hello, My Name is DAVID." He had been instructed to write his name in large letters so that others would be able to call him by name. He milled about the gathering crowd, waiting for this to happen.

A lovely young woman conducted the opening worship, held in the church's spacious sanctuary. She was a professional dancer and led the assembly in a series of movements while her "sister" — who did not appear even remotely related — beat out irregular rhythms on a Japanese gong. They reached up high, stretching on tiptoe to pick the ripe fruit from the branches of an imaginary tree. They swooped down low, bending deeply at the waist, to sweep the leaves off the ground with the backs of their hands.

David joined in without reservation, encouraged by the fact that no one knew him here. He stood with the rest, his eyes closed, following the leader's instructions, meditating on the space that surrounded him. He reached out with his fingertips toward the people who shared this space with him. He turned his body this way, and then that, feeling his own "personal space."

Then the group was invited to spread out to form a huge circle around the circumference of the sanctuary. They opened their eyes, joined hands, and sang, "How Wide is the World," taking in, by implication, not only this space and this island, but also this nation, the earth, and the entire known universe.

David was fascinated. Not once had God's name been mentioned, at least not in a way that was recognizable to him. Yet the worship was reverent and well-ordered. He did not feel silly and exposed as he had in so many ill-prepared "contemporary" services in his own denomination. He was content for the moment to be in the company of new colleagues, and eager to see the work of presbytery unfold.

The evening session, it turned out, was filled with bureaucratic preliminaries, with the calling of rolls and the tabling of reports, one after another, everything fastidiously noted in the minutes. David gave them their due: parliamentary procedure — the watchdog of democratic process — required a certain amount of care and patience as the groundwork was laid for the real business which, he knew, as the session adjourned for the day, would begin the next morning.

David had had the option of being billeted overnight with members of the host congregation. But he chose to remain alone, taking a small motel room close by. He awoke the next morning and made his way immediately back to the church, ready to assume his strange new role as a United Church presbyter.

But the morning session was filled not with impassioned speeches and noble debate, but with procedural wrangling. First came the question of abstentions: Were people allowed to abstain from voting, or were they compelled to vote on every issue? The United Church Manual was consulted, a sort of secondary scripture, it seemed, just as the Prayer Book is for Anglicans, while speaker after speaker rose to correct the previous speaker regarding the true guiding principles and precedents that would answer this thorny question. At last it was determined that, barring a conflict of interest — which must be declared to the house — all members were compelled to cast their vote, one way or another, for every motion.

Members were reminded in passing that if any one needed to leave the floor, hence missing a vote, they required the permission of the house. But someone rose to question the validity of this requirement, bristling at the encroachment it represented on their freedom to come and go as they pleased.

This opened a new and particularly rancorous debate on the balance of democratic responsibility and individual freedom. Those who favoured responsibility took nasty swipes at those favouring individual freedom, accusing them of childishness; while the freedom fighters accused the others of being anal-retentive. Finally, a motion was made to table the issue, but an amendment was quickly moved to forestall that motion, a debate ensuing about whether a motion to table could be amended.

The lunch break arrived without presbytery having addressed a single issue of substance; though now, it was true, they possessed a clearer understanding of how they might conduct themselves were such an issue to arise. David was confused and not a little crestfallen.

Over lunch, he ventured to point out to a table mate, an older woman from Nanaimo, that the debate thus far had seemed a little virulent, especially considering its substance. Turning to him, realizing he was a newcomer, she said, "See how we love each other?" And she flashed him a wide grin, a piece of lettuce leaf caught between her front teeth.

It was all a wonderful diversion, these brief forays into the church's curious decision-making realms. It provided much food for thought and reflection. The Anglican Church could certainly be accused of having been, for generations, a male-dominated, priest-ridden, hierarchical institution — a church culture sometimes described pejoratively as, "Father Knows Best." But its actual machinations seemed more archetypally feminine, battles being waged with subtle delicacy through innuendo and inference, more than through direct combat.

By contrast, the United Church was far more egalitarian, having welcomed women, gays, and lesbians to the ranks of the ordained long before other denominations. In its protectiveness of those marginalized by society, it seemed almost motherly. Yet, if this meeting were any measure, their decision-making was archetypally masculine: in terms of substance, presbytery was excessively procedural; in terms of style, it was nothing short of brutal, having little regard for either feelings or finesse.

So for all their respective vanities — the sacramental theology of the Anglicans; the social concern of the Uniteds — neither church seemed particularly effective at breaking through its own rhetoric to actually *do* something. Thank God for the local church, David found himself thinking as he drove home the next day, glad for the signs that told him he was nearing Ucluelet.

But in the end, it was no use, none of it. For when David drove the stretch of highway that ran into town, out past Daphne's place, he slowed the Frog Prince to a halt. The houses of Mill Stream appeared through the trees, set back from the road in clearings at the base of tall stands of Sitka spruce and red-cedars. A sudden break in the weather allowed the momentary parting of the clouds, the sun penetrating the forest to light up the clearings as if from within.

Daphne's home and office glowed in a shaft of sunlight that lit the grounds while leaving the roadside, where David sat, in shadow. A wooden sign at end of her driveway identified the veterinary practice of Dr. Daphne Hart, DVM, the letters carved in raised relief. He could see through the trees a compound made by the intersection of three buildings, likely trailers originally, which had been arranged in a U-shape and covered with cedar shakes and shingles so that they appeared as a single cottage, long and low, with paned windows, sculpted eaves, and painted shutters. Flower boxes adorned the window sills, and trellises framed the front door. The effect was magical, as if it might be the hidden lair of the queen of the forest people.

Everything else was now forgotten. Such taste, such simple elegance, such self-possession as this small cottage in the woods conveyed to David, while he sat watching from the roadside — these were the very qualities he would desire for himself. Could their destinies — his and the *Messiah's* cellist — long remain separate?

. . .

As the days and weeks passed, David grew frightened by what was happening to him. His obsession with Daphne raced through his veins like a drug, heightening his every thought and emotion, vandalizing the minutia of his days with bold strokes and wild vivid colours, overtaking his common sense and, along with it, the balance and order upon which so much of his life depended.

Everyday tasks became charged with energy. He would overreach a glass on the counter, sending it flying to the floor. He would turn too suddenly through a doorway, cracking his shoulder against the frame. The daily ritual of shaving required such Herculean effort of self-control that he often relinquished it altogether and found himself scratching at the rough stubble of several days' growth on his chin.

Basic life skills were slipping away. On one afternoon drive to Tofino, David ran out of gas near Long Beach and had to knock on doors in Esowista, the nearby reserve, until someone let him use their phone to call for help. He would forget to shop, scrounging through his empty cupboards as suppertime approached, only to give up and drive over to the Pen. There he would sit alone in a booth with a beer and a mock turkey platter, gazing out through his sad reflection in the window.

As a last desperate measure, an antidote to this foolish lovesickness, David drew himself up and focused all his energy on the one project that remained unfinished — the food bank. He called up all the possible players or stakeholders — the town's doctors, the social workers and counsellors, the Catholic priest, the evangelical pastor, the public health nurse, and anyone else he could think of who might be able to shed some light on the material needs of the town's poor and unemployed.

This helped, but still it wasn't enough. Randy noticed it right away.

"Letting ourselves go a little, are we?" he teased as David leaned back into the hair-washing chair. "Are we growing a beard, or are we just not shaving?"

"I don't know," David mused, raising his hands to stroke his face. "How does it look?"

Randy studied the patchy growth on his customer's cheeks and chin. "Too soon to tell," he said. "But it definitely changes the look. So what's happening?"

David was about to dodge the question, to be predictably circumspect about his personal life. But he suddenly realized that walls had come down, silent inner walls, and he felt no qualms now about opening up to Randy. When did this happen, he wondered.

"Randy?" he said, an excited tremor in his voice. "I think I'm in love."

"Really?!" Randy said, looking quizzically down at the middle-aged minister whose head was in his hands beneath the flow of warm water. "In love!" he repeated.

"Yes," David said, "in love," hearing the words come again from his own lips. It was a strange sensation, and thrilling in a way, like allowing a dark secret out into the light where, caught now in a stunning array of hues and colours, it was even more beautiful than before. Love is meant for the light, he thought, smiling to himself.

Randy was trying to take in this new information, but was having some difficulty. He was frowning as he led David over to the barber's chair. "So, um ... what does the church say about this?" he asked.

"The church?" David asked. "This isn't about the church," he said, annoyance rising in his tone. "This is about me. I may be ordained, but I'm still human, you know."

"Right, of course," Randy said. "Of course you're human. But you *are* married, aren't you? And presumably you are not talking about being in love with your wife ...."

"Damn!" David cut him off. "Can't a priest have feelings like anyone else? I mean, I'm not celibate, you know!"

"Of course not," Randy replied evenly. "So what is it you're telling me? You're in love, and ...."

"And ..." David took up the line, "And I don't know. I don't really know what this means." He nodded at this truth.

"So ... you're in some trouble, I would hazard a guess," Randy said. "You're married, you're in love with someone else, you're a minister — in fact, you're in a lot of trouble, I'd say!"

"What do you mean?" David shot back.

"Well, think about it." Randy put his scissors down and came around to look at David directly, not through the mirror's reflection. "This is not good. We've talked before, you and I, about passion — though not exactly meaning this. Well, here it is again. What did you say, that passion has something to do with suffering? I see a lot of suffering in this scenario, my friend. Is that what you want?"

David dropped his eyes. He couldn't find a clear line of thought. "But I'm not saying I'm going to *do* anything about it," he said. He felt like a squirming child caught with the cookie in his hand, but not yet actually in his mouth.

"Passion doesn't lend itself to moral boundaries," Randy said, "that's for sure." He returned to his position behind David's head and began snipping. "Anytime I've followed *my* passion it's got me into trouble. Not that I wouldn't do it again. But I'm not married. And I'm not a minister. So be careful, that's all I'm saying." He snipped with the scissors several times in the air. "Now, what do you want me to do with the back?"

David was annoyed by his conversation with Randy. But he had nothing to regret. He was simply talking about his feelings — something that, in his case, ought to have been met with at least some measure of encouragement. He was not talking about, well, anything really, lust or infidelity, nothing dangerous. They were just feelings, that was all. Everything was fine.

It was not until he was driving by Daphne's cottage on his way home, slowing the car to peer through the trees to get a better look at her compound, that he realized he had walked out of Randy's shop without having paid him. Okay, perhaps everything was not fine.

Over the next few weeks David concentrated on pulling together a report for the town council based on his conversations with the various community representatives. What became evident to David was a need for both a food bank and a used clothing depot, though the town doctors had disagreed. They insisted that education ought to come first, not hand-outs. People on limited incomes, they argued, were making bad choices, buying pop and chips and candy rather than healthy food. For their own money, they'd put effort into education, not a food bank. Others, however, had been slightly more encouraging.

David categorized all the answers to his questions, assembled statistics about actual numbers and percentages of unemployed, prepared charts and graphs, and wrote and re-wrote an interpretive narrative until it sounded as if he knew what he was talking about. Then he sought and was granted a place on the agenda for the next town council meeting.

Town council met the following Wednesday evening. David arrived early and found his way to the council chambers, up a narrow stairwell above the town offices. He was surprised at the formality of the room's set-up. It was arranged like council chambers elsewhere, but all the dimensions had shrunk. The councillors' table, raised and curved so that the councillors could eye one another during debate, was a half foot above the criticism of the public part of the room, with its orderly rows of stacking chairs. A podium faced the long table, the place from which the public could rise, when called on, to address the council. Even in Ucluelet the tricky workings of democracy were being safeguarded.

David shuffled his papers in his lap and re-read crucial sections he planned to emphasize in his presentation. Two other members of the public joined him in the visitors' section, one whom he recognized as the reporter from the local newspaper. David was overdressed, having finally shaved and put on his black suit and clerical collar. But this was intentional. He wished to make an impression, even to offer a little reverse intimidation of his own; to achieve this, few things worked better than the sombre look of a priest in his black suit.

A door opened behind the councillors' table and the town clerk entered. Officiously, she seated herself at one end of the counsellors' table, glancing out at the public gallery overtop of her reading glasses. She then began immediately taking notes, though there were as yet no proceedings. The door opened again and Murray, the mayor, entered in mid-conversation with a councillor whom David did not recognize. Another councillor entered. And then, without warning, Daphne Hart appeared, taking her place among them at the table. David gasped. This was something Grace had neglected to mention.

David's head dropped. He squeezed his eyes shut. Now everything was at risk. His mind raced as his carefully constructed composure slipped away. He could no longer call to mind the opening remarks he had prepared so labouriously. If he did not get a hold on himself, the town's first food bank would also be its shortest lived. But even worse, any impression he might have hoped to create for Daphne was now bent out of all shape. He had not imagined, for instance, impressing her with his clerical suit. Now she would see him for what he was, and not in his finest hour. So two enormous failures loomed immediately before him, one professional, one personal, and both very public.

He tried concentrating on his breathing as minutes were read, motions made, reports received and tabled. He could not look up, but fixed his stare instead on the pressed creases in his pant legs. When his name was called, he felt faint as he rose and made his way to the podium. He placed his notes on its flat surface, and held on with both hands as he began to speak. His voice was uncharacteristically subdued and he was unable to find his inner volume control.

Without looking up from his notes, he mumbled something vague about the recent downturn in the local economy, realities of which the council hardly needed reminding. He spoke of the church and its traditional care for society's most vulnerable members. He spoke of the need to do something, even if it were not specifically the food bank and clothing depot he was proposing. He referred them to the detailed report they had in front of them and, though he had prepared so much more to say, heard himself concluding his remarks, asking if perhaps they had any questions. Finally, dazed and disoriented, he allowed himself to look up.

There was a general shuffling of papers as the councillors sifted through the documents before them. Finding David's, they began perusing it. Only Daphne was looking at him. He smiled thinly at her. But she appeared to be lost in thought, trying to put some pieces of a puzzle together in her mind.

A councillor cleared his throat to speak. Still looking over David's document, he asked if the church was behind this, or was this David's initiative alone. The church had given its general consent, he answered, as the councillor glanced up at him. David said he would be taking Council's comments back to the church before proceeding further. The councillor seemed satisfied with this.

Murray addressed David now, displaying for the benefit of the room the page of appendices. He noted that there was no Native representation among the people David had interviewed. Did he intend to talk to anyone from Ucluelet East, for instance, the local reserve, or did David think the food bank and clothing depot would not apply to them?

It was a nasty question, a line with a hook on it. David had to admit that his limited experience in this part of the world had simply prevented him from thinking of the Native community. But he would be pleased to follow up the mayor's question by contacting people from the reserve and including their comments in a future version of his report.

Murray looked up and down the table of councillors. Seeing no one else preparing to speak, he thanked David for his report and said that Council would look forward to the updated version David would provide them, including input from the Ucluelet Band. In the meantime, he reminded David, the church was free to do whatever it wanted. But if it was seeking Council's approval, that would have to wait until the proposal was complete.

Council would be pleased to look at the matter again at that time.

David was dismissed. He gathered up his papers and quickly left the room, making his way down the stairs and out onto the street overlooking the harbour. Mercifully, the wind and rain had let up and David stood for a moment on the sidewalk, taking in the fresh ocean air. A door opened and closed behind him, but he hardly noticed. He felt a touch on his arm. He turned around and found himself looking into the dark eyes of Daphne Hart.

"I just wanted to thank you for your presentation," she said. "Council isn't usually the place for encouragement, not with Murray anyway. But I really appreciate what you're trying to do. In fact, I'd love the chance to talk with you some more about it sometime."

David didn't know what to say. He was amazed just to find himself in her presence there under the glow of the harbour lights. She dug into her pocket and produced a small bundle of business cards. She drew one out.

"Here," she said, pressing the card into his palm. "Call me. I'd like to hear more about your plans." As he took the card from her she reached out and touched his arm consolingly. "I've got to go back in. But thanks again."

Then she turned and was gone.

. . .

The thorns tore at his clothing as David thrust himself farther into the thick bracken. His feet scrambled for a foothold in the wet undergrowth but met only twisted roots and sudden sink holes. He lurched forward, step by clumsy step, his feet slipping wildly beneath him. He could hear the ocean now, it was close, but the tangled bramble was too dense; he still could not reach it. When finally he gave up, he simply let his body fall forward. He was caught by the weave of the thicket and he lay, breathing hard, propped up by the undergrowth.

How hard could this be, he asked himself. The wide Pacific Ocean spread out to the western horizon, rolling on for thousands of miles, vast and uninterrupted. All he had to do was break through this narrow strip of shoreline underbrush, and he would be at the water's edge. But this was proving impossible.

After his breathless encounter with Daphne Hart, David had spent a sleepless night, confused thoughts of love and loss tossing over and over with half-dreams and floating images: Beverley and Jill, themselves tossed together on an open sea of twisted sheets; Paul and Catherine in their youthful innocense, knowing nothing, yet possessing everything he himself now desired, so free of responsibility, so open to an unwritten future. Finally he had risen, splashed water on his face, checked the clock, and realized he wasn't going to sleep at all. He made himself some coffee and took it up to the attic where he gazed out at the coming dawn.

He had tried all morning to get some work done, pouring over the readings for the coming Sunday. But he couldn't hold a single thought in his head for more than a few seconds at a time. He'd say to himself, *okay, we're dealing here with* — and then he'd realize he had just read an entire passage without having a clue what it was dealing with. So he'd go back and start over, only to once again lose his concentration half-way through. He was getting nowhere.

By afternoon, he had given up trying to make any headway on anything remotely approximating work. He should lie down, he thought, catch up on the sleep he'd lost. But by now he had drunk far too much coffee, and his body was buzzing with electric energy. His hand trembled as he stroked the stubble of a new day's growth of beard.

So he had headed out in the Frog Prince to make a fresh assault on the blowhole, determined either to break through to the shoreline or to exhaust himself trying. He managed only to achieve the latter. At the fork in the road, under its tall dead cedar guardian, David had followed the trail to the left, just as Cecil had said, tramping through run-off water that sloshed up over the tops of his boots. When the trail narrowed and there was still no sign of a path leading down to the shore, he had simply plunged himself, headfirst, into the thick underbrush, intent on blazing his own trail to the sea.

The forest had another idea, however, and now, in small consolation, it supported his weight with its matted branches, twisted and thorny, rather than swallowing him whole. He yielded completely, his energy spent, letting his body go limp while his head took stock of his situation.

He was a faithful family man, a priest in the church of God, a man of integrity. What was he doing now flirting with danger, opening himself to a tempest that could sweep him away forever from everything he knew and loved? Did he think he was somehow immune to the consequences of irresponsible behaviour? If he pursued this thing with Daphne, was he really prepared to lose everything?

No, he had to take hold of himself. He had to get his feet back on the ground, he had to return everything to its proper perspective. He had only six weeks left now in his stay on the Coast. That was all the time he had to keep at bay the terrifying temptations, to begin putting things back in their place, and then to return to his life. He was too close; he could not afford to blow it now.

Slowly he extricated himself from the thick bramble, backing through the small tunnel of broken twigs and branches he had created, crawling through. His feet finally found something that felt half solid. It was the soggy path from which he had made this mad lunge toward the sound of the surf. He stood upright, brushed himself off, and turned away from the ocean, passing beneath its ghostly cedar guardian, making his way back to the Frog Prince, and home.

He would have to do something, he realized. Inner resolve would not be enough. He needed some sort of symbolic action to free himself from these demon tempters. He recalled something he had learned from Regional Dean Barbara's workshop on stress management. Sometimes it is helpful to write things down, she had said, to compose a letter, to get the inner feelings out, and so to put distance between ourselves and our demons. He considered this. It could be a therapeutic letter, not real correspondence, something tangible he could then offer up in prayer, burning it perhaps, like incense, or letting the angry rip tides of the ocean carry it away.

He got home, exchanged his wet clothes for his sweats, sat down at his desk and pulled out a pad of paper. He sat for the longest time, unsure how to begin. He got up and paced the house, up and down, trying to formulate his confusion of thoughts and feelings. What was it, exactly, he was required to sacrifice to the gods in return for his peace of mind?

It was turning to late afternoon, but the low February sun was working to penetrate the cloud cover. The wet season was ending. Soon the sun would succeed and crocuses would start poking up through the soft earth. There was something he had to bury in the soaked sod of winter, something to leave behind as springtime now drew him forward to the life he had left at home.

He found himself in the kitchen, still unsure how to start, but determined to break through. He reached above the refrigerator for the bottle of Laphroig. Maybe a wee dram would inspire him. He dropped a few ice cubes into a glass and poured himself a healthy shot, then added a splash of water. He carried it down to the study and sat again at the desk. He picked up his pen.

*Dear Daphne*, he wrote, surprised to see her name on paper. He sipped at the whiskey. He looked out the window. *Dear Daphne*, he said aloud dreamily, excited by the sound of her name on his lips.

*Thank you for your kindness to me the other evening at the Town Council meeting.*

He called to mind the touch of her hand upon his arm, her consoling words, her dark eyes looking with such understanding, with such compassion, into his own. He took another sip. Again he put pen to paper.

*I am afraid my presentation was not what I had intended it to be. The issue of unemployment is important to me, but I failed to do it justice. I suppose it was just nervousness, but I left feeling that I had made a botch of the whole thing.*

True, he thought. That's exactly how he had felt. This was good, this confession. He took another sip, inspired now to probe deeper.

*The thing is, I have wanted, in every ministry I have had, to make my mark. It's something I learned from my father, who was also a priest, and he never failed to make his mark wherever he was, whatever he did. So it might be true to say that, in spite of my good intentions, my motives were mixed. I am concerned with the plight of those who struggle to make* *ends meet. I am moved by their victimization by economic forces over which they have no control. But, truth be told, I am equally moved by the thought of my passing through this town — or through this life, for that matter — unnoticed. I want to make a difference; but also I want to be <u>seen</u> to make a difference.*

He leaned back and re-read what he had written. True, he said to himself, all too true. He turned on the desk lamp against the descending dark and took another sip of the whiskey. He pressed on.

*My sense of failure, then, had as much to do with failing to make my mark as it did with disappointing the hopes of those who might have benefited from a food bank or a used clothing depot. I hate to admit this, but it is nonetheless true. I am indeed a wretch. But it will soon be Lent, the season of repentance. My confession is made in faith that new life will spring forth from it.*

A little too ecclesiastical, he thought, a little too dramatic. But what did it matter — he wasn't sending the letter anyway. He went upstairs and re-filled his glass, this time adding the ice but not the water. He returned to the next matter at hand.

*In fact, this whole trip, this whole adventure, has been about me. I have been moved not by concern for others, but concern for myself. My wife had an affair. With a woman. Did I care to find out what had led her to do this? No, I did not. Did I listen to her when she tried to share with me her own pain and confusion? No, I did not. I turned and ran away. I came out here. Caring for the people of my new parish was not even part of my intention. Even today, I hardly know their names.*

David suddenly remembered his first Sunday up at St. Columba's, in Tofino, and the deaf lady arranging flowers on the altar. He had not given her another thought, even as the weeks went by and she never again showed herself in church. He did not ask anyone who she was, or what she had been doing. She had simply slipped beneath his notice, outside the blinkered vision of his own selfish concern. He raised the glass to his lips and took a another drink. The pungent aroma of the whiskey did not bother him now. Even its burning bitterness slid down his throat with ease.

*So, Daphne, when you followed me out from the meeting, offering me encouragement, it meant far more to me than you could have known. It was like a sweet balm, a salve, for a wound that had been festering for some time, perhaps all my life. It was like forgiveness. It was like, in spite of my selfishness, in spite of everything, someone still cared enough about me to do what you did, to touch my arm, to look into my eyes, and say, "It's okay, everything is going to be all right."*

Tears came to David's eyes now as he wrote these words. Everything would be all right, he repeated to himself, everything would be all right. He sniffed, wiped his eyes, and took another drink of the scotch, replacing the glass roughly on the desk, the whiskey splashing up and onto the paper. He blotted it dry with the cuff of his sleeve and carried on.

*But that's not all I want to say. I want to say too that something has happened to me that is at once both the most exciting and the most fearful thing I have ever known.*

He gulped at the scotch.

*I have fallen in love, hopelessly in love. With you. Please don't be taken aback by this. It probably happens to you all the time. But not to me. From the first moment I saw you, at the Christmas concert, I have been unable to think of anyone — or anything — else. Watching you give yourself to that performance, with such serenity and grace, so lovely in the soft glow of the stage lights, I fell in love with you in an instant, and have not been the same since.*

He wiped his mouth with the back of his sleeve. Onward!

*When I saw you at the restaurant, I just about went out of my skin. Though trying to appear aloof and self-controlled, I attended to your every move and gesture: you chose sweet vermouth as an aperitif; you ordered the halibut; you hold your fork in your left hand; you sweep the bangs from your forehead with your right. You see, I was completely swallowed up by your presence there. I was barely able to remain in my seat, with the bishop and his wife going on about something or other, I don't even know what. You were my entire universe that evening, Daphne.*

True. All true.

*I would ask your forgiveness, but what is there to forgive? Passion knows no morals, no ethical standards, no bounds of any kind. It just sweeps you away. And, Daphne, I have been swept away — by you.*

David leaned back in his chair to consider the words on the page but, losing his balance, he had to make a fast grab for the edge of the desk to catch himself from falling backward, chair and all.

The room was beginning to spin. He rose and placed both hands on the surface of the desk to steady himself. He turned and climbed the stairs to the kitchen, snatched the bottle of whiskey by the neck, and brought it back down with him to the study. Pouring himself another glass, this time with neither ice nor water, he placed the bottle within reach, took a gulp from the glass, and returned to his confession.

> *And now, what I should be saying is that I can never see you again, that I cannot allow myself to search your eyes, your wonderful lively eyes, for hope that perhaps there was more to your touch on my arm than the desire to console the miserable presenter of an embarrassing report. But, my love, I do hope. I cannot help but hope. If I could not hope I would be but a walking dead man.*
>
> *Oh, Daphne, tell me you love me too. Tell me everything's going to be all right. Tell me I am not a fool. Tell me ...*

David trailed off. He couldn't think what else he wanted her to tell him. He took a swig right from the bottle. He signed the letter, stuffed it in an envelope, put her name on it, and drove to the post office without thinking to turn his headlights on, weaving in and out of the circles of light cast by each street lamp.

There he stood, rocking on his heels, at the mail box. An alarm bell seemed to be ringing somewhere. An inner voice, very deep and far away, shouted out to him: *WHAT ARE YOU DOING?! STOP! STOP!!* He pulled open the door and dropped the letter inside.

As the sprung door slammed shut, he stood for a moment, trying to focus on a thought. What was it he had just done? He had told the truth, came a slurred voice from inside his head. It's just the truth, that's all, the truth. And he got into the Frog Prince and wove his way home through the darkness.

# Chapter Six

David was wakened, bathed in sweat, by involuntary movements in his gut. Propelled from his bed, he shot into the bathroom and lost the contents of his stomach into the toilet. As he stood up, the room spun round as if he were at sea. Unable to find his sea legs, he tumbled backward against the sink, falling to the floor. There he sat, dazed, slumped against the vanity. The room continued to spin. He lowered himself to his hands and knees and began crawling from the bathroom.

He became aware of the sound of a ringing telephone. How long it had been ringing, he did not know. But he forced himself to make a left turn at the bathroom door and crawl the full length of the hall. When he got to the kitchen, he sat upright on the floor beneath the ringing phone. He reached above him, gripped the edge of the counter with his fingers, and pulled himself up on unsteady legs. Holding onto the counter with one hand, he lifted the handset from its cradle with the other. He brought it to his ear and listened, breathing heavily.

"David?" came the tentative voice at the other end. "Is that you, David?" He recognized the voice of his mother.

"Hello, Mother," he tried to say, though the words coming from his mouth sounded to him barely human.

"David!" His mother sounded alarmed. "Are you all right? What's wrong?"

David tried to swallow, but a foul taste rose up from the back of his throat. Propping the phone between his chin and his collar bone, he clung to the counter with both hands now, trying to stop the room from spinning round and round. He closed his eyes and concentrated on forming his words, but his tongue lay thick and furry in his mouth, like something dead.

"I'm, ah, I'm okay," he lied into the phone.

"David — no, you're not!" he heard his mother say. "What's wrong? Are you sick?"

David tried to focus. "Yes," he said slowly, deliberately, "I am ... sick."

Then, as momentarily the fog in his head began to lift, certain scenes from the previous night started unravelling from the unfocused corners of his memory. He saw his desk, white sheets of paper spread out before him, an empty bottle of whiskey at his elbow. He was writing ... he was careening down the road beneath arcs of light ... he was standing at the mail box ... he was dropping a letter inside.

*Oh, my God*, he whispered. *Oh, my God.*

His mother was talking. "... And in the dream you were trapped, you couldn't get out. It was very upsetting. So I need to know that you're all right."

"I'm hung-over," he said into the phone.

"What?" she said. "You're what? Hung-over?!" He could hear her smile clear across the country. "Oh," she said. "Well, this is not like you. But otherwise you're all right?"

"Otherwise, I don't know," he said. "I think I've just done something incredibly stupid. Oh, God," he said again.

"Well, you know what you need?" His mother was always ready with helpful advice. "You need to get some sugar into your system. Can you make a cup of tea, and put lots of sugar in it? Do you have any pop? You need to drink something sweet. Can you do that?"

David nodded silently, obediently.

"Well," she said. "I'm surprised at you, David. But I'm glad that's all it is. Now you go back to bed and take care of yourself. Call me later. And get yourself a pop or something."

"Bye," he said, letting the handset slip from his chin, bounce off the floor, and dangle by its coiled cord.

Using both hands, he edged himself along the counter to the fridge. As he opened the door, the blinding light hurt his eyes, but he caught sight of a single can of Coke in the door rack. Steadying himself against the fridge with one hand, he made a grab for the Coke with the other. Success. But then he turned away too fast. The floor rose up to meet him, and he collapsed in a heap.

Rolling over on his side, he pressed the cold metal of the pop can to his forehead. It brought immediate relief. His mother was right, he thought, as he tucked his knees up under his chin and fell back asleep. The telephone handset made tiny squawking noises as it hung by its cord above the floor a few feet away.

His memory was sketchy when he began to come round later in the day. He was back in bed, the sheets twisted around his legs. He could recall dizzying lunges to the toilet, dry heaves, and the sickly bitter taste of the black bile that was wrenched from his convulsing gut. But now, as he lay still, mainly he could recall that fateful moment as he held open the sprung door of the mail box, the letter suspended for an instant inside the box itself, above the yawning cavern, and then … the feel of the letter slipping between his fingers, floating down, out of sight, gone.

He re-enacted the scene over and over in his head, trying to alter destiny, trying to wrestle the letter out of the hands of a staggering drunk. But he could not succeed. The deed was done. His only hope was that he had neglected to address the envelope properly, or to place a stamp on it. But the trouble with small towns is that they are just as likely to send it on anyway, knowing both the intended recipient and the sender, by the handwriting alone, if nothing else. Denise would probably have put a stamp on it herself, knowing she could catch up with him the next time he was in.

Just how much damage had been done? Slowly, carefully, he mulled this over. He could recall how the letter had started. That part was okay. It was what followed. But he couldn't recall clearly just what it was he had said. He knew he had confessed his love for her. Even that might be salvageable, if he had not gone too far. But then he remembered, hazily, as if through a swirling mist, writing the words, "my love." He saw the words appear on the page: *my ... love*. He squeezed his eyes shut. "Oh, God!" he moaned aloud. *That* would be unsalvageable.

He pulled the covers up over his head. Damn that Barbara and her stupid, *stupid* stress workshop! Write a letter and get a few things off your chest! He could write a few things to *her*, that was for damn sure! How could he *ever* have been so *stupid*?!

How long could he remain in bed, he wondered. Would someone from the East, Harv perhaps, sent on a mission by his mother, fly out and rescue him, stealing him away under the cloak of darkness? Because otherwise he still had six weeks to live in this town: six weeks to preside at public worship; six weeks to face Denise at the post office; six weeks to push the cart up and down the long aisles of the Co-op; six weeks to drive past Daphne's place, speeding up, turning his head away, so as not to be recognized.

But the food bank. What about the food bank? He peeked out from under the covers. He couldn't just drop that whole enterprise, not when he was so close to having a plan in place. Considering the options, he nodded to himself. He would go ahead and meet with the Native community of Ucluelet East. He would complete his report. Presenting it to Council in person was now out of the question. But he could submit it in written form, and perhaps appoint a parish representative to be there. Yes, that made sense. He would be passing the actual work on to the parish anyway. He could finish the groundwork and then just step out of the way. He could do this much.

He sighed heavily, shaking his head. He covered his face with his hands. "Oh, God," he said again.

. . .

In the days that followed, David felt suspended from the usual dimensions of time and place. He stayed in the house, sleeping, roaming from room to room, gazing out across the harbour, waiting. He was not sure just what he was waiting for — a phone call, a knock on the door, a word from Daphne herself; perhaps some sort of public humiliation, the *Westerly News* reporting on a rash of recent crank mail, a grainy photograph of a hand-scrawled letter held up to the camera, the signature — his signature — indecipherable, the public being asked for its help. He didn't know. But surely something would happen. The sacred laws governing the universe had been broken, and David himself had been the lawbreaker.

He waited two full days before venturing down to the post office. Strategically this might have been a mistake, he knew. His twice-daily visits were sure to be missed and perhaps commented upon by Denise to the other postal workers or, worse, perhaps even to parishioners. Still, he could not bring himself to face a reckoning for his actions.

When he finally crossed the threshold of the post office and approached the counter, he wore the wary expression of a man who was about to be hit. Denise was at the counter, busy with a customer, filling out forms for an express package. She caught him in the corner of her eye and left the counter for a moment. He waited, holding his breath. Returning, she placed two small bundles of mail on the counter. "There you go," she said, and she turned back to the forms spread before her.

As he walked out into the sunshine he allowed himself to exhale, uncertain whether or not to believe his good fortune. Had the letter gone through undetected? Had it perhaps been relegated to the dead letter pile, the scrawled code on the envelope unbroken, where it would languish for months, perhaps years, undelivered? Or ... or did Denise seem just a little too brusque, a little distant, as if she *knew,* but was not going to let on she knew? In which case, he was already a marked man, a pathetic figure, capable of the stupid desperate acts of lonely men everywhere. Well, so be it, if that was the case. He could cut his visits to the post office back to once a day, avoid Denise, and lose himself in the small crowd of locals picking up their mail in the mid-afternoon.

But in truth, he just didn't know. And this became a worse sentence than if the letter were now all over town, photocopied, posted on telephone poles; worse than if he were the target for derision, the butt of jokes, the town fool. The utter silence he encountered over the next days and weeks played on his mind, like trip wires in the grass, like mines buried in the road ahead, lying in wait for that moment when his guard was down, when, unsuspecting, the toe of his boot would trip off a tiny device, and he would be blown sky-high, leaving a crater the size of a small car. But nothing.

The days became weeks, and Denise, if anything, seemed as friendly as ever. No mail was returned to him, marked, "Insufficient Postage." His parishioners did not meet his Sunday greetings with smirks on their faces. He did not turn down an aisle in the Co-op and find himself face to face, shopping cart to shopping cart, with Daphne herself. Life went on, the cloud slowly lifting, the spring returning to his step, the sun breaking through more often now, the soft crocuses pushing their way up to the surface.

He turned his attention to the completion of his report to Town Council, which meant arranging a place for himself on the agenda of the next meeting of the Native Social Services Committee in Ucluelet East. He prepared a one-page brief. It summarized the consultations he had done to determine the need, and it described the vision of a community food bank and used clothing depot that would be set up at St. Aidan's. Would this be of use to the band and its members? he asked in the brief. Did they have questions or concerns? Was there anything he seemed to have missed?

The committee, it turned out, was all women. Lucille, the chair, and the Native Social Services staff person, wore a business suit, which put David at ease. He had considered, for the first time in his career, representing the church in corduroy pants and a casual sweater. The Coast was a casual place, and the Natives seemed to be a casual people. But this *was* an official visit, he reasoned, so had chosen again his clerical suit and collar, though he felt uncharacteristically self-conscious about it. The rest of the committee members, however, looked on in jeans, sweat suits, and hockey jackets.

They had him wait out in the hallway while they dealt with a few preliminary issues. Then he was invited in and given a seat at the table. Lucille made introductions. Many of the members present shared the same family name, but their actual relation to one another was not explained. At the opposite end of the table sat Millie, an Elder, small, deeply lined, inscrutable. She looked out upon the proceedings without expression, watching this priestly visitor without comment as he passed out the brief and launched into his presentation.

The committee read over his summary as he spoke. Some had questions. Was the food bank just for Ucluelet, or could Natives on the reserve use it too? No, no, that was the whole point, he said, that it would be a resource for the entire community, for both Natives and non-natives alike. How were band members to get over to town to access the food bank, someone asked him, as many of them did not have cars? They talked for a few minutes about bussing or pre-arranged car pools, perhaps on certain given days of the week. Someone expressed doubt that members of their community would use such a thing, preferring to keep their needs to themselves and to their own people. David said he hoped that, over time, they would feel welcome, as the food bank really was for everybody.

After everyone had their say, the group fell silent, and the committee members began glancing down the table at Millie, who thus far had said nothing. "What do you think, Auntie?" Lucille asked her.

Millie folded her mouth into a frown. Then, in a small voice that cracked with age, she spoke in a language foreign to David. She did not look at him as she spoke, but gestured with her hands in his direction, so that the subject of her comments was clear. She paused, as if considering what she had just said, and then nodded to indicate she was finished.

Lucille turned to David. "My auntie says she doesn't understand what you are doing here. We don't know who you are. You wear the collar of a Catholic priest, yet you have a wedding ring on your finger. You live alone in the church's house. Where are your wife and family? These are the things she wants to know."

They all looked at him. He had been expecting questions, perhaps even opposition. But this he had not expected. He smiled and scratched his head, embarrassed.

Well, he began, he was not a Catholic priest, but an Anglican priest, the difference being that he could marry and that, yes, he himself was married, with two children. He also served here as the United Church minister, he explained, because St. Aidan's was a shared ministry of the two denominations. He hadn't realized that people didn't know this and apologized for not having made it clear.

Lucille did not interpret this to Millie, implying that she understood English, but was choosing not to speak it. The table looked back at her.

She nodded, then spoke again in her native language, a deft combination of guttural sounds and tongue-clicking noises that flowed easily from her mouth. A few of the women smiled at what she was saying, catching one another's eyes.

When Millie nodded, Lucille interpreted for David. "Auntie wants to know why your wife and family are not here with you. Why do you live alone? It is not right that you are here and your wife and family are not."

David nodded that he understood the question. "It's sort of complicated," he said. Millie was looking at him. He was not going to get off that easily. He knit his brow as he considered how to say this. "My wife and I have been separated," he said, looking down at the table. "But when I finish my time here in another month or so, I'll be going home and we'll be together again as a family." He considered his words, hoping they remained true.

When he looked up, Millie was still looking down the table at him. Their eyes met, her gaze easily penetrating his. He looked away. She understood. She looked at Lucille and nodded again.

Lucille addressed David. "Thank you," she said. "We'll consider the proposal you have brought to us." He was being dismissed. He rose from the table, thanked them all, and turned to leave. But Millie's voice stopped him at the door.

"You go home," she was saying in heavily accented English. "You go home now, it is time. Your family waits for you." She was not smiling, but she nodded at him as she spoke, like a grandmother would. He nodded solemnly in return, comprehending in a deep place what she was saying. "Thank you, Auntie," he said, "thank you." And he left.

She was right, of course. It was time now. He would tie up the loose ends and begin the process of pulling out. His replacement had been chosen, a United Church minister, a woman, and she would be taking over at the end of the month, beginning on Palm Sunday. He had several weeks left of services and sermons, all Lenten in theme, and then he would be gone.

His last week Paul would be joining him, flying out on his March break and driving back across the country with his dad in the Frog Prince. David could begin letting go now. Even the food bank. He would write up a report for Town Council, although he had no idea what the Ucluelet East Social Services Committee was going to do with his presentation, or how he would find out. He would simply report that the consultation had happened, and that no serious objections had been raised. But Millie was right, it was time to go home.

The next day, David wrote up his report. He would ask Mimi to type it up. Perhaps she would agree to stand in for him at the next town council meeting as the report was tabled; symbolically he would be passing the mantel to the congregation. Perhaps this thing would fly, perhaps it would not. But it was time for him to lay it down.

Which brought back to mind the ingloriously unfinished business of Daphne. It was something from which he could not just walk away. If she had not received the letter, all was well and good. But if she had ... David could barely think of it. If she had, he owed her something, an apology, an explanation, something. Walking away would only leave him haunted. Had the cry of his heart been heard? Was there any response at all? Even her scorn would be better than this devastating silence, this void.

David needed advice about this, he needed someone else's wise counsel. So he made an appointment for a haircut with Randy.

There was another man in the shop when David arrived, not a customer but a friend, it seemed, a young man a little too well dressed to be a local, leaning against the glass display case that served as the sales counter. He and Randy were chatting between the rooms as Randy finished with a customer, an older woman, whom he had given a perm. The stranger eyed David as he entered, but continued to claim Randy's attention in conversation.

As the woman paid and left, David settled himself into the hair washing chair. The visitor asked Randy if he wanted a coffee. Randy, in turn, asked David, who shook his head. He himself would have a cappuccino then, Randy answered, low-fat. The young man went out.

"So?" Randy asked, when the young man had gone.

"So?" David responded. "So ... what?"

"So, how's your love life?" he said, a broad smirk spreading across his face.

"You're bad," David said. "You know that."

"Yes," Randy answered. "But you ... well, what does that make you?"

"Okay," David said. "I did something really dumb. REALLY dumb!" He sighed. "I wrote her a letter, just to get things off my chest."

Randy nodded.

"And I mailed it," David finished.

Randy raised his eyebrows. "And?" he asked.

"And ... nothing." David said. "I haven't heard a thing. Which is probably good, because it was just a letter. I didn't want anything to come of it anyway." He breathed out, hard. Randy led David over to the chair in front of the mirror. As he pumped the chair with his foot, raising it to cutting level, he appeared to be thinking.

"So what will you do now?" he asked.

"I don't know," David answered. "I'll be leaving in a few weeks. I'm wondering if I should do something, make contact with her somehow. But I'm getting ready to go home. I'm returning to my wife and family. So I don't know."

Randy nodded. "It's hard, isn't it?" he sympathized. He was a natural at this sort of thing: non-judgemental, affirming, keeping the door open for more.

"What do *you* think?" David asked him.

Randy had started clipping with his shears, but he stopped. "I don't know," he said. "What is it you want?"

"Closure," David said. "That's all. Closure."

"I'm not sure it's that neat," Randy said. "It's all a risk, isn't it? You walk away and wonder what might have been; or you make contact with her, and you find out. Which would be worse? Maybe you don't want to know. But maybe you do." He looked at David in the mirror. Smiling, he said, "But you do, don't you? You do want to know."

David smiled sheepishly back at him.

"Well, good luck," Randy said, "that's all I'll say. Good luck."

Randy's visitor returned with his coffee. The conversation gave way to small talk between the two of them until David was at the counter, paying up. Randy put his hand over the till.

"This one's on me," he said.

"That's not necessary," David protested.

Randy shook his head, resolute. "And would it be so wrong for an agnostic to say: 'God bless'?"

"No, it wouldn't," David said, "Not from you. Thank you, Randy."

They shook hands and David walked out into the bracing morning air. The sun shone brilliantly off the snow-capped inland mountaintops. He strolled down to the bluff overlooking Tofino's harbour and stood watching the fish plant workers down below, hauling crates of packing ice across the yard in their long blue smocks and tall rubber boots. Gulls circled overhead, piercing the mid-morning stillness with their cries.

Life seemed to be opening up for David once more. The thought of finishing off here was not a sad one, though he would forever miss the daily wonder of this, God's coastal creation. There was life — new life — for him back home, and he drew a deep and grateful breath. He was almost ready.

. . .

Although there were still several weeks to go, David found himself rehearsing in his head his farewell sermon. It would come on the fifth Sunday in Lent, a day traditionally known as Passion Sunday, containing the scriptural themes that prepared the way for Palm Sunday which followed the week after.

It occurred to David that the theme of Christ's Passion was especially fitting for his last Sunday among these people, if not so much for their sakes then at least for his. For what was life without passion, his new word? What was life without risk and suffering? Had he not been learning this himself? Christ's agony on the cross had less to do with our sinfulness than with God's love, with the willingness of the Creator to enter into that which he had made. It had been a risk, and it cost him dearly. But without that sacrifice, would it have been love? God so loved the world, Christians were fond of repeating, that he gave his only begotten son. *That* was the point, surely.

David looked back upon that fateful night he had spent alone in the church, his life unravelling around him, gazing into the tortured face of his Lord, who was able to offer David no consolation other than his own suffering and death. It had seemed to David like no consolation at all.

But now, mindful of his own recent descent into darkness, he felt a renewed bond with this suffering Saviour. At the very least, he knew now that the One on the cross understood him, forgave him, perhaps even sympathized with him. And that somehow altered David's own experience, validating it. He and his Saviour met at the cross. There, they recognized one another. It was a mutually respectful recognition.

Somehow this was filling David with a renewed appreciation of life and of living. He recalled the words of Jesus, the Good Shepherd: he came that they might have life, and have it abundantly. Such living seemed now inextricably bound up with the cross, because it opened one up to risk; and risk led one back to life. In fact, he now concluded, there was no abundant life without abundant risk.

It was along these lines that his final sermon was forming in his head. It no longer bothered him that he would not be using a single quote from the early church Fathers to back him up.

But it did bother him that he still had something to attend to, one more loose end, albeit a humiliating one. This itself was a risk, an enormous risk, and he was not sure how to prepare himself for it.

Mimi had typed up his report to Town Council, as he had asked her. It represented the only certain link between himself and Daphne, the only excuse he had to visit her and face the consequences, if there were to be any, of that stupid drunken letter. He would deliver the report into her hands, he decided, and so stand before her one last time.

David drove the Frog Prince out to her home, pulling into the small gravel parking lot that pointed the way to the main doors of her veterinary clinic. There were no other cars in the lot. He parked and turned off the engine. His hands were shaking; so he hung on to the steering wheel. He sat for a few minutes, breathing out, trying to let go of the anxiety, opening himself to this new risk and possibility. Finally, still breathing from a shallow place high in his chest, he forced himself out of the car and up the steps to her office.

A bell atop the door announced his arrival. He could feel his pulse racing, the blood draining from his head. He exhaled, telling himself not to panic, to remain calm.

Daphne entered from a room off to the side of the waiting area. She wore a white smock and was drying her hands with a towel. She had a smile prepared for her new customer but, as she recognized him, it was replaced by a look of surprise, and then of slight alarm, as if he might be a crazy person, a stalker perhaps, or worse, as if she might be in some danger.

His heart was pounding, but still he tried to remain focused.

"I'm sorry to bother you," he stammered. "I, um ...." He couldn't remember what his next words were supposed to be. His mind raced, ransacking his memory, opening closet doors, throwing things onto the floor, desperately trying to find the right words. He was losing precious time. "I guess I was just wondering," he blurted out," if you received my letter."

Daphne raised her eyebrows as if to say, "Letter? What letter?" Then, tentatively, she seemed to change her mind. She nodded.

"Oh God," he said, more to himself than to her. "I'm so sorry, Daphne," he said, her name sounding strange and presumptuous on his lips now that he was standing before her. "I never meant to send it. Really. I was just trying to get some things off my chest. I got drunk. I never meant to send it."

Daphne stood perfectly still, watching him.

"I'm sorry if it caused you any embarrassment, or any discomfort." David was relieved that he was able to find at least a few of the words he had prepared to use. "I didn't mean to ...." But now, again, his memory tripped him up. Let it go, he told himself, just let it go. A heavy silence hung between them.

Daphne moved over to the reception counter, placing one hand flat on its surface, as if to steady herself. "Well," she said, taking a deep breath, "I *was* a bit surprised." She tried to smile, but it was an awkward crooked smile.

"I'm so sorry," David said again.

"I can see that," she said. She frowned. "I just wondered what it said about *me*."

David was taken aback. "Oh, no," David said. "No, it didn't say anything about ... I mean ... it wasn't about you, it was about me. No, don't think for a minute .... " He cursed himself inwardly.

"Daphne," he said. "I hope you won't take this the wrong way, but you really are a lovely person — if only you knew. I've just been really confused lately, and that sort of got mixed up with seeing you at the concert, and then again at the restaurant, and then again at the Town Council meeting. Things all got a little crazy for me. But I never meant to ...." His voice trailed off.

He allowed the slow shaking of his head to finish the sentence for him.

She nodded. They fell silent.

"I don't suppose," David said, "I don't suppose that you would want to go for a coffee or something. Do you want to talk?"

She shook her head. "No," she said. "But I think you mean well."

Another silence.

"I've had this sort of thing happen to me before," she offered. "Well, never a letter, exactly." The first faint traces of a smile appeared in the corners of her mouth, an amused, self-deprecating smile. "But still, this sort of thing. I wonder if you can imagine how that might feel. I live on my own here. I have friends, but basically I'm on my own. Most of the time, this is the way I like it. I like what I do. I like my life. I don't go out of my way to get involved in other people's lives. I just live my own. Then, when something like ... that ... comes along, it can feel a bit, well, overwhelming, a bit scary even. I mean, I didn't do anything to lead you on, did I?"

David remembered the soft touch of her hand on his arm down by the government docks after his presentation to Town Council. She had only meant well. And he had violated those intentions.

Whatever rampant fantasies David had entertained about Daphne, it was now abundantly clear that they were not shared by her. He was a complete stranger to her, just as she was to him, minding her own business, living her own life. Until these ... these *creeps* like him come along and wreck everything. *Oh God*, he thought to himself. He had nothing to say. He just shook his head in response.

"Well, anyway," she said, "I don't think you meant any harm.

You are probably a good person, aren't you? I think you are. So ... I do thank you for stopping by." She smiled at him. "That *is* why you stopped by, isn't it?" she added, eyeing him warily for a moment.

David smiled and nodded. He tried to find his tongue. But no words were forming. He just stood inside the doorway, awkward and dumbstruck. "I *am* sorry," was all he could get out. He tried to smile again. He had an urge to reach out and take her hand, perhaps to shake it, perhaps to raise it to his lips, this incredible woman who deserved so much better than to get tripped up by some idiot's clumsy, *stupid*, schoolboy crush.

But he turned and took his leave. As he passed through the doorway he caught the toe of his shoe on the stoop and stumbled. "Are you all right?" she called after him. He waved over his shoulder and kept moving.

His head felt light, his body numb, and he walked stiffly, like an automaton, back to the car. Its splotchy lime-green brightness seemed all the more ridiculous to him now, a clown car for a clown. He climbed in and started it up.

Glancing back at the clinic through his rear-view mirror, David saw that Daphne had come to the door. It was a sight he hoped he would always remember: the *Messiah's* cellist leaning against her doorpost, her arms folded across her chest, her head lightly cocked to one side, brushing her bangs from her eyes with her right hand, watching him drive off in the Frog Prince. He thought he detected a smile.

David pulled out onto the highway. His neatly typed report to Town Council lay beside him on the passenger seat. He had not even thought to mention it.

. . .

With the balmy turn in the weather, David was now able to resume his explorations of the shoreline. People were appearing on the beaches now, sauntering hand in hand, jogging or riding bicycles, tossing sticks for dogs who splashed headlong through the surf. New life was returning to the earth. Even the bald eagles seemed suddenly plentiful, screeching from their perches high in the treetops, or chased through the air by the squawking crows and gulls whose nests they were raiding.

Daily, life was opening up in new and exciting ways. After one particularly exhilarating climb along the rocky headlands around Ucluelet, David arrived breathless at a remote outcrop overlooking the ocean. He was surprised to hear a faint but familiar sound on the wind. Following it over a rugged promontory, he came upon a young woman sitting cross-legged on a blanket, her long thick hair wafting in the breeze. Oblivious to him, she was playing a flute to the open seas; and she was completely naked.

Ucluelet's annual Whalefest was a celebration of the return of the gray whales that marked the beginning of spring. All the tour operators were starting up, offering half-day excursions out among the Broken Group Islands, or up and down the open coast in search of whales. A parade down Peninsula Drive offered homemade floats and children dressed up in clown costumes though, oddly, no marching bands; the squeals of children and the banter and clapping of bystanders were somehow sufficient.

The Chowder Chowdown on Sunday afternoon, over at the Rec Hall, featured nine local restaurants, each putting their best soup forward. For three dollars, visitors were given a small Styrofoam cup, a plastic spoon, and a ballot. They then toured the room, sampling as many chowders as they could handle, or stopping for seconds, thirds, and fourths when they found the one they liked best. The voting was a mere formality, for it was understood that no restaurant could win two years in a row and that, over time, each contestant would have a turn winning the grand prize, which was honorary mention in the *Westerly News*, the sponsors of the event.

The whole place was waking and stretching after the winter rains. Colour rose in people's cheeks and, implausibly, hope ran high that this would be a good year, that the salmon would flood the creeks and streams, that the tourists would turn out in droves, and that wealth and good fortune would come back to the area. Like the year of the herring, back in the early 1880s, when a suddenly insatiable Japanese market drove the prices up through the roof, and fishermen around town were dropping thousand-dollar bills for a twenty dollar purchase, buying spanking new trucks and repainting their boats in bright reds and yellows. Like that year.

David himself felt cleansed. He was but a few weeks now from heading home. He was disengaging, letting go, finishing off his work here; he was feeling strong and healthy and ready for whatever the future would bring. It was a visit with Cecil that introduced the only cautionary note in his spring fever.

He called on Cecil frequently now, not from compunction, but because he had grown to enjoy the old man's dour company, sitting at his kitchen table, listening to stories from his days in the bush, first as a trapper, then as a logger. For years he had also fished with his brother up the coast. It was those memories that were now beginning to stir as they sat, swilling Cecil's strong black brew.

"This is some beautiful place, isn't it?" David had asked him.

Cecil nodded.

"You've been fortunate to spend your life here," David went on.

Cecil nodded again.

The two sat in silence, as happened often. David no longer found it an awkward silence. They were sharing their company even when they weren't sharing their thoughts, creating space enough for friendship to grow between them. But David could tell that Cecil's mind was fixing on something. His small dark eyes grew clouded and a bushy brow drooped over one eye.

"What are you thinking, Cecil?" David asked him. "Are you remembering something?"

Cecil spoke without looking at David. "It's a terrible beauty, this place," he said. "A terrible beauty."

"What do you mean?" David asked him.

"It tricks you. It waits for you, for when you're not looking," Cecil said. "When you're standing there looking out to sea. You think, 'Ah, now that's a beautiful sight' — and you don't see the rogue wave swelling up, right there in front of you, coming in to get you. I've seen men pulled right from the rocks, men who've lived here all their lives. I've seen men die trying to save them." He looked over at David. "That kind of beauty."

It was more than Cecil usually had to say. David waited.

"It was this time of year, a little earlier maybe," he said, continuing a narrative that seemed to have already started in his head. "We was up the coast, my brother and me, fishing. The seas had been good. We'd seen lots of things that trip — dolphins, Orcas, things you wouldn't believe. We were headed back, a beautiful evening. That's when the wind, she swung around from the south-east. Y'see, winter wasn't through with us yet."

He sipped at his black coffee, holding on to his mug with both hands as he replaced it on the table, like he was anchoring himself for the tale he was about to tell.

"So the sea was up, and we were getting beaten back pretty bad. We was coming in, but we was making no headway. Night time came, black as coal, and we were still at her. And that's when the ice struck."

"The ice struck?" David asked.

"Everything begun icing over. The lines, the deck, everything." He looked up at David to see if he was following. "We had to chop at the ice or she'd have sunk with the weight. So my brother, he'd take the wheel while I chopped. I chopped until I couldn't feel my hands no more, even with gloves over my gloves. Then I'd go in and take the wheel and he'd chop. We had only the one axe."

David was trying to imagine the terror of being tossed about by a violent wind-swept sea while chopping at ice that was forming faster than they could rid the boat of it. He frowned at the desperate images that Cecil was conjuring. He waited. Cecil was frowning too. David thought he detected a tremor in his lip.

"So my brother was chopping and I was in the wheel house. He came in and handed me the axe with his one hand. But when he went to take the wheel with the other he couldn't grab her." Cecil stopped, his jaw quivering. David saw tears in his eyes now. He looked straight at David. "You know why he couldn't grab the wheel?" he asked him.

David shook his head.

"Because he'd chopped his fingers off," Cecil said, spittle running from the corners of his mouth.

David's face registered with horror. "Oh, my God!" he whispered, recoiling at the image. "He chopped his fingers off!"

"Didn't even know it, either," Cecil said. "Too damn cold."

"Oh, my God!" David said again.

The two sat together at the table for a long time, not speaking.

Finally David looked over at Cecil. "You've sure seen some things, haven't you, Cecil," he said.

Cecil nodded. Things that played in his head now, David figured, as he sat day after day, looking out upon the world. Things that haunted him. Things that told him that the created world, however beautiful, was not kind, was never kind. That life was filled with danger; and living, with risk.

. . .

In his last week it occurred to David that there was still, in fact, one more loose end. Three times he had tried to find the elusive blowhole and three times he had failed. He had to try one last time before he left the Coast — for Cecil's sake, for his own sake, for the sake of the new life flowing through his veins.

It was overcast, late on the Saturday afternoon before David's last Sunday. Everything was in readiness for his final services. He had delivered the bulletin information to Mimi, which she had received with a detached professionalism that had come to characterize her dealings with her minister since the Christmas concert. Ernest had agreed to the list of songs and hymns David had provided him, including one he was willing to learn from scratch. The sermon had fallen nicely into place and David was determined to deliver it without having to look at his notes, sort of a tribute to this freer conversational preaching style he had learned since coming to the Coast.

David drove the Frog Prince out to Mill Stream and parked it at the side of the highway. He glanced up at the thick gray sky and decided to bring along his slicker, which was in the back seat. He pulled up his collar and headed into the bush, along the trail that promised to deliver him at last to his goal.

He passed easily through the new growth nearest the road and rounded the bend where the bear dung had turned him back the first time. There was no sign of such obstacles now, though it was the time of year that fresh ones could well appear. The low forest gave way to a broad meadow, where the mighty Sitka spruce had once stood proud and tall. A bald eagle, perched on the high silver limbs of a long-dead cedar, watched David's progress.

At the fork in the road, David peered up toward the distant crown of the Old Guardian, its upraised limbs still bearing the hulks of his two fallen comrades. It appeared that the tree was gazing off to its left, to David's right. Was the Old Guardian giving him leave, granting him safe passage? Was he pointing the way? David smiled. He tipped an imaginary hat, and set off along the track to the right.

At first the way was wet and strewn with slippery fallen logs, but David deftly negotiated the tricky obstacle course. He then had to bend down low as thick bracken began closing in on the trail. The only way forward narrowed to the dimensions of a small tunnel. But he could hear the ocean now, the pounding of waves on a distant beach. He could also hear the wind picking up, as it whistled through the tall trees high overhead.

He got down on all fours and began crawling through the trail that was now no more than a deer run. Thorns picked at the seams of his slicker and poked at the exposed flesh of his hands and neck. David's world was reduced to the two or three feet he could see directly in front of him. He felt the slight panic of a rising claustrophobia as he crawled along, hemmed in on all sides. But the run grew no smaller, so he carried on.

The trail, such as it was, climbed a bluff and, on the other side, as the forest floor fell away, it opened up again, allowing David to stand. Overgrown with ferns and tangled branches on either side, the trail sliced a narrow passage through the dense foliage. By turning his body sideways, David was able to slip slowly forward, his hands parting the leafage in front of him, his face bearing the assault of the twigs and branches as they swung back into place. The ocean was loud now.

For a while, David plodded downward, unable to see his feet for the thick vegetation. Then, suddenly, the forest parted before him to reveal a scene of spectacular beauty. It was an expanse of pristine beach, almost free of driftwood, littered only with small piles of seaweed and bull kelp. Rocky outcrops at either end enclosed the beach in a little bay. A small island protected the mouth of the bay from the direct impact of the surging tide, but still the crashing of the surf, pounding again and again onto the sand, was almost deafening. David leapt over a fallen tree trunk and stood triumphantly on the beach, breathing hard, his hands on his hips, his face flushed.

The rock face to his right rose up sharply at the northern end of the bay, discouraging his approach. So David turned to his left and traversed the beach with purpose in his stride. He took a running leap across a stream of run-off that spilled from the thick undergrowth that lined the bay. He made his way to the rocky outcrop at the beach's southern end and began climbing its glistening face, using the splintered cracks and fissures for toe holds.

The rock formed the base of a large headland that pointed to sea. Farther out, it broke up for a stretch into gravel and surf-grass, overhung with twisted shore pine and red cedar. The rising tide pounded relentlessly along the shoreline; but out to sea it was even more forceful, hurtling itself against the rocky outcrops and craggy sea stacks, sending immense clouds of spray up into the mounting wind. Surely, he was close to the blowhole; the violent energy of this place only filled him with determination to find it.

He continued along the broken shore as it led him farther

out on the headland. He was startled to hear up ahead a mighty *wump*, as somewhere a surging wave shot into some narrow rocky enclave. He could feel the percussive effect under his feet. He was close, very close.

He navigated his way around an outcrop of forest that brought him right to the water's edge, the roiling tide on one side of him, impenetrable bush on the other. As he made his way around the outcrop, and jumped down onto a pebbly beach, he suddenly found himself at the mouth of a mighty cut in the rock, a surge channel, rock cliffs rising fifty feet on either side. The ocean rushed in from the other side of a steep pile of boulders that divided the channel about half-way along. He entered the channel, picking his way between the small tidal pools, and clambered up the rock pile. It was wet and slippery with moss. High above him on both sides towering hemlock and cedars gazed down, their embattled branches swishing back and forth in the rising wind.

As he gained the top of the rock pile, he beheld an awesome sight. The surge channel, caused by an ancient splitting of the headland, cut a deep splice in the rock that pointed directly out to sea. But an enormous boulder higher up had split off and fallen, wedging itself half-way down the narrow walls of the channel. So the waves, rushing forward from the other side, first smashed against this rock lintel, then surged beneath it.

David straightened to take in this natural wonder just as a wave hit the wedge — *WUMP!* The raging waters, forced through the low narrow passageway, rushed headlong into the broken rock on which he now stood. They hit with such force that it threw David off balance. Salt spray shot straight up into his face. Reflexively, he stepped back and, for an instant, found himself suspended between heaven and earth; then he plummeted downward.

His fall was broken by the jagged rock that rose sharply from a tidal pool at the base of the rock pile. David heard a crack as his right leg buckled beneath him and his body crumpled in a heap into the shallow pool. He came to rest, half-submerged, in the brine.

David immediately tried to leap to his feet. But white-hot pain shot from his leg up through his body and straight into his brain. It was like a bolt of lightning, and he fell back into the water, stunned, where a second bolt struck, bringing him to the edge of unconsciousness. He sucked air into his lungs, winded. A third bolt shot through him as he writhed in the pool.

David forced himself to lie back in the freezing tidal water, gasping for breath. His mind raced to assess his situation. He was wet and cold. He was in pain. His leg was likely fractured. He peered down into the dark water to inspect it. To his horror, his leg actually went off at an odd angle just above the knee, a complete break. He turned his head to the side and vomited. Tears came to his eyes.

Could this really be happening? Surely this was a dream, a nightmare. Because if it were not, he was in trouble, serious trouble. This is how people died. Not just of injury, but of exposure. And who would find him out here? If nothing else, he had to get himself out of this pool, or he stood no chance whatsoever. The tide was coming in and he was lying right in its path. An enormous WUMP from the other side of the rock pile shook the ground beneath him. This spurred him into action.

Taking hold of his right thigh, just above the break, he braced himself for the pain, and then stood upright on his good leg, raising his body out of the water. The pain shot through him again, but he managed to thrust himself onto the ground. His back arched, his body twitched, as the nerves in his leg ignited and sparked in blinding flashes, like live wires. He could not catch his breath. But he dared not give up. So again he stood and, lurching forward, hurled himself into a crevice in the cliff wall. He screamed out in agony, but lost consciousness as he hit the rock, his body wedging itself more or less upright into the crack, his broken leg coming to rest atop his good leg.

His loss of consciousness was momentary. When he came to, he knew for certain that he would not be able to move himself again. Here he would have to remain for as long as it took for someone to find him ... or for him to die waiting.

David considered this for a moment. Things really were that bad. He could die here. He bit his lip, trying to find a manly solution. *Think, think.* A smoke signal? A flag of some sort? A loud noise? Another wave rushed up the surge channel, hitting the rock — *WUMP* — the sound echoing off the high walls that rose up around him. It was futile.

Something took hold of him — something he had never known before. It was fear; but it was more than fear. He began to weep uncontrollably, his breath coming in shallow gasps, bitter tears burning hot down his cheeks. *O God,* he cried out into the din of wind and waves. *O God, help me! Help me, O God, please! I don't want to die!*

The pain from David's broken leg was constant, a throbbing reminder of the flesh and bone that ground together and of the nerve endings that sparked with every twitch of his muscles. But he found that if he kept perfectly still, he was spared the more excruciating shock waves. So he did not move, permitting himself only a slight rolling of his head and neck.

A light rain began to fall, driven by the onshore wind. While David was protected from the shower by the rock cliffs and by the boughs of trees that spread out high above him, his body began to shiver in the damp and cold. He tried to contain the involuntary movement this created, but his shaking grew worse, wild and convulsive, causing pain to shoot up again from his leg. His teeth clattered together, even as he tried to tuck his head deeper into the collar of his slicker, locking his jaw in place. His right arm was pinned beneath his body, but his left arm was free; so he reached over and grasped his elbow, holding it tightly, a small consolation.

*Stupid, stupid, stupid!* he upbraided himself. How could he be so stupid! Now everything was at stake, everything. He allowed himself to think of Paul and Catherine. His voice broke into soft moans, calling out their names. *I love you,* he cried. *I love you.* Beverley's face appeared before him. *O Bev, I'm so sorry,* he said through sobs, *I'm just so sorry. Please forgive me. I'll never do anything this stupid again. Just don't leave me, don't leave me here.* Her visage dissolved in the descending dark. He was alone again. He wept openly into the wild night.

There was no measuring the minutes or the hours as David tried to gain control of himself, to focus his thoughts on things positive and hopeful. Perhaps someone would happen by, walking their dog. Ha! In the middle of the night? In the middle of a storm? Out here on this remote outcrop? He changed tack. Perhaps he could keep his spirits up by sheer force of will. He wanted to return home, didn't he? He wanted to celebrate Easter, with his family all gathered round? But the only image that presented itself to him was of his family gathered round his coffin, looking down upon him, sad and confused, shaking their heads as he is lowered away from them down into the dark earth. He gave up. It was no use. He let his mind drift.

The tide was coming in now, sloshing around the soles of his shoes. There was nothing he could do about it. He only hoped that he was far enough up the channel that the water would not rise much above his ankles.

Now and again it seemed that his shivering might subside.

David allowed himself to think that maybe everything was going to be all right; maybe he was going to make it. Then it would start up again, worse than before, his entire body convulsing uncontrollably, igniting nerve endings up and down his leg, sending him into new paroxysms of agony. He cried out as the pounding waves and driving wind rose up to sweep his voice away.

David began to slip in and out of consciousness. It grew hard to tell which was which. In an agitated dream-like state he glanced up to see someone standing before him, a middle-aged man in a clerical collar, wearing a red life-jacket. David reached out his free hand in supplication. Beside the man, there appeared another; it was David's father. David called out to him. *Dad,* he said. *I'm in a bit of trouble here. Can you see that?* But the two figures looked on without expression, his father present, but distant, just as he remembered him.

David drifted off again only to be awakened by soft movement all around him. He was mildly surprised to realize that a large black bear had manoeuvred herself between him and the cold rock, enfolding him in the furry folds of her underside, wrapping her arms around him like a blanket. He nestled into her soft belly, pressing his cheek against the beating of her heart, the fishy smell of her breath warming his own, as he fell back into sleep.

He awoke again in the night to realize that he was no longer shivering; in fact, he could no longer feel his body at all. There was no pain, but neither was there movement as he tried twitching a muscle to test his reflexes. It seemed that his mind had become dissociated from his body, unable to command it to do anything. *Good,* he reasoned. *Perhaps it's healing itself.* It was a comforting thought that allowed him to drift peacefully back to sleep.

He continued to wake at intervals, not entirely sure where he was anymore, having no feeling to indicate whether he was wedged into the side of a rock wall on the rugged shores of a wild and rocky coast, or just dreaming that he was there. But there seemed to be people moving about him now. A few hovered above him, looking down as if from some great distance, yet close enough that he could discern definable features in their faces. They seemed to be bathed in some sort of light, though the source was not clear, as if they themselves were one and the same with that light. Other darker figures spoke in harsh voices; he could hear them calling out to one another. There was more light, then more voices.

He found himself floating high above the scene — serene, detached. He looked down and saw himself crumpled into the rock crevice, figures moving furtively about him, in and out of the darkness. What were they doing, he wondered. And why was he able to see himself? Strange.

Then the *wump* of the surge channel startled him. And again. *Wump. Wump, wump, wump.* Like a motor, cutting the air. And now he raised his head to witness a marvellous sight: he could see all the way up and down the ragged coast. The sun was rising on the distant horizon, shining its healing rays out from beneath a low bank of clouds.

He fell back again into a deep sleep.

. . .

It was the sounds that David noticed first: squeaking soles on waxed floors; voices echoing down bare corridors; the hum of electric lights. He sensed a presence.

"Am I dead?" he asked into the void. The sounds stopped. A voice above him said, "No, no, you're not dead. But just a minute

... I've got to tell ... wait just a minute...." And again he heard the squeaking of shoes, running off down a hallway. He drifted off again.

The next thing he noticed was a pain in his chest, a barbed hook that caught him every time he inhaled. He took another breath, just to be sure. The pain stabbed him again just about his sternum. He held his breath, then slowly let it out. At least he could breathe. This was a good sign. He hurt, and he could breathe. These were both good signs. He drifted away again.

Voices floated above him now, unlikely voices, familiar voices, but strange. Was this another dream? He had only to open his eyes to find out. But he was reluctant, suspended for the moment between awake and asleep. There would be no turning back once he opened his eyes. He would be making a choice, a choice he was not yet ready to make. But he heard, quite clearly now, the voice of Cecil, his neighbour. And another, younger voice, but deeper than he remembered.

He opened his eyes and sat bolt upright. "Paul?" he tried to say. But a seal of phlegm broke in his throat and the word became a guttural cough. David leaned forward and erupted into a coughing spasm, the pain in his chest catching him with each convulsion. A nurse rushed in and, stepping up to the bed, placed her hand on his back, helping him bend forward. Finally, gasping, he caught his breath and fell back into the pillows, spent. He was certainly awake now.

The nurse reached for his wrist. "Are you all right?" she asked. David nodded.

"Your body's had a bit of a shock," she said, holding his wrist. "We almost lost you — several times, in fact. So you just need to take it easy. You have some resting up to do."

Paul's face came into view.

"Paul," David called out weakly. "Paul ...."

The nurse looked down at her watch and released David's hand, placing it beside him on the bed, giving it a pat. "You're doing just fine," she said, smiling.

"What happened?" he tried to mouth the words.

"There'll be time for that later," she said. "You had a fall, you've broken your leg, and you suffered serious hypothermia. They air-lifted you in. You're a lucky man, Reverend Corcoran." She patted his hand again, smiled, and turned to leave. "Not too long, gentlemen," she called over her shoulder as she left the room.

David felt his right leg now, at least he felt the dead weight of it, wrapped from thigh to toe in a thick plaster cast and suspended above the bed by some sort of line and pulley system.

Paul moved in closer and looked down at his dad. "Hi, Dad," he said.

"Oh, Paul," David said, his eyes filling with tears. He lifted his hand off the bed. Paul took it into his own. David smiled up at him, so big, so grown up now.

There was someone else here. Cecil sat slumped in an armchair in the far corner of the room, like a child, his hat folded in his hands, his small dark eyes surveying the father-and-son reunion. David smiled and nodded in his direction. Cecil lifted his cap in greeting.

David lay back and closed his eyes.

When he woke again, he learned it was Wednesday. Three days lay behind him, unaccounted for. Paul and Cecil were gone. A nurse entered the room. He recognized her instantly — it was Ruth. She sat him up, puffing the pillows and propping them behind his back. He was filled with questions.

He was in the Tofino hospital, he knew that. Now he learned that he had been rescued from the headland by a team of volunteer firefighters, along with some risky manoeuvring by the search and rescue helicopter. They feared that his heart had stopped — they couldn't get a pulse — so they had administered CPR all the way back. This accounted for the pain in his chest. At the hospital they had warmed his blood intravenously and kept him breathing with a hand-held respirator. That had been her job, Ruth said.

He smiled up at her. "Thank you," he said. But how had they known? She shrugged, shaking her head. She said he should rest now, and she left the room.

How had they found him? How did they know he was there? His heart had stopped? He had been brought back from the brink of death? Amazing. A beguiling mystery, filled with so many unanswered questions.

Released now from slumber, David's mind was a video of floating images: the faces of Beverley and his children as they had appeared to him in the dark; the curious man in the red life-jacket; his father, standing before him, stern and resolute; a black bear? — preposterous! — yet ... yet why could he recall so vividly the smell of its breath; the human figures — some real? some imagined? It was all a great mystery indeed — but a miraculous mystery, for here he was, alive.

*Thank you, Lord*, he whispered. But it sounded so thin, so inadequate, the words little more than a formality. He tried them again. *Lord, I just want to thank you.* No, it wasn't working. It wasn't going to be enough.

He had no doubt now that God was listening to him, perhaps even smiling down on him. It felt good to be able to pray again. But his real thanks, he suspected, would have to find some other way out than words. The faint glow of a new understanding flickered across his mind. Why else would he have been spared?

The next time Paul and Cecil came in, David was sitting up. He pumped them with questions. Paul had arrived on Monday, as planned, but there had been no one to meet him at the airport in Nanaimo. He had to get a bus — three buses, actually — and was lucky to arrive in Ucluelet before midnight. He had found the house but, with no one there, had gone next door and knocked on Cecil's door. Together, they pieced together the puzzle and then drove over in the Frog Prince to find David at the hospital. "Nice car, by the way," Paul chided his father.

But what about the rescue, David wanted to know. How had they found him?

Cecil smiled. "It's that goddamn car of yours," he said. "Everyone knew it was yours."

"So, someone spotted the car on the highway?" David asked.

"Some doctor from Mill Stream," Cecil said. "She called it in. I suppose seeing the minister's car parked by the bush — parked by *that* bush, anyways — in the middle of the night, it didn't look natural."

Who? David wanted to know. What doctor?

Cecil shook his head. He didn't know.

*Incredible*, David thought to himself.

"Well, anyway, I found it," David said.

"Found what?" Cecil asked him.

"The blowhole," David exclaimed. "I found the blowhole! I was standing in it! That's where I fell."

Cecil looked puzzled. "You was standing in the blowhole?" He raised his hand to his head and gave it a good scratch. "You was standing in the blowhole?" he said again. He shook his head.

"I don't think so."

"Sure," David said, and he explained in detail how he had turned right at the fork, found his way through the deer run, come out onto the beach, and then made his way out along the headland to the south. He described the surge channel with its high walls, the rock pile plugging it half way along, and the fallen boulder wedged between the walls, farther up.

Slowly, a wide toothless grin spread across Cecil's face. "Well, I never," he said, and he started to laugh. Laughing, he started to cough, so that he was laughing and sputtering at the same time. David motioned with his head for Paul to go over to him. "You okay, Cecil?" Paul asked him.

Tears were streaming down Cecil's face as he laughed and laughed. "Oh-h-h, that's a good one," he said finally, as he began to breathe again. "That's a good one, all right."

David and Paul were looking at him. "What?" David asked him, annoyed.

Cecil fixed David with a stare across the room, a glint in his eye. "You wasn't in no goddamned blowhole," he said. "That thing's no more'n about three or four foot across, no more'n a crack, for God's sake. You still never found it." And again he began to laugh.

David's face fell as Cecil's words sank in. He hadn't found the blowhole? He'd almost lost his life to that thing, and it wasn't the blowhole?

"Goddamn it," David said. "Goddamn it!" and he pounded the bed with his fist. He looked up at Paul, and across at Cecil. "Well, goddamn it, anyway," he said again, until he too succumbed to the awful absurdity of it, and began to laugh, clutching at his chest.

. . .

The next day David sat on the bed, fully clothed, waiting for Paul to pick him up and take him back to the rectory. The phone rang on the bedside table. He had received several calls and visits from parishioners, including Mimi, who had brought him a house plant. But he was reluctant now to answer the phone. The truth was, he was ready to go; he was looking forward, not back, and he did not want to prolong his good-byes.

He picked up the handset. "Hello?" he said.

"Hello, David."

David smiled with recognition. "Bev!" he said. "It's so good to hear your voice!"

"How are you?" she asked. "We've been worried sick since Paul called. He said you almost died."

"I guess so," David said. "But I'm here now." He didn't want to talk about it. He just wanted to connect with her across the great distance that had been separating them. "My leg's mangled, and my chest hurts every time I breathe, but other than that I'm okay — really," he said. "How are you?"

It sounded like she was not ready to have the tables turned so quickly. "Me?" she asked. "Okay, I guess. We're looking forward to having you home. Catherine is preparing some nice surprises for you. So ...."

David could not suppress the wide smile spreading across his face. It was just so good to be talking with her again. What was different now, he wondered.

"David?" she was saying.

"Yes?"

"When you come home, there are some things we will need to talk about."

"I know," he said.

"Well ... I'm not sure you do," she cautioned.

"That's okay," he said. "The main thing is that — Bev? I love you. We can work it out."

She was quiet for a moment on the other end of the line. "A lot's happened," she said, "hasn't it?"

"Yup," he said. "But mostly I've been acting like an idiot. I know that. I don't know how much damage I've done. Maybe some of it was necessary. But I just know I want to come home, and be a family again. It could be a new beginning." A sudden shadow fell across his thoughts. "Or am I missing something?"

"Well ...."

She was hedging. David's heart sank. Maybe she didn't want a new beginning. Maybe the damage he'd done was irreparable. Maybe she only wanted a dignified ending. He waited.

"If you want to talk about new beginnings," she said slowly, her voice sounding almost coy, "then I want you to be thinking about two words."

"All right," he said, sitting up, bracing himself, wondering if divorce had a two-word synonym.

"Foster care," she said.

For a moment his mind went blank. The words were so foreign to anything he might have imagined her saying, that at first they had no meaning at all. He repeated them to himself, and then aloud to her. "Foster care."

"That's right," she said. "You could just do a little thinking about those words."

Slowly, an image began emerging on the photographic paper of David's brain. He saw a house filled with children, children who were not his own: little girls in smocks standing by the stove; little boys with gap-toothed grins running up the stairs;

listless teenagers with bad skin lounging in doorways, tossing their hair out of their eyes.

"Foster care," he said again. "Hmm. What a concept."

"David," she scolded him, "now don't you dismiss this. I've been giving it a lot of thought. It's important that we simply think about it."

"I'm not dismissing it," he said. "I think it sounds, well, it sounds ...." He was not sure *how* it sounded, whether it was a good or a bad thing. But there was one thing he now knew beyond a doubt: he loved his wife. If she wanted foster children — well, why not? "Wonderful," he said at last. "It sounds wonderful," and he smiled, feeling a little giddy.

"Think about it, David," she said, unconvinced.

"I love you," he said.

"Did you hit yourself on the head when you fell?" she asked.

"If I did, I'm sure I needed it," he answered. "I'll see you soon."

It took a couple of days for David and Paul to pack things up for their journey home, David hobbling around the rectory on crutches. They were in no hurry, though; the open road was patient and waiting. Paul would be missing a few days of school now, but it was not an issue for either of them. They would get there when they got there.

When the car was packed, they closed the front door to the rectory, leaving the keys on the kitchen counter, and drove down to the government docks. Sitting on a park bench, they watched the boats come and go, more tour operators and sport fishermen than commercial vessels. Squawking gulls rose and fell, quarrelling among themselves. Sea lions rolled about beneath the dock, keeping one glistening eye on the hulls of the boats that were tied up, above them. Bald eagles circled high overhead. A gentle breeze wafted up the harbour from the wide ocean beyond.

"You know, Dad," Paul said, "things aren't going to be the same when we get back."

David, his arm draped behind the back of the bench, looked at his son. "So I gather."

"Ya," Paul went on. "Mom? She said that when you got back, it would be her turn."

David nodded.

"But that was before you got all banged up," Paul added. "So this might change things." He gazed down at his father's swollen leg, wrapped in ten pounds of plaster, the stubby shapes of his toes peeking out the end of a thick woollen sock. "This might help," Paul said approvingly. "This definitely might help."

"Knowing your mother," David replied, " I don't think this'll change a thing."

The two nodded, chuckling together.

"Let's go," David said finally, gripping his son's shoulder.

Paul helped his dad into the passenger seat of the Frog Prince, wedging the cast diagonally through the door, and then climbed in himself behind the wheel, a lanky teenager, all arms and legs, folded up into a spray-painted lime green compact. As they drove up the main street and onto the highway, David hummed to himself an old familiar hymn, singing the words inwardly, to himself:

> *Were the whole realm of nature mine,*
> *that were an offering far too small;*
> *Love so amazing, so divine,*
> *demands my soul, my life, my all.*

**Path Books**
A LIGHT TO MY PATH

We hope that you have enjoyed reading this Path Book. For more information about Path Books, please visit our website at **www.pathbooks.com**. If you have comments or suggestions about Path Books, please write to us at publisher@pathbooks.com.

## Other Path Books

**The Habit of Hope: In a Changing and Uncertain World**
*by William Hockin.* Reflecting on the anxieties that deeply trouble us today, William Hockin offers spiritual guidance and reasons for hope. With keen insight and a deep knowledge of Christian faith, he helps us value our own experience and approach the source of our hope.
*1-55126-325-4 $14.95*

**Practical Prayer: Making Space for God in Everyday Life**
*by Anne Tanner.* A richly textured presentation of the history, practices, and implications of Christian prayer and meditation to help people live a rewarding life in a stressful world. Offers clear instruction on different forms of meditation for beginners and the experienced.
*1-55126-321-1 $18.95*
*Meditation CD: 1-55126-348-3 $18.95*
*Audio cassette: 1-55126-349-1 $16.95*
*Leader's Guide: 1-55126347-5 $18.95*

**Prayer Companion: A Treasury of Personal Meditation**
*by Judith Lawrence.* A personal prayer resource providing a rich variety of stories, reflections, prayers, and meditations to help us cope with difficult times as well as good times. A friendly companion to those searching for greater meaning in everyday experience.
*1-55126-319-X $18.95*

*Available from your local bookstore or*
*Anglican Book Centre, phone 1-800-268-1168*
*or write 600 Jarvis Street, Toronto, ON M4Y 2J6*